UNFORGIVABLE LOVER

A WARRIORS OF LEMURIA NOVEL #5

ROSALIE REDD

UNFORGIVABLE LOVER
A Warriors of Lemuria Novel #5

By

Rosalie Redd

For permissions contact: Rosalie@rosalieredd.com
Cover Design: Melody Simmons
ISBN: 9781944419219
United States of America

CHAPTER 1

"*N*ikki! Not so close!" Worry laced Jasmine's words, bringing Nikki to a halt. A few loose stones skittered over the cliff's edge and pinged against the rocks.

"Don't worry, Jas, I got this." Nikki closed her eyes. The warmth of the spring sun on her shoulders was in stark contrast to the cool, damp spray prickling her cheeks. A moment's respite, that's all she wanted, and the waterfall's roar did its best to drown out the lonely voice in her head telling her she wasn't good enough.

"Please, Nik, come back."

With a soft sigh, Nikki opened her eyes and glanced at Jasmine. She wore a red bandana around her head, the knot tied at her temple. Her brown hair flared around her ears, framing her features and accentuating her deep green eyes etched with unease.

Nikki tightened her fingers around her backpack straps. A couple of rhinestones on her bracelet caught the light, sending a cascade of brilliance over Jasmine's white tank top. "Wahclella Falls is beautiful this time of year. I wish I could dive in."

Jasmine pursed her mouth and laugh lines formed around her eyes. "Of course, you would. Just don't stand so close to the ledge, okay? You make me nervous."

"I'm fine, Jas. Really, I am." Nikki stepped back from the rim.

Jasmine gripped Nikki's hand, and she drew away, her shoulders tightening at the contact.

A slow, resigned sigh eased from Jasmine, and she wrapped her fingers around her hiking stick. "Let's go. We need to leave if we're going to make it back before nightfall. You want to do a marathon session of the *Underworld* movies?"

Nikki rubbed the back of her neck. Surprised at the hike invitation in the first place, she wasn't sure why Jasmine would put in the time to try to get to know her better. They were work buddies, nothing more. The hike was a nice diversion, but a few more hours of studying were on tonight's agenda.

"Sorry, Jas. As much as I like all things paranormal, I have a major test tomorrow. If I don't pass, I don't graduate, and I'll have to return to classes in the fall. No way do I want to see Professor Chandler again." Besides, without the master's degree, she couldn't apply for the open management position at Zumitel, the software company she devoted her life to these days.

"Aw," Jasmine scrunched her nose, "all right, but I want a rain check."

"Sure, no problem." Nikki glanced at the majestic waterfall one last time then followed Jasmine down the path.

The heel of Nikki's sneaker skittered over a wet stone protruding from the mud, and she placed her hand along a tree trunk to steady herself. This part of the trail hugged the precipitous hillside, skirting down a vast ravine.

Jasmine peered over her shoulder. "I'm glad we came here today. I didn't think the rain would ever end."

"Yeah, springtime in Portland can be a drag sometimes, but the summers are so worth it. At least I can check the first waterfall of the season off my list like James and I..." Nikki's throat tightened. James had shared her love of waterfalls and last year they'd put together a list of the best ones in the Columbia River Gorge, marking off each beautiful cascade they discovered.

Jasmine huffed. "Forget about James. He's not worth another moment of your time."

Handsome, smart, and kind, James had showered Nikki with affection, but it hadn't lasted. Soon after, she'd discovered his binge drinking only to watch it morph into a daily occurrence just a few months into their relationship. After her father's addiction destroyed her family, Nikki couldn't handle another alcoholic in her life, so she'd said her goodbyes and moved on. "Don't worry, Jas. I'm all about my career—"

A loud rumble shook the ground. Pebbles rained along the dirt.

One hit Nikki on the shoulder. Another grazed her ear. She glanced up.

Trees, plants, and rocks tumbled toward them at breakneck speed.

Nikki shoved Jasmine forward, down the path, and toward a large boulder. Jasmine screamed, and Nikki lost her footing. She buckled to the ground. Her knees jarred painfully against rocks littering the path.

"Nikki!" Jasmine's voice echoed, competing with the crashing of tree branches and rolling mud.

The deafening roar ricocheted in Nikki's ears, eclipsing her scream. She scrambled backward, up the trail in the direction they'd come. A stone pelted her on the shin. Blood pooled from the cut. Fear snaked its way into her stomach, coiling into a tight ball. She continued to scramble up the path, forcing her limbs to move despite the rocks digging into her palms.

A Douglas fir, followed by a rhododendron bush, slid down the mountainside chased by several more giant trees with spear-like branches that rushed toward her. Boulders from the size of toasters to refrigerators crashed and rolled along with a wave of mud. She winced, her heart racing, and braced for the possible impact.

The landslide roared past her and slowed. A few pebbles bounced over the debris.

The trail no longer existed.

Nikki's pulse pounded. She scanned the trees on the other side of the wreckage. "Jas!"

Jasmine rose from behind a boulder. Her fingers, bloody and raw, gripped the edge of a tree that remained rooted in place.

Relief flooded through Nikki's bloodstream.

Jasmine's features tightened. "Nikki. Be careful. Back up slowly."

So focused on Jasmine, Nikki hadn't assessed her situation. One foot dangled over the trail's broken ledge. She gripped a tree root, the gnarled ends eerily similar to long pointy claws. At the bottom of the ravine, trees rested in a tangled, broken heap. She shivered.

It was one thing to stand at the edge of a cliff overlooking a waterfall, quite another to stare into the depths of an abyss up close and personal. The hair at her nape rose. "I can't move."

"Look at me, Nik," Jasmine commanded.

Nikki peered at her workmate.

Jasmine nodded in encouragement. "You can do this. Hold on to that tree and move back. I'll be right here."

Nikki reached further into the exposed tree's roots and curled her fingers around the sturdiest one. The muscles in her arms shook. She forced her gaze to return to Jasmine. "I'm scared."

"I'd be surprised if you weren't. Now, scoot back, slowly."

A bead of sweat slid down Nikki's cheek. She'd had to rely on herself for so much of her life, she could do this, too. Pulling on her inner strength, she crawled up the path.

A few small pebbles dislodged from the edge and pinged against a downed tree. The sound ricocheted through the still air.

Nikki held her breath. Beneath her feet, the ground remained solid.

Thank you, thank you, thank you.

With careful, measured movements, she scooted up the trail. She reached level ground and stood, leaning against a tree. A tremble started in her calves and spread up her thighs.

"I did it," she choked, the sound morphing into a relieved laugh.

"You're not hurt anywhere, are you?"

Nikki exhaled, long and slow. "No, I'm okay."

"Nik, there's no other way out. I'll return to the car and find a ranger. I won't be gone long."

Nikki glanced into the sky. Tinged pink, a few small clouds reflected the setting sun's rays. *I may have to spend the night out here.* The errant thought traipsed through Nikki's mind like an unwanted visitor. She forced herself to smile. "I'll be okay. There's some trail mix, water, and a mini flashlight in my pack."

"I saw a few trees in a thicket not too far up the path. Wait there, but don't go any farther. I'll be back as soon as I can." Jasmine gave her a thumbs-up then took off down the trail.

As the pounding of her sneakers receded, an eerie quiet settled over the forest, a peaceful contradiction to the landslide's violent chaos. Goosebumps rose along Nikki's arms.

"There are worse things than spending the night in a cold, dark forest." She'd hoped saying the words would ease some of the tension in her shoulders. It hadn't. Instead, she tightened her grip on her backpack strap, drew her courage around her like a cloak, and headed toward the small thicket of trees. Despite her forced bravery, the twilight descended, and she couldn't quite shake the sense of fore-boding that tingled the hairs along her nape.

CHAPTER 2

*G*aetan leaned over his cane, forcing the staff to bear his weight. His knee buckled beneath him, and he braced himself against the rough stone wall. The hard volcanic rock bit into the skin on his palm, scraping deep into the flesh. Tangy and bitter, the scent of blood wafted through the Portal Navigation Center.

He welcomed the pain. After what he'd done, he deserved far worse.

Rin, the Portal Navigator, placed his hand on Gaetan's back. His red hair jutted from his head in tufts, a sharp contrast to the worry lines rimming his eyes. "What did ya tell Noeh and Melissa?"

Gaetan focused on the little Jixie's wild hair. The sudden urge to laugh bubbled up his throat, and he clamped his jaw tight. There was nothing funny about their situation. Prince Anlon—Noeh and Melissa's son—had disappeared through the portal only a few minutes ago. To where, they didn't know.

Self-loathing coiled in Gaetan's gut, twisting his insides into a ball. This was his fault. The royal couple had placed Anlon in his care.

All four of Gaetan's markings, the ones that signified his personal values—responsibility, benevolence, empathy, and patience—burned hot on the back of his hand then faded from a dusky charcoal to a light gray. He wasn't surprised. Guilt, bitter and dark, ate at his soul.

A bout of pain travelled up his leg, the agony so great white spots formed in his vision. He slipped his fingers into the satchel tied at his belt and withdrew a pill. Round and white, the medicine was as much a curse as a blessing. He popped the pill into his mouth and dry swallowed. "I sent a cryptic note through the sunstones. Indicated we needed to see them right away. I expect they will arrive any—"

The pounding of heavy feet accompanied by the swish of soft-soled shoes echoed from the corridor. A moment later, Noeh entered the chamber. He wore a thin shirt, a pair of dark pants with his dagger attached at the belt, and a pair of boots.

Melissa, wearing a loose blouse and slacks, drew to his side.

Noeh's attention passed from Gaetan to Rin and back again. "What was so urgent you needed—"

"Where's Anlon?" Melissa's voice wavered.

Heat raced up Gaetan's back and burned his ears. His throat tightened, but he forced himself to answer. "That's why I called you here." His gaze flicked to Noeh. "I don't know how to tell you this, my king, but Anlon, he's gone."

"What?" Noeh's stern voice boomed around the room.

Melissa gasped.

Pulling on his empathy and natural ability to calm others, Gaetan gripped Melissa's hand. "I'm so sorry, my queen. Anlon was so fast, I couldn't stop him—"

Noeh gripped Gaetan's shoulder and spun him around so they were face to face. In the heat of the melee, Gaetan had forgotten Noeh was deaf.

"Where's my son?" Flashes of gold flicked through Noeh's eyes. His nostrils flared, the beast dangerously close to the surface.

Rin stepped forward and pointed to the platform. "Anlon disappeared through the portal."

Melissa cried out and bolted for the large stone platform. Noeh wrapped her in his arms, stopping her. She struggled against him, squirming in his embrace. After a long moment, she glared at Gaetan. Tears rimmed her eyes.

A low growl rumbled in Noeh's chest. "How did this happen?"

Gaetan lowered himself to one knee, bowing in front of his king. His bad joint protested, but nothing could match the ache in his heart. He'd hurt the one male that meant more to him than anyone, the male he'd raised like his own son after the death of Noeh's father. There were no words to describe the anguish in his soul. "I set Anlon down to talk to Rin. The babe, he levitated a sunstone through the portal and pursued it. This is my fault. If I—"

"We tried ta stop him, but the newb, he was too fast." Rin strode up to Noeh and bent down on one knee. "Yer Majesty, we had no idea—"

"What were his coordinates?" Noeh released Melissa and brushed past Gaetan without a glance. "Show me my son's location."

Gaetan rose, using his cane for support.

Noeh refused to look at him. The king couldn't have injured Gaetan more if he'd taken his dagger and stabbed him in the chest. Deep inside, Gaetan's beast howled.

Rin held out his hands in supplication. "I...I can't tell ya. I don't know where he went."

"What? How can you not know?" Noeh's voice ricocheted around the chamber.

Rin slowly rose to his feet. "I'm sorry, Yer Majesty. There was no signature mark among the *Porte Stanen's* red sunstones."

Gaetan gripped his cane, and the cracked sunstone at the tip reflected the light across the stone walls. He'd come to the Portal Navigation Center to fix his sunstone, the one Ginnia had given him long ago. His sister bore the brunt of Gaetan's biggest childhood mistake, leaving her forever stuck in her childlike world. He was bad luck, just like the cracked sunstone, and now he'd harmed or even killed the little prince. Vicious hatred of his own vile self filled his lungs with every breath he took. He deserved no mercy.

Melissa stepped forward, tears streaming down her face. "Noeh, please. We must find him. What if the Gossum..."

"Ah, *craya!*" Noeh ran his hand through his hair and paced the room.

A chill crested over Gaetan's shoulders and down his back. Gossum were their enemy in this war over Earth's water. Placed here by their goddess, Alora, the Stiyaha fought to keep Earth free and to barter with the humans for their precious resource. The Gossum, and their god Zedron, wanted to enslave the humans and take the water by force. If the Gossum, or Mauree, their leader, found Anlon...

No, that couldn't happen. Gaetan's mouth went dry and a shudder of dread wracked his body followed by a guilt so heavy he almost buckled under the weight.

Noeh stilled. The muscles in his shoulders visibly tensed beneath his shirt. He pointed to the porte stanen, the giant stone lined with red sunstones that ignited the portal. "Open a gateway. Send me to the last known coordinates."

Rin's mouth fell open. "But, Yer Majesty, what if ya run across Gossum?"

"Which is why I must leave," Noeh's gaze flicked to Gaetan, "to find my son."

Noeh's words buried into Gaetan's soul. How far he'd fallen. So, so far.

"Yes, Yer Majesty." Rin ran to the porte stanen as fast as his little feet would carry him. He swirled his hands over the sunstones lining the surface, faster and faster, until a thin mist gathered along the platform, forming into a ball.

Melissa clutched Noeh's arm. They peered into each other's eyes, but didn't speak, at least not verbally. Ever since Noeh saved Melissa's life, they shared a soul and could communicate telepathically. Gaetan and Saar were the only ones aware of their special bond.

Noeh tugged Melissa to him and gave her a rough, bruising kiss. She wrapped her fingers in his hair, holding on for a long moment before pulling away. "Bring our son back to me."

Noeh glanced at Gaetan, his mouth drawn into a grim line. Anger, bitterness, and pain reflected in the depths of his blue eyes. Like a spear, his gaze tore into Gaetan, shredding him from the inside.

Gaetan held out his hand, guilt and love for Noeh pushing him forward. "I will accompany you."

Noeh's jaw tightened. "No. Stay here. You've done enough already."

Gaetan's cheeks heated as if Noeh had physically slapped him. The pain in his leg flared, burning all the way to his heart. The urge to slip his finger into the lining of his pants pocket and take a painkiller washed over him. Disgust burned the back of his throat. Unable to meet Noeh's hard, disapproving stare any longer, he glanced at the stone floor.

Noeh exhaled. "Have Saar put together a search party and follow me."

Before Gaetan could say another word, Noeh disappeared through the portal.

Melissa choked on a long sigh. Her red-rimmed eyes glimmered with unshed tears. Gaetan wanted to go to her, use his ability to provide comfort, but by the set of her jaw, she wouldn't appreciate the effort. Not from him.

"You were my mentor, my father's best friend, and the one Stiyaha I can count on above all others. If anything ever happens to me, I want you to raise Anlon. Raise him as you did me until he's ready to rule. Will you do that for me, my friend?" Not long ago, Noeh had said those words, and Gaetan had pledged his commitment to his king without a second thought. Gaetan prayed this wouldn't come back to haunt him.

"I can't let Noeh go alone." The decision lit a fire in his chest. The Keep and all its inhabitants couldn't afford to lose their king. Gaetan would do whatever he could to save his friend. "Rin, reopen that portal then continue to search for Anlon."

"I figured ya'd say that." Rin swirled his hands over the stones once again.

A tear slid down Melissa's cheek, but she nodded, hope reflecting in her eyes. "Please, find my son."

The desire to please his queen, make some small amends for his deed, rocked him to his core. "I will do whatever I can. Tell Saar what happened. He'll send others." Gaetan hobbled up the steps and through the mist, following his king and his heart. *Gods help us all.*

CHAPTER 3

*N*ikki nestled further into the crook between the pine tree's trunk and the fallen log. The breeze had picked up a few minutes ago, right after sunset, and there was enough room to provide protection from the wind.

She bit into her granola bar and focused on her crossword. With the sky bathed in dark shades of purple, she had to squint to see the page. "A four-letter word to believe something desired may happen or events will turn out for the best."

The first letter in the puzzle was already filled in—the letter 'H.' Nikki tapped the rubber end of her pencil against her bottom lip. *Hmm, how about 'hope.'* "How fitting, that's just what I need right now."

She wrote the remaining letters in the corresponding boxes then shoved the small paperback into her pack. Working the crossword had helped occupy her mind, but now, the reality of her situation teased at her subconscious.

She glanced into the darkening forest. Were there wolves out here? Bears? Coyotes? Dread, cold as ice, snaked over her shoulders. Her muscles tensed, tightening at the base of her neck. Trailing a fingertip over her bracelet, she followed the links from her wrist over her hand and around the ring on her middle finger. The familiar movement often calmed her nerves, but not tonight. "C'mon Jasmine, bring the cavalry. I need to study for my test."

Jasmine...

Although they'd recently moved from polite acquaintances to work friends, Nikki didn't know that much about Jasmine. Not even where she lived or who was in her family. What if Jasmine never returned?

A gust of wind rippled through the boughs. The limbs brushed against each other, sighing in the dusk. Goosebumps prickled along Nikki's arms, and she rubbed her skin, trying to maintain some warmth from the relentless chill in the air.

With temperatures in the eighties during the day, she'd dressed in a thin top and a pair of shorts. A sweater hadn't even crossed her mind. She huddled further against the tree, but the wind was relentless, beating at every exposed piece of skin.

Between the treetops, the full moon and a few stars became visible in the sky. Toby, her little brother, would've enjoyed a night in the woods. Born with Down Syndrome, he hadn't grown past the mental age of five and had loved camping. Unable to handle Toby's special needs, their father had fallen down the long road of alcohol addiction until one day he'd taken them on a little joy ride and smashed the car into a tree.

Nikki was the only survivor. Since her mother had passed during Toby's birth, Nikki had no family left. The familiar loneliness echoed within her as if she were a hollow cave. She'd lost so much. How she missed her little brother.

She rummaged in her pack, her fingers grazing against her water bottle, another granola bar, the baggie of trail mix, the puzzle book, a pen. Her small flashlight seemed intent on eluding her. To be caught out here in the woods after dark was a completely different experience than hiking the trail during the day. A tendril of fear wound inside, squeezing the breath from her.

With a quick jerk, she upended her pack, dumping the contents in her lap. The water bottle rolled off her leg and the trail mix, the granola bar, and the pen flew through the air. Her puzzle book slid between her foot and the fallen log. Something cold and metallic caressed her bare thigh. She grasped the penlight. The muscles in her arms shook from relief.

She depressed the button. Light shot from the bulb in a thin stream, illuminating a few feet in front of her. She shined the beam over her surroundings. Her water bottle lay nearby. She stretched to retrieve it.

A twig snapped.

Hisssss...

Every muscle in Nikki's body tensed. A scream lodged in her throat. The beam of light was like a beacon, announcing her location. Fingers shaking, she flicked off the light.

Not accustomed to the blackness, she was blind. A soft whimper threatened to escape, and she clamped down on it, snuffing the sound.

A strong astringent scent like rubbing alcohol wafted by on the breeze. Brush under nearby trees rustled.

Her pulse pounded at her temple, racing at breakneck speed. Yet, she remained frozen, like a mouse hiding from a predator.

"The putrid scent of humans from the nearby trail clogs the air. Why do you wish to go this way, my lady?" a man's voice echoed from the trees.

Nikki's first impulse was to jump up, yell for help, but something held her in place, an even deeper instinct perhaps, one of self-preservation.

A loud female tittered, the sound uncanny and unnatural. "Eldon, please. Your intelligence is sorely lacking. I suspect Saar will send troops this way, and I'd like some revenge."

Nikki turned her head to peer toward the voices. Her eyes had adjusted to the dimness, and she caught movement between the trees. A woman, with a patch over one eye, wearing a blouse and short skirt, traipsed through the woods, a bald man at her side. How odd...

Loud chuffing sounds burst from the man. "I smell Stiyaha." His long tongue whipped from his mouth. The tip snapped in the air.

Nikki screamed.

The sound was swallowed by a roar so loud it shook the trees.

A man with a dark shirt and black pants emerged from behind a boulder. He raised his fist, the long dagger blade extending from the hilt in his grasp.

Other bald men dropped from the trees. Like a pack of wild dogs, they circled the armed man.

Nikki scrambled against her hiding spot, burying herself as deep into the copse as possible.

"Don't attack! Not yet." The woman held out her hands, commanding the strange creatures. She adjusted the patch over her eye. "Noeh, what a pleasant surprise. What brings you—"

"Where is my son? What have you done with him, Mauree?" The large man took a step forward, toward the lone woman.

Caught up in their own confrontation, they didn't notice Nikki. Afraid to make any noise, she inhaled and exhaled with slow, deliberate breathes. A part of her feared they would hear her racing heart.

"Your son?" Mauree tilted her head. "Is he missing? How interesting. Perhaps I'll have to find the little tyke."

A loud, anguished howl tore from Noeh. Dagger outstretched, he lunged toward Mauree.

"Kill him!" Mauree's shrill voice echoed between the trees.

The strange bald men attacked the solitary man, this 'Noeh.' Long, knifelike claws extended from their fingers. Lengthy tongues snapped from their mouths.

Nikki flinched. Had she fallen down the rabbit hole? Was she in some kind of bizarre, delusional nightmare? Another shriek built in her throat, but fear paralyzed her and kept her rooted in place.

Noeh changed, growing to a towering height of nine feet. Long, shaggy hair grew over his limbs. His clothes magically disappeared beneath the fur. Tusks emerged from his mouth, along with a feral growl of pure rage.

Nikki gaped at the unbelievable sight. Yep, it was official, she was in Wonderland. Her silent scream ricocheted in her mind.

∾

Gaetan tracked through the forest, following the trail of broken branches, bent ferns, and utter destruction Noeh had left in his wake. Even without his preternatural ability to see in minimal light, Gaetan couldn't have missed the carnage. He couldn't keep pace, and he'd lost sight of his friend a few minutes ago. A spurt of energy lit by fear urged him onward.

Noeh's loud roar echoed through the trees. The beast was loose.

Gaetan tightened his grip on his staff. The sunstone on the end flared to life a moment before resuming its usual orange luster. Pulling on his inner determination, he hobbled over the beaten path and prayed he wasn't too late.

Snarls, growls, and the slashing of claws through flesh filled the night air. Gaetan crested a small hill, and the moon's soft glow provided enough light to reveal several Gossum surrounding a beastly Noeh. Black sludge, deathly evidence of more of the vile creatures, coated the ground at his feet. The Gossum attacked, ever relentless, one after another. Blood dripped from several of Noeh's wounds, but he never relented.

Noeh gripped a Gossum by the tongue and flung it far from him. The creature smacked against a tree. A loud crack rent the air, its back broken. It slid to the ground in a pile of goo.

Not far away, Mauree placed one high-heeled foot on a nearby downed tree. A black patch lay across one eye, the other sparked with killing intent. She clapped her hands. "Kill him! Kill him! Kill him!"

Anlon was nowhere in sight. A strange combination of relief and panic flitted over Gaetan's nerves.

He gripped his staff and, forcing his deformed leg to bear his weight, pushed himself into a hobbled run. Pain rippled up his calf, and he used the energy to fuel his drive. He must aid Noeh. Nothing else mattered.

Gaetan closed the distance, and a glint of light shifted his focus.

Mauree slid a dagger from a pouch along her thigh. Her attention riveted to Noeh. With a quick flick of her wrist, she launched the weapon.

Gaetan was too far away. He slowed to a stop behind a tree, the realization freezing his muscles in place. He couldn't save his king.

Helpless, Gaetan watched from the shadows, the back of his throat stinging. The blade flipped end over end through the air, catching the moon's glow with each revolution. With a soft thunk, the tip embedded in Noeh's throat.

Noeh tensed, the muscles in his arms and legs turning rigid. A strangled gurgle emitted from his lips. Blood gushed from the wound, pulsing with each beat of his heart.

A Gossum stung him on the face, another on the arm, a third raked its claws down Noeh's back. Each strike made Gaetan flinch. They swarmed over the great king, and Gaetan could only see glimpses of his bloodied body. Before Noeh landed on the ground, he disintegrated, turning to sand in an instant. Gaetan held back a gasp. Oh gods, no.

His best friend and king was dead.

Grief, powerful and strong, tore through Gaetan, shredding his heart. For a long moment, he couldn't think, his brain refusing to acknowledge what his eyes so clearly revealed.

"If anything ever happens to me, I want you to raise Anlon."

The memory of Noeh's words reverberated in Gaetan's mind, and his promise to Noeh bore down on him like a serpent twisting around Gaetan's soul. The unbreakable bond would drive him to find the babe as much as his guilt. If he didn't honor his commitment, when he died, his soul wouldn't return to Lemuria, but instead, it would disappear into the ether, the space between space. That was worse than death.

He didn't care, not for himself, but he couldn't let the babe suffer, lost and alone, or worse, fall into the enemy's hands. Anlon was somewhere. Gaetan just needed to find him. He curled his hand into a fist. Nothing, absolutely nothing, would keep him from his commitment.

CHAPTER 4

*K*aelyn bit into the crunchy bread, and the sweet taste of garlic butter rolled across her taste buds. She groaned at the wonderful flavor. Seated across from her at the end of the long dining table, Saar raised an eyebrow, and his smile created that small dimple she so adored.

He chuckled, the familiar growl audible even above the cacophony of voices from the other warriors in the Grand Hall. "No need to waste pleasure on bread, little bear, when I can make you moan like that."

She placed her hand over Saar's, rubbing her fingertip over his middle finger in long, sensuous strokes. "Do you have something to feed me that tastes better?"

The fork he held in his other hand slipped from his grasp and clattered against his full plate of spaghetti. A bit of sauce splashed onto the worn wooden table. "Maybe we should return to our quarters where—"

Tense, heated voices rose above the din. Melissa stood at the Grand Hall's entrance, her features strained. Quentin, one of the warriors, gripped her arm. She jerked away, breaking his grasp. "Where's Saar? I need to speak to Saar."

An eerie sense of foreboding sent a chill over Kaelyn's arms.

Saar rose, and the bench scraped against the stone floor. "Melissa, what's wrong?"

Others got up from their seats. All conversation ceased.

Melissa ran to Saar, her eyes glimmering with unshed tears. She choked back a sob. "Anlon... Noeh..."

Saar's brow furrowed. "What happened? Are they injured? Where are they?"

Anguish, cold and hard, tightened Melissa's features.

Kaelyn ran her hands up Melissa's arms. "No need to rush. Take a big breath."

Melissa inhaled then let it out slowly. Her gaze flicked from Kaelyn to Saar and back again. "Something happened to my son..."

A collective gasp erupted from the crowd, quickly followed by raised, worried voices.

"Quiet!" Saar boomed, silencing everyone.

Kaelyn gripped Melissa's hand. "Please tell us what happened."

Melissa blinked several times, as if taking the time to collect her thoughts, then nodded. "Gaetan took Anlon with him to visit Rin. Somehow, my son...he crawled through the portal before Rin or Gaetan could stop him."

"Where did he go?" Saar's words came out terse, his mouth tightening into a scowl. The warrior in him emerged full force.

A tear slid down Melissa's cheek, and she shook her head.

Kaelyn glanced at her mate. "Saar, you're upsetting her. Please, let me do this."

He studied her for a brief moment, worry lines etched around his eyes. Kaelyn ached for her strong, sensitive mate. She ran her hand down his arm, leaned in, and whispered, "Sometimes a softer touch is better."

He exhaled. "You're right. I'm just so worried."

"As we all are." Kaelyn returned her attention to Melissa and stroked her arm, trying to provide some kind of comfort to the distraught queen. "Please, continue."

Melissa's chin trembled, but determination glinted in her eyes.

"Rin didn't know where Anlon went. The coordinates were blank. Noeh," she swallowed hard, "went after him to the last known coordinates. Gaetan followed, and Rin still searches. I've already lost one child to the Gossum, I can't bear to lose another…"

Melissa stilled. The muscles in her entire body stiffened. A soft, garbled cry emerged from her lips. Eyes widened in terror, she slid to the cold stone floor in a pile of sand. Kaelyn gasped at the mound at her feet, staring at what used to be her queen.

After a brief, stunned silence and a few loud gasps, cries rose from the merchants and council members.

Warriors yelled and drew swords. The zing of metal against metal pinged loud in the room.

Kaelyn's mind whirred. She was unable to process or make sense of it all.

"No!" Saar gripped the edge of the table and flung it against the wall. Plates shattered. Wood splintered. Spaghetti sauce, red and foreboding, left a long trail across the floor.

Dread snaked over Kaelyn's spirit, teasing her with the promise of death. Fear pushed her into action. She brought her bear's head whistle to her lips and blew. A shrill, piercing trill burst into the air.

Everyone stilled. All turned to face her.

Kaelyn met several of the warriors' gazes. "Don't panic. Calm yourselves."

After a long moment, the tension in the room eased. Low and uncontrolled sobs lingered in the air.

Saar's face was a mask of rage, his scar pulled tight against his features.

She placed her hand on his arm. "I sense you know something. Tell us."

His deliberate gaze drew to meet hers. A tic pulsed in his jaw and tension lines formed around his eyes. "Noeh and Melissa were bound together. During childbirth Anlon lived, but Melissa died. Noeh saved her life by sharing his soul with her. Gaetan and I were the only ones who knew."

"Oh, no. Does this mean…" Kaelyn couldn't finish her words.

Saar's mouth tightened, and his eyes glistened with a mixture of fury and anguish. "For Melissa to perish like this can only mean one thing. Noeh is dead."

"No..."

"This can't be!"

"We are doomed."

"Alora, please help us," someone wailed.

The warriors' words filtered through the crowd. A heavy weight settled in the room, oppressive and unbearable.

Kaelyn straightened her back and lifted her chin. The warriors must have something to focus on, a purpose to channel their energy. Hope, they needed hope. She drew in a large breath and raised her voice. "Prince Anlon and Gaetan are out there. We must find them."

A murmur of assent rippled through the crowd.

Saar gripped Kaelyn's fingers and brought them to his lips for a gentle kiss. His eyes gleamed with appreciation. "Thank you. Your level head is what we need."

Her heart swelled, an ache born of love for him.

Saar turned to the warriors. "Quentin, split the soldiers into groups and meet me in the Portal Navigation Center. Our prince and our *haelen* need us. We search until we find them or until the sun's burning rays scorch our hides."

CHAPTER 5

*G*aetan held his breath. Unable to move, to breath, to think, his mind whirred with the impossible reality. Noeh was dead. That was his fault, his responsibility to bear. Emptiness like he'd never known invaded his chest, the weight so heavy it almost brought him to his knees. If not for his staff, his constant companion, he'd be on the ground.

An eerie silence filled the forest, punctuated by multiple Gossum raspy breaths.

"I did it, Eldon. I killed the king." Mauree's words snaked into Gaetan, eating away at his soul like acid.

A Gossum Gaetan had seen before approached Mauree. "You certainly did, my lady, you certainly did. All hail, Mauree!"

The Gossum gathered around Mauree. Their excited cheers echoed into the night.

Gaetan curled his lip. The urge to run headlong into their midst, take out as many as he could before they killed him, too, flared to life.

"Please, find my son." Melissa's words echoed in his mind. As much as he wanted to mete out his own retribution, he had to find the babe.

"Well done, my lady. Now that Noeh is dead, what are your plans?" The male Mauree had called Eldon bowed before her.

Mauree tapped her finger against her chin. "As a Stiyaha, I know how the Keep's residents will react. They will reel from the loss of their king. Disorganized and out of control, they will send many troops to avenge his death." She wrapped her arm around Eldon's shoulder. "It won't be long before we win this war for Zedron and claim Earth as a slave planet. Then you and I will take our place as ruler over the humans. I think it's time you took a little trek to Portland, pick up a few more recruits."

"As you command, my lady, but what of the child? Noeh's son?"

Gaetan stiffened. *No, not the babe...not the babe.*

"Find him, if you can, but don't waste too much time on the search. If the little brat is out here, he won't survive once the sun comes up. Let's go. We have much to do." Mauree wiped her hands down her skirt and headed into the forest. One by one, her troops followed.

Fear wound around Gaetan's heart, squeezing the precious organ. They would search for Anlon.

Pain flared and rippled in his leg, sending a flicker of need through his veins. With shaky fingers, he reached for the pain meds in his pouch, and his knee knocked against his cane with a loud rap.

A Gossum, the last to depart, stopped in his tracks. He peered around his surroundings, his dark ink-black eyes flitting from tree to tree. His tongue snaked from between his lips. The barbed tip whipped to and fro, spittle landing on a nearby fern with a soft splat.

Gaetan tightened his grip on his staff. If the need arose, he'd battle the Gossum. The creature wouldn't be his first kill.

The Gossum approached, and his gaze flicked to a thicket of brush surrounding a downed tree. "I smell your fear. No need to hide. Come out, come out, wherever you are."

Fear? Gaetan didn't fear this lone creature. Quite the contrary, but his hatred and the heaviness inside would never ease, no matter how many Gossum he killed.

The Gossum closed the distance. "I see you, little human."

A soft feminine sob eased from the small copse.

Gaetan's pulse quickened. A distinctly human aroma permeated the area from a nearby trail, but no human would remain here at night.

"I'm afraid you saw too much. Your life must end. So sorry." The vile creature lunged into the underbrush.

A female's shrill scream rent the air.

Gaetan bolted toward the commotion.

The slick, wet snap of the Gossum's tongue hitting flesh ricocheted off the trees.

As Gaetan closed the distance, the Gossum's dark form hunched over a human female. She struggled beneath him, kicking, punching, battling for her life. Respect for her will to live whisked over Gaetan, fueling his sudden need to save her, to save someone tonight.

He swung the blunt end of his staff, hitting the creature across the back. A loud snarl erupted from the Gossum and it whipped its head to look at him.

Before the creature could react, Gaetan whirled the end of his cane with all his strength. The sunstone embedded in the end cracked against the creature's skull. Stunned and knocked off balance, the Gossum fell away from the human.

Gaetan yanked his dagger from his belt. He tightened his grip around the hilt and slit the creature's throat. The creature slid into a pile of black goo.

The human female lay on a few matted ferns, her chest heaving with each panting breath. Beneath the sleeves of her thin top and the hem of her shorts, lacerations marred her arms and legs, evidence of the brutal attack. Blonde hair cascaded around her shoulders, a few wisps caught in her long lashes. Eyes the color of the sea bore into him, and he held his breath, mesmerized by their beauty.

She's breathtaking.

He shook his head to clear away his errant thought and assessed her injuries to determine the best course of action. As the Keep's healer, he might be able to save her. "I won't hurt you. I'm here to help."

She didn't move, but her panting breaths continued to rush from her in heavy heaves. Blood trickled down her neck and pooled at the small juncture at her throat.

Craya. Had the Gossum bitten her?

He drew his hand toward her face.

A soft keening sound rushed from her lips. Her fingers jerked, as if she tried to defend herself, but she didn't have the strength. Light reflected off her bracelet. Small jewels tracked around her wrist and along a chain attached to a small ring on her finger. Her adornment was eerily similar to the marking on his hand. His mouth went dry.

He focused on her features once again.

Fear reflected in the depths of her eyes. He'd scared her, and that he couldn't deal with.

His marking for empathy burned on the back of his hand. He placed his palm on her forearm, sending a round of soothing warmth into her skin. "I'm a healer. Let me assist you."

Her breathing calmed and something akin to trust reflected in her eyes.

With gentle care, he swiped her hair away from her shoulders. Ragged and raw, four puncture wounds marred the skin along her throat. Blood oozed from the damaged tissue.

Gossum were all male for a reason. Human females didn't survive the transition.

Anger, bitter and hot, swelled through Gaetan. This was his fault. Too many had suffered because of him. He smashed his fist into the soft loam.

She parted her lips, and a soft rasp escaped. "H...help me." Her soft words called to him on a level he didn't quite understand.

A thought sparked, bringing with it a tinge of hope. The idea grew, solidifying in his mind. He met her gaze, focusing on the brilliant swirls of green. "I might be able to save you, but you can't return to your former life. You'll have to come with me. Do you want to live?"

Nikki struggled to move her arms, her legs. Pain, hot like fire, burned at her neck. With each breath, her strength waned. *I'm dying...* The realization sent a shot of adrenaline through her veins. Perhaps this was some kind of bizarre nightmare. Yet, deep inside, she understood this was all too real.

"Do you want to live?" The strange male's deep voice filtered inside, calming her.

Everything had happened so fast. The fight between the preternatural creatures in the woods, the brutal attack, and now this strong, fearless man, offering her a chance to live. Yet, he'd said she'd have to give up her life, go with him. Her mind raced, searching for answers and alternatives. There were none.

With the moon behind him, his features were cast in shadows, yet she had the sense she could trust him. "Do I...have a...choice?"

"A choice is what I'm offering you. You must decide, now, before your preference is no longer an option." His soothing words settled into her soul.

Numbness teased at her thoughts, dragging her down and drowning her in its undertow. More than anything, Nikki wanted to experience love. She inhaled a ragged breath. "I want to...live."

He slid his arm around her waist and drew her to him. His muscles bulged under his shirt, and a wave of security and peace crested over her. Gently, he stroked her hair away from her face. His fingers brushed against her cheek, thoughtful and tender.

"What is your name?" His breath tickled her ear.

"Nikki."

"Nikki. Such an unusual name, one I haven't heard before. I'm going to seal your injury with my saliva. It will help you heal." His lips caressed her skin and his tongue, warm and wet, slid over her wounds. The sensation lit up her nerves, and she melted into him, wanting more of his sweet kisses.

"Nikki is short for N...Nicole." She choked on her words, unable to focus on anything but his mouth, his tongue, his soft, affectionate ministrations.

"Nicole." His voice rumbled in his chest. The vibration travelled between them, and beneath her thin shirt her nipples puckered. "Such a beautiful name. That suits you much better."

His lips returned to her throat. A soft pulling sensation at the wounds made her head swim. With each tug, the pain lessened. He swirled his tongue over her injury once more then drew back to look at her. "How do you feel?"

Like I died and went to heaven. That, however, wasn't an appropriate response. "Alive."

"That's good, very good indeed." The rumbling of his voice reverberated between them, settling into her chest, warming her. This man, this stranger, made her feel more alive than she'd ever felt in her life, and she didn't even know his name.

Unable to see him clearly, she trailed her finger over the rough stubble on his chin. "What's your name?"

He wrapped his fingers around hers, stopping her exploration of him. "Gaetan."

"Gaetan. I've never heard that name before."

"Then I guess we're even." He held her close for a moment longer, studying her. "It's time to go. Can you stand?"

"I'm not sure."

He gripped a long staff with a large gem at the handle and rose to his feet. A cringe crossed his features, and he rubbed his knee. After uncurling his fingers, he held out his rough, calloused palm.

The urge to bolt flushed through Nikki's veins, yet she remained nestled in the small copse, surrounded by the trees and this man who had touched her so tenderly. On a level deep inside, she understood she was different, changed. Her old desire to apply for the management job and move up in the company seemed so distant, like it was someone else's dream. There was no going back. He'd given her an option, life or death, and his requirement was clear. She must go with him.

Her throat tightened. Here was the moment of truth—her new life. Taking a leap of faith, she trailed her fingers alongside his until their palms rested together. Even in the dim light, the smile that bloomed on his lips was visible. Oh, how those luscious lips curled.

He drew her to her feet. Cool night air wafted around the exposed skin on her bare arms and legs. The scratches burned, reminding her of the creature that had attacked her not long ago. She tensed and glanced into the forest. "What were they? Will they return?"

Dizziness, part born of her weakened state, part born of her fear, clouded her vision. Her knees buckled. With a quick tug, Gaetan pulled her against him. Her cheek rested against his chest. "It's okay. I've got you."

The warmth of his skin against hers was a welcome balm. She felt needed, wanted, cared for in his arms, and despite her independent nature urging her to push away from him, she longed to stay.

"You're not out of the woods yet, figuratively and literally." He stroked her hair, and she burrowed deeper into his chest. "We need to get you to the infirmary. Come with me, this way."

With one hand on his cane and the other wrapped around her waist, he led her away from the small copse and the fallen log. Not far away, mist gathered between the trees. More appeared, swirling into a ball. Enraptured by its beauty, she couldn't look away.

Tugging her forward, he approached the strange mist. Images within the vapor appeared—cave walls, a platform, and a small man with red hair and a matching goatee. He swirled his hands over a large stone, a soft orange glow emanating from the surface. His eyes widened. "Hurry, Gaetan, hurry."

Behind them, tree branches jostled. Eerie, familiar chuffs filled the air. The creatures...

As a scream ripped from her throat, Gaetan jumped into the mist and the vast cave beyond, taking her with him.

CHAPTER 6

*G*aetan landed on the cold stone floor. Pain spiked through his leg, sending a wave of bright lights flitting across his vision. The urge to cry out bubbled in his throat, but he clamped his mouth shut. He had a patient to help who would soon become a Dren.

Cool and damp, the portal's remaining mist swirled around him, coating his skin in a wet sheen. He welcomed the brief respite. Even now, he couldn't believe he'd given Nicole his saliva, but she'd needed it to counteract the Gossum's venom and seal the wound.

If he hadn't made a noise, the Gossum would never have found her. The weight of his deed settled over his shoulders, heavy and firm. She was his responsibility now, just like Ginnia. He'd taken Nicole from her life, brought her into his, with its war and death. Bile rose in his throat, bitter and hot.

"Gaetan! I couldn't believe it when I got yer message…" Rin stood next to the porte stanen, the red sunstones still glowing on the surface. His scrunched brow accentuated the lines around his eyes. "Say, who do ya have there?"

One arm wrapped around her for support, Gaetan drew Nicole from the platform. His cane tapped along the stone with each step, echoing against the chamber walls. She trembled in his arms, no doubt from her ordeal and the remnants of the Gossum venom. The need to get her to the infirmary urged him onward.

"This is Nicole. I don't have time to explain, but she needs medical attention." He glanced toward the corridor. "Is there a warrior nearby that can transport her?"

"I...I can walk." Nicole struggled against him, but her efforts were weak, ineffective.

He refused to let her go, fearing she'd fall and injure herself further. In truth, he enjoyed how her warm, soft curves pressed against him. He leaned close to her ear and whispered, "You're still suffering from the Gossum bite. Please, let me help you."

She relented, sagging into him further. "I'm so...tired."

A strange flutter beat in his chest. He didn't have time to analyze the emotion.

Rin stepped closer, his large blue eyes widening. He studied Nicole. "She's human. What did ya go and bring a human into the Keep for?"

Gaetan smacked his cane against the floor. "Rin, call a warrior. We need assistance."

"The warriors left. Gone. Out searchin' for Anlon and yerself." Rin's mouth quivered. "I heard about Noeh. He's dead, along with Melissa."

Gaetan's vision pinpointed. In the rush of the battle and rescuing Nicole, he'd forgotten about Noeh and Melissa's special bond. They shared a soul. When Noeh died, so did Melissa. A pain, greater than any he'd ever experienced, pierced his heart. Their deaths were his fault. If he'd watched Anlon like he was supposed to none of this would've happened.

"Gaetan?" Rin touched his arm. "Are ya all right?"

He forced himself to focus on the little Jixie. The concern reflected in Rin's eyes just about broke him. He didn't deserve anyone's sympathy. With a soft tug, he tightened his grip around Nicole's waist. She moaned, but otherwise didn't stir.

"My friend, do we still have a wheelchair here?"

Rin straightened his shoulders, and his eyes brightened. "Yes, I'll get it for ya." The small male scurried behind an alcove. A moment later, he wheeled a chair toward them as fast as his little legs would go.

Gaetan helped Nicole into the seat. Her head lolled to the side, and her blonde hair covered her face, hiding her features from him. Before he could think better of his actions, he brushed the fine, golden strands away.

Long, luscious lashes graced her cheek. Beneath them, the heat of a fever tinged her face pink. Plump lips begged for a male's kiss, and he had the sudden urge to bend down, find out if they were as soft and supple as they appeared.

A tic started in his jaw. A male like him, with his disfigured leg and addiction, was not something she needed. Although he'd given her some of his saliva to slow the venom, if she were to survive, she required the special herbs and medicines in the infirmary.

He placed his cane over the chair's handle and pushed her toward the exit. At the room's entrance, he peered at Rin. "Any luck on Anlon's whereabouts?"

Rin shook his head. "Not yet."

Gaetan's throat thickened. "Keep me posted." Without a glance, he headed for the infirmary, praying he didn't lose Nicole as well.

The rich, deep baritone of a man's voice filtered into Nikki's mind. Soft and comforting, his words settled into her psyche, sending a gentle warmth through her entire being. She'd never felt so relaxed, so content, so at peace. All she wanted was to stay in this blissful state, enjoy more of his comforting tone.

Light, faint at first, but growing brighter by the second, warmed the skin on her face. An orange glow penetrated through her eyelids. Jerking awake with a start, she inhaled, and the scent of tarragon swept across her senses. As she opened her eyes wider, her vision focused on a tall, handsome male.

He had short brown hair with a spot of gray at his temple. A broad nose and a strong jawline defined his features despite the few age lines etched in his cheeks, but his pale blue eyes, the soothing color of aquamarine, drew her in. He smiled, and laugh lines formed around his mouth, accentuating his full lips.

Deep inside, on a level she didn't quite understand, she recognized him. Still lost in her blissful state, she glanced over his shoulder. Tension formed at the back of her neck, and she looked around.

Walls, made of stone, enclosed them in a room filled with long tables. A tall cabinet rested against the wall. Bottles, beakers, and an assortment of herbs lined the shelves. A woman with shoulder-length blonde hair leaned over a cabinet strewn with bandages, surgical knives, and medical supplies.

Stones embedded in the walls flared to life, brightening and warming the room. This wasn't like any place she'd ever been before. *Maybe I'm still in my dream.* Yet, she didn't believe that. She returned her attention to the man.

"Wh… Where am I?" Her words squeezed out her parched throat and came out hoarse.

"You're in the infirmary. How do you feel?" The man's consoling voice sounded familiar. He was the one who'd calmed her.

She peered at him. "Thirsty. How did I get here? Who are you…"

Memories flooded her mind. The mudslide…hiding by a downed tree…the strange creatures…the attack…her rescuer… A shot of adrenaline flooded through her, and she kicked out, fear overriding all common sense. Unbalanced and unaware of her surroundings, she slipped from the table. A sheet twisted between her legs, sending her careening toward the ground.

The man wrapped her in his strong arms, preventing her from crashing to the stone floor. He held her in his embrace, and his minty breath caressed her cheek.

"I've got you. Don't be afraid." His soothing voice filtered over her like a cool breeze, calming her racing heart.

Gaetan... His name flashed through her mind. "You're Gaetan. You're the one who saved me from..." She choked on the words.

"Come. This must be unsettling. You'll have all your answers and more." He pulled her to a standing position, and her hands landed on his broad chest. Even through his woven shirt, his warmth lit up her fingertips. Before she could process her reaction to him, he released her. All she wanted was to crawl back into his arms.

Nikki ran her fingers over her throat where the creature had bitten her. The skin was smooth and unblemished. She glanced at her arms then at her legs. All the cuts and scratches were gone. "How did my injuries heal?"

The woman she'd seen before stepped forward and handed her a glass of water. "The water should help with your thirst. My name is Sheri. I'll do everything I can to make you feel comfortable here."

That small gesture eased some of Nikki's anxiety. She took a sip of the water, her fingers still shaking from her ordeal. When she was done, Sheri took the glass and gave her arm a gentle squeeze. "You don't look too worse for wear. As for your injuries, Gaetan is our master haelen, or healer, the best in the Keep."

"The Keep?" She glanced from Sheri to Gaetan.

His beautiful eyes bore into her, as if he could see into her soul. "You've slept for several hours. What do you remember from last night?"

"Everything," she whispered. The sudden urge to feel his touch again whipped through her. Before she could stop herself, she placed her hand on his arm. "You saved me."

A flinch crossed his features. He stepped away and headed over to the counter, his cane knocking against the stone floor in counterpoint with each step.

"Do you regret saving me?" A lump formed in her throat.

He whirled around faster than she thought possible. His eyes sparked with flecks of amber. "I'm a healer. Saving others is what I do."

The lines along his cheeks deepened, speaking of an anguish so profound his pain was palpable in the air.

Sheri touched her arm. "Gaetan tells me your name is Nicole."

Nikki dragged her attention away from Gaetan and focused on Sheri. "Please, call me Nikki. You said I'm in a 'Keep.' When can I go home?"

A knowing look flashed between Sheri and Gaetan. Dread trickled down her spine. She gnawed on the inside of her cheek. "Tell me."

Sheri patted her hand on one of the medical tables. "Come, sit down. There's a lot you need to hear."

Nikki assessed both Sheri and Gaetan. Both had rigid postures, their mouths set in stern lines. She'd get faster results if she complied with the request. With a quick huff, she slid onto the bed. Carved from the stone, the cool, smooth surface was a welcome relief to her overheated skin. Her legs dangled over the edge. Nervous energy had her kicking her feet to and fro. "I'm ready anytime you are."

Gaetan sat on the edge of a stool, the seat worn on one side. "The creature that attacked you was a Gossum. Once human, he was changed by another of their kind through a bite." A tic formed in his jaw, and he rubbed at his knee. Four dark lines, like tattoos, ran from each knuckle, merging at the wrist then disappearing up his arm beneath his shirt sleeve.

She traced the rhinestones in her bracelet. They seemed eerily similar to the dark lines on the back of his hand.

He cleared his throat. "One bit you. Human females don't survive the change. I took a chance, giving you some of my saliva in hopes you'd live long enough to arrive at the Keep where I could treat you with my special medicines and herbs. I was successful. As for you returning to your human world..."

Her thoughts froze and it took a moment for his words to sink in. "I remember now. I can't go home. What I saw wasn't my imagination. Monsters really do exist, don't they?"

He nodded, and the compassion in his eyes tugged at her heart. "They aren't the only...non-human creatures on this planet."

An image of the large, hairy beast she'd seen in the forest crossed her mind. She sucked in a sharp gasp and gaped at him.

"What do you mean? Are you one?" A part of her didn't want to hear his answer, and she held her breath.

His mouth thinned. With great effort, he pushed away from the stool and strode toward her with his cane. He stilled, mere inches away from her. Warmth radiated from him, cascading over her, drawing her in. "Sheri was human once, but I wasn't and, now, neither are you."

Blood pounded in Nikki's ears, drowning out all sounds. Her vision pinpointed and she focused on his eyes, using them like a lifeline to reality, holding on for dear life. "What am I?"

"You are like Sheri, a Dren—" His attention drew to the wall. One of the yellow stones blinked, flaring to life with a rhythmic pulse. "*Craya!*" He held up one finger. "One moment."

She glanced at Sheri. With her blonde hair, pale skin, and hazel eyes, Sheri appeared human. What made her a Dren? She opened her mouth to ask, but Gaetan cleared his throat.

"I'm sorry. I have to leave." Over his piercing eyes etched with worry, his brow furrowed.

"Is everything okay?" Sheri raised an eyebrow.

"The warriors have returned. Saar called a council meeting. I must attend." He shuffled to the door, the muscles in his shoulders bunching with each step.

Although Nikki couldn't see his injured leg covered in long pants, there was no outward appearance to indicate there was anything wrong with him. Yet, there must be a reason he used a cane. What had this proud man gone through in his life? Whatever he was to others, to her, he was her savior. She longed to understand him better.

He halted and turned to Sheri. "I'd appreciate it if you filled Nicole in on the details and find her a room."

"Of course. I'd love to. It's nice to have another Dren among us." Sheri studied Nikki's clothes. "Besides, it looks like we're about the same size. I have just the outfit in mind."

Gaetan met Nikki's gaze once again. For a brief moment, heat flared in the deep recesses of his eyes. Warmth filtered through Nikki, as if he'd caressed every nerve in her body. Unbidden desire, strong and powerful, pooled low in her core.

He broke the contact and walked through the doorway. His hobbled gait echoed down the corridor. Despite that she knew little about him, Nikki longed for his touch with a desperation that rattled her to her soul.

CHAPTER 7

"*This* must be overwhelming for you. I've been there. It gets better. Trust me." Sheri's welcoming smile did little to tone down the swarm of butterflies in Nikki's stomach.

"Overwhelmed is an understatement." Still seated on the medical bed, nervous energy nagged at her, and Nikki kicked her feet.

Sheri held out her hand. "C'mon. I'll take you to your room and explain what I can."

Impatience had Nikki gnawing on the inside of her cheek. "You said we're both Dren. What does that mean? What am I?"

"I'll explain along the way. There's a shower waiting for you, I promise." Sheri winked and crooked her finger, encouraging Nikki.

Nikki laughed despite herself, but the tension in her shoulders didn't ease. She sighed and peered at her tattered and ragged clothes. Getting out of this outfit would be a good thing. "A shower sounds great." With more courage than she felt, she slid from the bed and gripped the other woman's hand.

Sheri tugged her toward the exit. Nikki glanced around the infirmary one last time. The beds lined up in rows spoke of much illness or…war. Goosebumps formed along her arms.

They passed through the open doorway into a long corridor.

Yellow gemstones lined the walls in an intricate pattern. One flared to life. She stopped and touched the stone. Warmth emanated from the gem. "What are these?"

"Sunstones. They provide heat and light in the underground Keep."

"They're beautiful." Nikki couldn't help but smile at the small wonder.

"They are also used for communication. The Stiyaha use the stones to send messages throughout the Keep."

"Sti-ya-ha?" The word sounded foreign on her tongue.

"Stiyaha are the shape-shifting warriors that live here. They fight for their goddess, Alora, in a war over Earth's water, but...I get ahead of myself. Let's—"

"Is Gaetan a Stiyaha?" The question slipped from her lips before she could stop herself. Her cheeks heated.

Sheri peered at Nikki, a knowing glimmer in her eyes. "Yes, he's a Stiyaha. As you now know, he's also our healer, and the Keep's oldest resident."

"How old is he?" As much as she wanted to know about herself and what she'd become, she wanted to understand Gaetan, the man who'd saved her.

"Over seven hundred years old."

Nikki gasped. "Wow, that's a far cry from my twenty-five years. How long do they live?"

"Well over two thousand years. C'mon, let's keep moving." Sheri headed down the long corridor.

Nikki caught up to and walked next to Sheri, her mind reeling from what little she'd heard so far. "I have so many questions."

"Let's start with the Dren. That's what you will become soon, once Gaetan's saliva works its way through your blood." Sheri glanced at her. "You will receive a special power, one unique to you."

"A special power? Like what?" Maybe being Dren wasn't such a bad thing after all.

"Well, let me show you mine." Sheri stopped and held out her hands. "Step back."

Nikki took a step backward and focused on Sheri's hands.

37

Sparks of electricity crackled from her fingertips, lighting up the corridor in a brilliant, blinding light. Nikki gasped, excitement tingling along her nerves. "Wow! That's impressive."

"I look forward to seeing your new talent, once you discover it." Sheri smiled and motioned for them to continue along their path.

"How long will it take for my power to show?" It was all so unreal, Nikki had a hard time accepting her new reality.

"That depends. It could show up anytime, but will increase in force and intensity once you feed."

"Feed? Do you mean 'eat'?"

Sheri's lips drew into a thin line. "No, I mean 'feed'."

A coil of dread curled inside Nikki. She stopped and gripped Sheri's hand. "Please, explain."

"You'll have to feed from a male, drink his blood, in order to survive."

Dizziness crested over Nikki, and she placed her hand along the stone wall to steady herself. "How? Why?"

"You'll receive fangs, and—"

Nikki's pulse spiked, and her breaths rushed in and out of her lungs. "I...I'm a vampire?"

Sheri gripped her shoulders. "It's not what you think. We're Dren, not vampires, and we don't kill."

"What if I elect not to 'feed,' as you put it?"

Sheri sighed and released her grip. She pinched the bridge of her nose. "If you don't feed, you'll go insane. The timeframe is different for everyone, but it can occur in as little as a week. Drinking blood is actually very erotic and pleasurable for both parties."

An image of Gaetan flashed through Nikki's mind. He held her in his embrace, his tongue licking her wound, his lips pressing against her skin in gentle caresses. Warmth spread over her skin. Was that what it would be like to 'feed'? If so, she could get on board with that.

"One other thing, you'll never have to worry about diseases as we are immune to human ailments. The one bummer though is that it's unlikely you'll ever conceive."

"Well, that's good to know." After being raised by her alcoholic father, Nikki had never wanted to have kids.

Footsteps echoed from down the corridor, approaching at a fast clip. Two figures came into view—one male, one female. Both had an air of grace around them, almost feline in nature. With an authoritative stride and determined features, the male's cold, hard stare sent a chill over Nikki's shoulders. Next to him, the female's fast-clipped walk made her chin-length hair bob, and the red barrette at her temple caught the light.

Sheri stepped forward to greet them. "Demir, Aramie, so good to see you. I want you to meet Nikki. Gaetan—"

"Saved her from the Gossum." A quirk formed along the corner of Demir's mouth. "News travels fast within the Keep, especially if Rin's involved."

"Welcome, Nikki. So pleased to meet you." The dark-haired female smiled, and the man next to her, Demir, wrapped his arm around her waist.

"Thank you. It's nice to meet you." Warning bells rang in the back of Nikki's mind. This was all so strange. Was she already insane? The idea zipped through her mind, but after everything that had happened between her, Gaetan, and the scary Gossum, she didn't doubt her sanity.

Sheri glanced from Aramie to Demir. "I'm taking our new resident to her quarters, but if you have the time, I'm sure she'd love to hear some details about the Panthera."

"Perhaps we'll see you in the Grand Hall for the evening repast. We're on our way to Noeh's...to the throne room." Demir placed his hand out in a gesture for Aramie to proceed. He gave a quick nod. "Until then."

As they disappeared down the hallway, Nikki turned toward Sheri. "Just a couple of the Keep's residents?"

Sheri stifled a laugh. "Demir is the Panthera Pride leader and Aramie is his mate. They are shape-shifting panthers and great warriors. C'mon, we're almost to my room. I've got some clothes that I think will fit you, and there's someone I want you to meet."

They walked in silence for a few minutes. Nikki's mind swirled with everything she'd heard, seen, and experienced since the mudslide on the hill. My, how her life had changed.

Several doors lined the wall in this portion of the corridor. Sheri stopped in front of one and gripped the handle. With a quick twist, she pushed open the door. Loud barking emerged from the room.

"Hey, Coop! Good boy." A large German Shepherd jumped up and placed its front paws on Sheri's thighs. His tail wagged with an energy that spoke of his happiness to see his mistress. "Coop's an ex-police dog, but he won't hurt you. Will you, boy?"

Nikki strode into the room, and Coop focused on her. He chuffed and glanced at Sheri. "She's a friend, boy."

As if he'd understood, Coop sat on his haunches. His tail thumped against the floor in rhythmic beats.

"Can I pet him?" Nikki's chest swelled. She loved animals. They didn't judge and were always there for comfort.

"Of course. He loves the attention." Sheri stepped away from Coop and further into the room.

Nikki held out her hand. Coop's wet nose tickled her fingers as he sniffed her. Satisfied she was a friend, he nuzzled up to her. She petted his soft fur, enjoying the simple, familiar action. Nikki peered around the room.

A bed stood to one side, the covers ruffled as if someone hadn't bothered to straighten the sheets. Two dressers rested against the wall. An assortment of bottles, make-up, and brushes scattered across the tops. A pile of clothes lay in a heap close by. Sheri stood next to a small table, a bowl of fruit placed in the center. The bright red strawberry on top caught Nikki's attention. Her mouth watered. Food...

Sheri snapped her fingers. "Coop, sit."

Coop whined then trotted to a pet bed situated near one of the dressers, a bowl of water nearby. He circled for a moment then settled into place. His sad eyes indicated he wasn't happy with being dismissed.

Sheri cleared her throat. "Are you hungry?"

She eyed the strawberry. "Yes, a little."

"Please, have something. The evening repast isn't for a few hours." Sheri sat down at the table and nudged the bowl, encouraging her.

Nikki couldn't resist. She pulled out the other chair, the feet scraping against the stone floor, and sat down. The bright red berry called to her, so she plucked it from the bowl and popped the small fruit into her mouth. The sweet juice lit up her senses. She had another and another. The gum line over her front teeth ached, and some of the juice dribbled from the corner of her mouth.

Sheri tapped the edge of the bowl. "Do your teeth hurt?"

Nikki stilled and met her gaze. "How did you know?"

Sheri smiled. "Don't forget, I'm Dren, too. I went through the change and know the signs." She pointed to the strawberries. "As much as you like the food and think you're hungry, what you really want is a male's blood."

Nikki wiped the wetness from her mouth. The juice reminded her of blood. A sickening twinge tugged at her insides. "You're telling me I really need to bite someone?"

"Yes." Sheri's voice was low, controlled, full of compassion. "...and not just someone. A male."

"You mean a man." A strange giggle rose in Nikki. Macabre, that's what this was.

"Men are human. They are called 'males' among our kind." Sheri's features were drawn, serious. This wasn't a game, not to her. "Let me see your palm." She held out her hand, her fingers curling, encouraging.

Nikki placed her hand in Sheri's, palm up. Sheri tightened her grip. "Look. What do you see?"

Nikki glanced at her palm. "Nothing."

Sheri held up her other hand. "Do you see the faint 'M'?"

Nikki studied her new friend's palm. Indeed, there was a faint outline of the letter 'M' etched there. She blinked.

"You see it. Good. Now, look at your palm. You have one, too."

The faint outline, not quite as clear as Sheri's, marred her skin. She jerked her hand away then rubbed at the mark. The skin burned, hot and fevered. "What is that?"

"I wish I knew, but I have one, you have one, and Melissa…" Sheri choked on her words. She stood up and placed her fist against her mouth.

Nikki rose from her seat, walked around the table and wrapped her arms around Sheri's shoulders, drawing her in for a hug. "I didn't mean to upset you. I—"

"It's not you. Here," Sheri pulled back and grasped Nikki's hand, "let's finish our earlier conversation. Although you can still eat normal food, you will need to feed from a male, soon. Would you like me to introduce you to some of our warriors? I'm sure there are several that would love to oblige you."

The thought of drinking a strange males, blood made Nikki's skin crawl. "You said this was an intimate, personal act between a male and a female."

"Yes, and you never know, you may even find a mate among them. At the very least you'll have a bond, a connection that will allow you to track each other—"

"Gaetan. I want Gaetan." Nikki blurted the words before she'd had time to think. Heat rushed up her neck and into her cheeks.

Sheri's assessing gaze burrowed into her.

Nikki glanced at the floor. "I mean, if he's willing."

"Well, I could certainly ask him for you."

"Yes, thank you." Nikki's chest swelled at the memory of Gaetan's lips at her throat, his tender kisses as he'd sealed her wounds. The thought of kissing him, tasting him, sinking her teeth into his soft flesh— She stilled. Her gums ached, and she ran her tongue over the sensitive tissue. No fangs. *Thank God.*

Sheri touched one of the sunstones embedded along the cave's walls and furrowed her brow. After several long moments, she turned her attention to Nikki. "Gaetan agreed. He said he'd meet you in your room before the evening repast. We should get moving, so you have time for a bath and maybe a nap beforehand."

Nikki smiled. "A bath sounds wonderful."

"Oh!" Sheri's mouth quirked at the corner. "I can't forget why we stopped here in the first place. Let me get you some clothes."

She tracked to the shorter of the two dressers and yanked on one of the drawers. It screeched open, in need of some oil. Sheri rummaged around then held up a pair of dark slacks and a beautiful blue sweater. "These should do the trick."

Nikki strode to the other female. "Thank you, Sheri. You've been nothing but kind."

"You're very welcome."

An overwhelming sense of gratitude washed over Nikki, and the skin on her arms tingled.

Coop barked and cocked his head.

The water in his bowl rippled. A few drops slipped over the rim dampening the stone floor.

Sheri inhaled. "Did you just have a strong emotion?"

Nikki's pulse picked up speed, and the water rippled faster. "Y... yes. I was grateful for your kindness and..."

Sheri wrapped her arms around Nikki's shoulders and drew her in for a quick hug. She pulled back. Happiness reflected in her eyes. "I think we just discovered your power. It looks like you have the ability to control water."

"Really?" Nikki's mouth went dry.

Sheri nodded. "Practice, see what you can do. We need to go, though. There's so much more I need to tell you, and we must get you dolled up for your meeting with Gaetan." Mirth danced in her eyes.

Gaetan...

Nikki's desire to see him again went against her independent nature. She didn't need a male, didn't want one in her life, yet she couldn't deny how she craved his touch, his voice, his gentle caress. She fisted her hand. This needed to be about nourishment, nothing more.

CHAPTER 8

Moonlight pierced between the Rolmdew trees' branches, lighting up the Lemurian landscape. Alora stepped onto the suspended walkway and the wooden planks swayed under her weight. She gripped the handrail and peered over the edge. Fifty feet below, a thick blanket of underbrush dotted Lemuria's surface.

A distant howl broke the quiet night, joined by another. Rhondo beasts.

Her pulse quickened. Thank goodness they couldn't climb. That's why all of Lemuria's population dwelled within the Rolmdew trees.

"What is it?" Carine's soft voice was in stark contrast to the evil beasts'.

Alora turned to face her friend. Carine's blue hair cascaded around her shoulders, the ends snapping to and fro, displaying her unease. Alora smiled to comfort her friend. "Did you enjoy Janalla's Place?"

A smile tugged at Carine's mouth, and she nodded. "Thank you for taking me. The food is fabulous. Zedron loves the place..." Her smile faltered.

Zedron... Alora tightened her hand into a fist. How she hated the *Kasard*. Her opponent in this game for Earth's water, she'd bargained with him for the Ursus queen Kaelyn and Carine, his slave, in exchange for his recording device, the one that proved he'd cheated in the game. Maybe she should've taken Veromé's advice and turned him in to the council, but she'd wanted to make Zedron squirm.

Alora placed her hand on Carine's arm and gave her a gentle squeeze. "Let's not talk about him. We're almost home. I'd love to have some of that muldoberry pie you made. How about you?"

Carine nodded, and her smile returned. "I'd like that very much."

As Alora continued along their path, her mind wandered to her rival. Zedron hadn't put up much of a fight, giving in to her demands all too easily. Veromé, her mate, and the one male she trusted more than anyone, had warned her the council might think she'd used coercion to get what she'd wanted and that Zedron would use that against her. The dinner she'd had churned in her stomach. She needed to strategize her next move.

Carine gasped. "Alora, did you hear that?"

Alora stopped, and the suspension bridge swayed in the breeze. "Hear what?"

A small cry, like the sound of a small child, filtered through the trees.

Carine blinked. "That."

The cries intensified, louder and louder, coming from the ground below. The hair at Alora's nape rose.

Before Alora could say a word, Carine sprinted along the bridge's slats to the platform built onto the nearby Rolmdew tree. She gripped the bark and scaled down the trunk. From the planet Arotin, Arotaar's were known for their strength, endurance, and climbing ability.

"Carine! Be careful!" Alora scurried to the platform for a closer look and to support her friend in any way possible.

Carine reached the forest floor and disappeared beneath the small bushes and plants that covered the surface. With each footstep, the dry leaves crackled under her feet. They would announce her location to the rhondo beasts, that is, if the babe's cries hadn't done so already. Alora tightened her grip around the railing.

A rhondo beast's howl echoed into the night, the pitch fevered, excited, and much closer. Another answered, then a third.

"Carine, hurry!" Alora searched the platform, searching for anything she could use as a weapon, but she found only the ropes that tied the platform to the tree. Dread's icy cold fingers traced a path down Alora's spine.

"I found him!" Carine's shout carried above the rhondo beasts' roars.

Not far away, the bushes rustled, the beasts approaching at a rapid pace. Alora shuddered. "Rhondo beasts! Run, Carine, run!"

The babe's cries echoed between the trees. Another couple on a nearby platform turned to stare.

Carine's dark figure emerged from the bushes, a small toddler cradled to her chest. Nestling him in the crook of one elbow, she used her free hand and her feet to scale the tree.

Alora gripped the wooden rail, her nerves strung tight.

A rhondo beast appeared between the bushes, the black, oily skin shining in the moonlight. The muscles in his hind legs tightened, and he lunged into the air.

Alora's pulse spiked.

Carine screamed and almost dropped the babe. The little tyke gripped her sleeve, holding on for dear life.

The rhondo beast's long pointy teeth snapped dangerously close to Carine's feet, but he couldn't reach her. Momentum and gravity drew him to the ground.

His distressed howl rang into the night.

Alora let out a relieved breath. That was too close.

Carine clambered up the Rolmdew tree. When she reached the platform, she handed the small child to Alora. A sudden tingling of surprise raced over Alora's shoulders. Short tufts of blond hair framed the babe's face, his cheeks red from his cries. His eyes were a deep blue, matching those of his father.

"Anlon." Alora choked on his name.

The babe smiled, tears still glistening in his eyes.

Alora's heart melted on the spot. She brought him to her chest and cradled him in her arms. His sweet cinnamon fragrance seeped into her senses. "You're safe now, little one."

Carine climbed onto the platform. Her breaths came out in shallow gasps. "It's been a while since I've climbed like that. Guess I'm out of shape."

Alora blinked then a relieved laugh emerged from her throat. "You risk your life to rescue a small child and that's what you say? Come here." Alora held out her arm, the one that wasn't cradling Anlon.

Carine met Alora's gaze. Uncertainty creased her brow.

Alora stepped to Carine and wrapped her in her embrace, the three of them together. "You're amazing, Carine. Thank you."

Alora released her, and Carine's eyes were damp. She glanced at the ground. "It's what anyone would do."

Alora placed her finger under Carine's chin, lifting her gaze. "Not true. Very few would've done what you did. Most Lemurians fear the rhondo beasts too much, including me."

Carine peered at Anlon. "He's cute. I wonder why he was down there."

"Do you know who this is?" Alora teased Anlon's chin, and he giggled.

Carine shook her head, and the blue ends of her hair sparked. "No. Do you?"

"This is Anlon. He's Noeh and Melissa's son." Alora peered at him. "He must've come through a portal, but nothing like that has ever happened before. Why are you here, little guy?"

As if he'd understood, he smiled and brought a red stone clutched in his hand to his mouth. With a long, wet swipe of his tongue, he licked the smooth surface.

A sunstone...

The need to return home and look into her visus bacin raced through Alora's nerves like a Lemurian tratee fly, quick and forceful. "Let's go. We need to see what's happened on Earth."

CHAPTER 9

Gaetan placed his hand against the door's polished wood. The cool, smooth surface brought back memories of the many times he'd entered the king's throne room and the discussions he'd had with Noeh. Never again. The weight on his shoulders bore down on him, plagued by a guilt he more than deserved.

Voices, heated and rough, penetrated through the crack under the doorframe.

He was late.

With more force than he'd intended, he pushed away from the door. His weight shifted onto his bad leg. Perspiration beaded along his brow. He held his breath as the pain crested then receded. Fingers trembling, he drew his pouch from his pocket, shook out a pill, and popped it into his mouth. The shaking in his hand lessened.

He pulled on his inner resolve and rapped his knuckles against the rough, wooden grain. The double doors swung open. Jax, Noeh's personal assistant, peered up at him. His short, curly hair framed his cherub cheeks and his blue eyes were rimmed red from tears.

"Ooh, Gaetan, yes, yes, please enter. You are expected. Yes, you are." The little Jixie motioned toward a chair. "I saved this seat for you, I did, I did."

Gaetan cleared his throat then stepped across the threshold, his cane leading the way. He settled into the worn, familiar seat. Tense quiet filled the room. The hair at his nape rose.

Saar and Kaelyn stood in the center of the room, tension tightening their features. Demir leaned against Noeh's desk, Aramie at his side. Tanen and a few council members sat in the limited number of chairs. Quentin and several other warriors lined the edges of the room, a couple standing next to the carved statues of warriors from long ago, the resemblance uncanny.

Against the far wall, the king's throne and the queen's chair were eerily empty.

Guilt, familiar, yet unwelcome, settled deeper into Gaetan. He forced himself to breathe and focused on Saar.

"Now that we are all here, let's get down to business. Since Noeh and Melissa are gone," Saar's intense gaze flicked to Gaetan, "we need to crown a temporary leader, at least until we find Anlon. I recommend Kaelyn. As the Ursus queen, she should rule."

Collective gasps erupted from the group. Silence expanded in the room, deafening in its stillness.

Someone coughed.

Saar's brow furrowed. A low growl eased from his throat.

Kaelyn raised her chin. "Do you hesitate because I'm female?"

One of the council members, Skylar, cleared his throat. "No, it's because you aren't Stiyaha."

A tittering of voices in agreement filled the large space.

Irritation flared along Gaetan's nerves. Whether Kaelyn was Ursus or Stiyaha shouldn't matter. Royalty was in her blood. Gaetan opened his mouth to voice his thoughts, but caught Skylar's disapproving gaze. The male tugged at his collar then glanced away, his lip curling with distaste.

Over the hundreds of years Gaetan had lived in the Keep, he'd earned respect from the Keep's residents. To see the blatant disregard in a male he'd known for so long was unbearable. A soul-wrenching ache built in Gaetan's chest. He adjusted himself in the chair and leaned against his cane, using the crutch for more than just his leg.

49

Tanen closed the book on his lap. The sound echoed around the room. "Why not you, Saar? You are our finest warrior and our Commander of Arms."

"I cannot sit here." Saar pointed at Noeh's throne. "For generations we've honored the royal family. Alora has made it clear she expects only royal blood to rule."

Demir cleared his throat. "Good thing I'm not royalty or my ass would be in that throne."

"Demir!" Aramie nudged him and shook her head.

He shrugged. "From what I can tell, Kaelyn did a fabulous job calming everyone when the news of Noeh's and Melissa's deaths broke. Her ability to rally the troops proves her leadership ability. I, for one, support the recommendation."

Uncertainty cloaked the room like a heavy mist. Council members and warriors glanced at each other. Now was Gaetan's opportunity.

He tapped his cane against the stone floor, drawing attention to himself. "Kaelyn is Saar's mate. Noeh trusted Saar more than anyone in the Keep." Gaetan's throat constricted, and he had to stop, swallow the bitterness in his mouth. Once he'd shared that revered place with the Commander of Arms. "If Saar believes Kaelyn should be our leader, then I support him and her."

Kaelyn nodded at Gaetan, determination glinting in her eyes. "My father and mother, King Arbane and Queen Entrania, taught me through example of what it means to rule. If you choose to accept me, I will lay down my life for each and every one of you. I vow it."

Saar stepped away from the throne and surveyed everyone in the room. "Let's vote. All in favor of selecting Kaelyn as our queen say 'aye'."

Several voices spoke at once, their assent filling the room.

"Anyone opposed, speak now."

Silence.

Quentin drew his sword and pressed the tip to the floor. He bowed on one knee. "Queen Kaelyn, I pledge my loyalty to you, now and forever." He slid his finger along the blade's sharp edge. Blood pooled along the cut, and he drew his finger across his forehead and down his nose in the traditional symbol of Lemuria.

The other warriors followed suit.

Gaetan rose from the chair and kneeled. As his knee connected with the stone floor, pain rippled up his leg. White spots flitted over his vision, but he forced himself to breathe. "My queen."

"Please rise, everyone." Kaelyn glanced from one to another, holding each male's gaze for a moment before moving on. "I make you a vow, a promise. I will not sit," she pointed to the throne, "in that seat until we find Anlon, the true heir, and then I will rule only until he comes of age to take the throne himself."

The atmosphere in the room shifted. Respect for her was visible in all their faces.

Gaetan smiled. She would make a remarkable queen, of that he had no doubt.

Tanen cleared his throat. "We should prepare for the death ceremony—"

"Tanen, as much as I understand your need to honor the dead, and believe me, I do, we must concentrate on the living. We'll postpone the ceremony until Anlon is found. The babe is our number one priority." Kaelyn pointed toward the warriors. "Get some rest, we leave at nightfall to resume the search."

The need to right his wrong burned inside Gaetan. "I'm coming, too."

"Stay here, Gaetan. We need you in the infirmary in case..." Kaelyn sighed. "I know you want to help, but your skills are better served here. Gaetan, you did nothing wrong."

Craya! Yes he had. He'd wiped out the entire royal family because of his mistake. His grip tightened around his staff to the point the wood creaked.

Sharp glances and a few terse grumbles emitted from the warriors as they headed for the exit.

Tanen turned his head, refusing to meet Gaetan's gaze.

Demir shrugged and motioned for Aramie to precede him.

Saar shook his head, his scar tight against his skin.

Heat raced up Gaetan's back and over his shoulders, burning his ears.

They all blamed him. He absorbed the guilt, let it fester in his soul, the pain building to an unbearable level. After exiting the room as fast as his leg would allow he leaned against the wall, his breath heaving from his lungs.

I must do something. He pounded his fist against his thigh. The edge of his palm smacked into the round, hard stone hidden in his pocket. *The blue sunstone...*

He retrieved the cursed gem from its hiding spot and studied it in the light. Shades of blue reflected off the walls with an eerie glow. Noeh had entrusted him with its care. In this, he would not fail. A passage from an old scripture dashed through his mind.

"Tenida raised the blue crystal into the night air. Its brilliance outshone the moon. The stone had healed Grian, the greatest of warriors, the one who'd sacrificed himself for another. Standing at the base of a large waterfall, the old haelen threw the crystal into the pool to hide it from the enemy. A brilliant flash of light erupted from the water, turning the color to a deep blue and stopping the waterfall's flow. The healer spoke, his voice booming through the trees. "The stone shall rest here until needed once again."

Gaetan's mission was to find Anlon, but if he got the chance, he'd throw that cursed stone back where it came from—Blue Pool. At sundown, he'd leave with the others, with or without their permission, but first, he had a promise to fulfill. *Nicole...*

At the thought of the young human female, turned Dren, a rush of adrenaline flushed through him. He was responsible for her, and he wouldn't shirk his duty. After what he'd done to Ginnia, his sister had given him plenty of practice with accountability. The marking for responsibility etched on his hand burned hot and fevered. As he peered at it, the line faded, along with his hope.

~

Kaelyn focused on Gaetan as the male shuffled past the two carved statues that graced the entrance to the throne room. His features were drawn, tension lines rimming his eyes. An ache built in the back of her throat. Although she hadn't known him long, she'd grown to care for the Keep's healer.

"You're deep in thought, little bear. What's on your mind?" Saar wrapped his arm around her waist and drew her to him. The comforting gesture eased the tension in her muscles. She snuggled against him, leaning her head on his shoulder.

"I'm worried about Gaetan." She pulled away enough to peer at Saar. "You know him better than I. Does he seem all right?"

A soft sigh eased from him. "This can't be easy for Gaetan. Noeh was like a son to him."

Kaelyn trailed a finger over his chin, along the edge of his scar. "...and Anlon. I know Gaetan adored the little tyke. He seems to blame himself."

Saar blinked. "I agree. It wouldn't surprise me if he misunderstood others' concern for him and interpreted it as condemnation. Anlon crawling through the portal could've happened to any of us. From what Noeh said, the newb got into everything."

"We'll keep an eye on him. I don't want Gaetan to suffer needlessly."

Saar kissed her forehead, his lips warm and soft. "Neither do I. Gaetan takes care of everyone else, but never himself. If anyone deserves a break, it's him."

The weight of being the queen bore into her. She was responsible for everyone now. "Still, I worry about him after what happened. I hope he doesn't do something to endanger himself."

CHAPTER 10

*A*lora floundered with the key, her fingers fumbling in the dark. With Anlon cradled in her arms, she couldn't see around his head to the door's latch even with the porch light blazing. She let loose an exaggerated breath and turned to Carine. "Here, will you hold him?"

"Of course." Carine held out her arms, and Alora transferred the little bundle of energy to her friend.

Anlon cooed, his adorable smile pulling at his lips. He pointed to the tall branches rising from the Rolmdew tree. "Tee." He giggled and the gentle sound skipped along the breeze.

Alora shoved the key into the lock and twisted the knob. With a firm push, she rushed into her home. The lights flicked on at the movement, illuminating her living quarters in a soft glow. Her attention tore to her visus bacin, and the hair at her nape rose. *Nothing's wrong, all is fine.*

Somehow, she didn't believe the mantra she'd told herself all the way home. After finding Anlon, her fear that something bad had happened on Earth had only intensified. She rushed to the edge of her scrying bowl and swirled her hands over the water. Nothing happened. Using more force than she'd intended, she pounded her fist against the stone rim, bruising her flesh.

"Can I get you a glass of water?" Carine set Anlon on the floor, and he crawled to the table, hauling himself to his feet. A look of triumph lit his eyes.

The little tyke was adorable, no question about it, but seeing him brought back her fear. Why was he here?

"Water will help, you know, calm you down." Carine's encouraging voice filtered through the room.

Alora leaned over the bowl, her hands still shaking. "Thank you."

Carine retrieved a glass from the cupboard and poured water from the chilled pitcher. She approached, an encouraging smile on her face. "Here."

Alora took the proffered glass and sipped the cool liquid before setting it aside. "I must see what's happened on Earth. What if..." Her throat tightened, and she couldn't complete her sentence.

"Your love for your characters will be your downfall." Like a dark cloud, Zedron's words sped across Alora's mind. Odd how the characters on Earth treated her with such reverence and respect, like a goddess, when she could be killed or die just like anyone else, but that's what had endeared them to her.

Closing her eyes, she drew in a long breath then let it out with a slow exhale, willing her heartbeat to slow. Concentrating on her characters and her love for them, her rhythmic breaths helped calm her nerves. "Let's do this."

Alora held her hands over the still water. With slow, deliberate movements, she swirled her hands, again and again, moving faster with each revolution. The water rippled. Small waves dashed against the bowl's edge. Water sloshed over the rim and onto the wooden floor. Still, she continued.

The rushing water grew louder, more intense, and drowned out Anlon's soft coos.

"Show me," Alora commanded.

The water stilled. In the center of the bowl, a vision appeared.

Alora sensed Carine approach from behind, but her friend kept her distance.

The image solidified. Cave walls, the Keep's porte stanen with its central portal stone, and the stone platform came into view in the Portal Navigation Center. Rin and Gaetan appeared to be in a conversation. Anlon crawled toward the portal, following a red sunstone floating through the air.

Alora drew her gaze away from her visus bacin and focused on Anlon. Even as he tottered across the table, he clutched the red sunstone in his palm. She returned her attention to the vision.

The sunstone levitated over the portal and a blinding red light lit up the scene. Gaetan and Rin shouted and rushed toward Anlon, but they were too late. He crawled up the steps and into the portal.

Alora sighed. "I guess that explains how he arrived here."

Carine placed her hand on Alora's shoulder. "Do you suppose…"

The water in the bowl swirled, the image blurring for a moment before a new one appeared. A forest at night. The scent of pine and dampness carried into the room.

Noeh battled several Gossum. A loud bellow burst from his lips, and he transformed into his beast. Alora flinched, her breath catching when Mauree came into view, drawing a dagger from a pouch at her thigh. Before Alora could blink, the traitorous female launched the blade. It twirled end over end and embedded itself in Noeh's throat.

Alora gasped. Her chest tightened, pain rippling through her as if the dagger had penetrated her skin.

Gossum attacked, tearing into her king. Noeh stiffened then slid to the ground and turned to sand.

Alora's thoughts froze. This didn't happen. It couldn't be real. Yet, her visus bacin never lied.

She raised her hand to swipe away the vision, but stopped herself. Gaetan, out in the woods, held a human female in his arms. She bore the telltale sign of a Gossum bite on her shoulder. Gaetan licked the wound, sealing it with his saliva. The vision faded.

Smooth as glass, the water in her visus bacin returned to its natural state.

Alora whipped around, and her bottom pressed against the bowl's edge. She stared at Carine. "Noeh is gone."

Carine shook her head. "I don't know what to say."

Alora pushed away from her scrying bowl and paced the small space. "It means I'm at a severe disadvantage in the war. Not that I wasn't already, but with Noeh dead..."

A lump formed in her throat. "Oh, no." She glanced at Anlon. Before she could stop herself, she rushed to the small babe and cradled him in her arms.

"What is it?" Carine's voice wavered.

"No, no, no." Alora paced to her character board and swiped her hand across the cover. The screen flared to life. With practiced skill, she splayed her hands over the board, searching the green dots for one in particular. The mark she sought was nowhere on the active board. Fingers trembling, Alora pressed the section for deceased characters and scanned the most recent additions.

There, last on the list, Melissa, Anlon's mother.

Tears blurred Alora's vision and she swiped the board, shutting it down so she didn't have to look at the results.

"Noeh and Melissa shared a soul. When he died, so did she, and they left Anlon an orphan." Alora tightened her hold on the toddler, but he squirmed in her arms, demanding his freedom.

She set him on the ground, and he crawled to the table, as if eager to conquer the obstacle yet again. "I should—"

A knock on the door made her flinch. Irritation flared in her chest. She didn't have time for a visitor.

"I'll get that." Carine strode across the room and opened the door.

A blast of cool night air wafted into the room, the taste of evil along with it.

"Carine." Zedron's low tone held a hint of menace. His attention slid past his ex-slave and focused on Alora. He winked, and the corner of his lip curled. "Hello, Alora. May I come in?"

"What do you want?" Alora spat the words at him.

"Is that any way to treat a guest?" He stepped over the threshold and into Alora's home. His gaze drew to Anlon. His brows rose and he peered at her. "A child? What are you doing with a young male like that?"

Alora strode in front of Anlon, blocking Zedron's view of him. "None of your business."

He released a low, predatory laugh. "Come now. Let's not play games, shall we? Except, of course, the one we play to control Earth's fate. You and I both know that is *Prince* Anlon. Although how he arrived here is a mystery to me, but no matter."

"What do you want?" Alora held her ground, unwilling to let him know how much he unnerved her.

Zedron glanced at Carine before his attention returned. "I'd like a little privacy with you, if you don't mind."

"I won't leave you alone with him. I don't trust him." Carine's words lightened Alora's chest, but she wouldn't put her friend in the middle. She'd already spent enough time between them.

"That's okay, Carine. I can handle the likes of him. Please, take Anlon upstairs. He could use a bath." Alora smiled, encouraging her friend to comply.

Carine didn't say a word, but by the set of her jaw, she wasn't happy with the arrangement. She nodded once then plucked Anlon from his spot on the floor and headed up the stairs.

When she was out of earshot, Alora faced her nemesis. "Spill it. Why are you here?"

He smiled, revealing his perfect white teeth and strode to her visus bacin. With deliberate intent, he ran his finger along the bowl's rim. "I've had second thoughts about our arrangement. I miss my slave."

A flash of anger rippled over Alora's nerves. She fisted her hand, her nails digging into her palm. "We had a bargain. You agreed to it."

He shrugged. "All right. If you'd rather I go to the council, that works for me as well. I'll tell them you manipulated me to release Carine to you. I doubt they'd look favorably on coercion." Using long, purposeful strides, he headed for the door.

Alora's heart pounded at her temple. She wanted to lash out at Zedron, beat her palms against his chest, his face, anywhere she could reach. Instead, she gripped his arm. "What do you want?"

He peered over his shoulder at her, victory reflected in his cold blue eyes. "I'm willing to withhold this bit of information, for a price. Care to hear?"

She released her hold on him and nodded.

He turned to face her and ran his finger down the side of her face.

She jerked away, her skin crawling from his touch. "Just tell me."

A low chuckle eased from him. "Well, I'll give you a choice, since that's what you gave me. I want one of three things—Carine, the babe, or...you leave Veromé and come to me."

Alora clenched her teeth. "Not a chance."

His smile widened. "You sacrifice yourself for your loved ones so often this should be easy for you. When you return from your dark place tomorrow night, I want your answer."

She shook her fist at him. "This has always been about revenge, hasn't it? You could never get over me selecting Veromé as my mate."

He seized her arm, his grip painful and tight, and yanked her against him. His vile breath reeked of muldoberry wine. "You should be my mate, not Veromé's."

"I will always believe you killed my friend Mitan. You wanted me to think Veromé was responsible, but I know, I know it was you." Spittle flew from her mouth and landed on his cheek.

Zedron's nostrils flared. "The council ruled Mitan's deck railing gave way, and he fell off the platform. I had nothing to do with his death."

She jerked against him, trying to free herself, but he was too strong. "I didn't believe you then and I don't believe you now."

He shoved her. She stumbled backward, and her hip rammed against her visus bacin. Pain bloomed at the spot.

Zedron's arrogant gaze raked from her hips to her breasts before focusing on her eyes. "Did that hurt? Good. You have one day to decide." He smirked then tramped from her home, slamming the door in his wake.

"You sick *Kasard*. I despise you!" Alora's fingers trembled. She curled them into fists, but couldn't stop the dread as it squeezed her heart.

CHAPTER 11

*N*ikki closed her eyes and rested her head against the edge of the bathing pool. The smooth stone surface was cool and in stark contrast to the warm water lapping at her chin. Steam rose into the air, invading her senses and calming her racing mind. She sighed and slipped further into the carved tub.

Sheri had shown Nikki to her room then dropped her off at the bathing hall. Geez, the things Sheri had told her—a planet called Lemuria, a war over Earth's water, their goddess Alora, Gossum, Stiyaha, Panthera, the great scourge, the list was endless. What a fantastical tale. At first Nikki hadn't believed Sheri, hadn't wanted to, but as Sheri continued to explain, all the details fit together.

Nikki gnawed on the inside of her lip. *I can never go back to my old life.*

A thickness coated the back of her throat. She opened her eyes to blink away the tears. Although she didn't have a lot of friends, she'd miss Jasmine. Did her work buddy find a ranger to search for her? They'd never find any trace.

Sadness beat at Nikki's spirit, but as she peered at the steaming tub, hope, small and brief, flared to life inside. Maybe she'd find a family here with a male. Then again, maybe not. She'd been alone most of her life. To think, hope, and dream this would be any different begged for trouble.

Swallowing the lump in her throat, she glanced around for a towel, suddenly eager to escape.

Tables set against the far wall contained stacks of linens and an assortment of personal cleansers, lotions, and perfumes. Preparing to get out, she placed her hand on the edge of the stone tub. The rhinestones in her bracelet shimmered in the light, reminding her of the mark on Gaetan's arm. Soon, she'd see him. A shiver rippled over her skin, and the water in the tub bubbled, slow at first, then faster and faster.

Adrenaline spiked along Nikki's nerves. She bolted from her seat and scrambled over the edge. Her bare feet landed on the stone tile with a loud, wet slap, and she had to grip the edge of the tub to maintain her balance. The water in the pool stilled, as if nothing unusual had occurred. *My special power...* She still couldn't believe this happened, but she couldn't deny what she'd seen.

Water dripped from her hair onto the stone floor. She carefully stepped to the towels and grabbed one. The cloth, soft and comfy, wrapped around her like a lover. She used another for her hair, wringing out as much water as she could.

Practice, that's what Sheri had said.

Nikki glanced into the tub. Small ripples bounced against the stone sides from when she'd jumped from the water, calming as each second passed. Could she make them bubble again?

She concentrated on the water, straining her mind. The waves on the surface continued to slow, barely a wrinkle. Frustrated, she exhaled and threw up her hands.

The water rippled. Sheri had mentioned emotion could be a trigger. Memories of Gaetan holding her close, his lips brushing against her neck, raced through her mind. A rush of heat ran from her chest and into her cheeks. Her breathing increased, and the water bubbled and frothed.

The door squeaked. Quick, padded footsteps approached.

Nikki's concentration broke. The water stilled, and she turned toward the source of the interruption.

A small female, not more than three feet tall, came to an abrupt halt. She was curvaceous, wearing a brown dress and held a stack of towels in her arms. Shoulder-length brown hair cascaded around her shoulders. Her coffee-colored eyes widened. "Oh, my, I didn't expect to find you in here, but no matter. It's a pleasure to meet you, dear. My name is Bet."

The small female curtsied then placed the towels on the rack. An inviting, warm smile curled her lip. "You must be Nikki. I've heard all about you."

Nikki stiffened. "You've heard about me?"

"Well, of course, dear. News travels quickly in the Keep." Bet moved closer, her small feet moving faster than Nikki would've thought possible. "Is there anything I can get for you?"

Self-conscious, Nikki took a step toward her clothes draped across a nearby wooden chair. "Just need a moment to, ah," she pointed at her pants and top, "get dressed."

Bet's gaze roamed over the towel then her eyes widened. "Oh, dear, don't mind me, I have a few chores to do." The small female turned her back and worked on straightening the towels on a nearby rack.

Nikki took the brief opportunity and threw on the clothes Sheri had given her. She wrung her hair, squeezing out more water, and peered at Bet.

Bet's shoulders tensed, and a soft sob slipped from her lips.

So caught up in her own private world, Nikki had forgotten that others also had problems. She flicked her wet hair over her shoulder and approached the little female. "What's wrong? Can I help?"

Bet sniffed and wiped at her eyes. She straightened, turned to face Nikki, and smiled, but the effort seemed forced. "It's nothing to concern you, dear. Oh, you need a brush," she grabbed one off a nearby table, "here. I picked this one up from a merchant yesterday, before I heard that—" A sorrowful wail escaped her lips.

Nikki bent down and wrapped the small female in her arms. Bet shook, her tears dampening Nikki's sweater. After a long moment, Bet pulled back.

"I'm s...sorry, dear. You didn't need to see that. I—"

"What has you so upset?" Bet's tears reminded Nikki of her brother, and a wave of empathy spurned a desire to help the female.

"King Noeh, he's gone...dead, and so is Queen Melissa." Her mouth quivered. "I don't know what we'll do without them, and, Anlon, our little prince, he's missing."

Nikki placed her hands on Bet's shoulders and gave the other female a gentle squeeze. "I'm sorry for your loss. I didn't know. Is there anything I can do?"

Bet blinked. "Perhaps there is. Many of us are worried about Gaetan."

Coldness prickled along Nikki's arms. Her grip tightened on Bet's shoulders. "What do you mean?"

Bet's eyes flitted back and forth as she searched Nikki's features. "He watched after Anlon when the newb disappeared. Gaetan is a very responsible male. He may blame himself for what transpired. Maybe you can talk to him, make him understand it's not his fault."

"Why me?" Although she felt this odd attraction to him, she didn't know him, not well anyway.

"He brought you here, so he must care for you." Bet's words weaseled inside Nikki. It wasn't possible. There was no way Gaetan cared for her. If her father couldn't, who could? Yet, she couldn't deny how her loneliness eased when she was around him.

"I don't know."

"Would you try? Please?" A hopeful gleam lit up Bet's eyes.

Nikki sighed. There was no way she could refuse those puppy dog eyes. "All right. I'll do my best."

"Thank you." Bet wrapped her arms around Nikki's waist. After a few moments, Bet pulled back. A soft giggle, filled with relief, eased from her. "Here," she held out the brush, "you still need this."

Nikki smiled and accepted the small gift from her new friend. "Thank you, Bet." Whether she could help Gaetan or not remained to be seen.

CHAPTER 12

*N*ikki sat on the edge of the bed and slid her fingers over the comforter. The silky material teased the pads on her fingers. After her bath, she'd retired to her room. The bed had called to her, beckoning with its comforting appeal. A nap had done her wonders.

An itch flared on her palm. With more vigor than necessary, she scratched her nails across the irritated flesh. The marking was darker and in the definite shape of the letter 'M.'

A shot of adrenaline infused with a mixture of fear, frustration, and unease propelled her from her resting place. She paced to the small table with its two matching chairs and wrapped her fingers around the back of one. How she wished this were all some sort of bizarre dream, but after all she'd seen and learned over the past two days, it was real, every bit of it.

A rap on the door, once, twice, three times, echoed through the room. She peered at the worn wooden door, the top curved to match the rough-cut stone frame. *Gaetan?*

Her pulse skyrocketed. She blew out a quick breath and headed across the smooth stone floor. As she opened the door, the hinge issued a loud squeak.

"Hello, Nicole." Gaetan stood in the doorway, one hand wrapped around his cane, the other pressed against the frame. The muscles in his shoulders bulged under his thin short-sleeved shirt. From under the edge, a long, dark line travelled over his taut bicep, down his thick forearm, and split into four lines that ran along the back of his large hand.

An overwhelming urge swept over her. She wanted to run her fingers over the taut cords and feel his strength beneath her touch. Instead, she curled her hands around her middle.

Gaetan cleared his throat. His pale blue eyes sparkled with flecks of gold. It would be easy to fall into their beautiful and mesmerizing depths. "Nicole, Sheri indicated I should stop by. May I come in?"

"Oh, of course." Nikki stepped aside. "But please, most people call me Nikki."

As he passed, the scent of tarragon eased into her senses, filling her with his warm scent. There was something in his quiet demeanor that grounded her, and she gravitated to him like a planet around a sun.

He smiled. "I rather like the sound of your given name. If you don't mind, I'd prefer to call you Nicole."

"Uh, sure." Heat raced across her cheeks. Damn him, he had her flustered already. She closed the door, the hinge protesting once again.

He motioned to the squeaky metal plate. "I'll tell Jax about the noise. He'll have one of the Jixies repair that in no time."

"Thank you. You've been very kind." She studied his features for a long moment. The gray in his hair accentuated the blue in his eyes. She swallowed hard. "Bet told me about Anlon. I'm sure you're worried."

"I am—" He winced. His fingers tightened around his cane, turning white with strain. One of the faint lines on the back of his hand lightened.

She gasped and touched her throat. "Why is your tattoo getting lighter?"

"*Craya...*" He wiped his palm over his face. "It's not a tattoo, but a damned curse."

65

The desire to understand him a bit more urged her on. "Please, tell me."

He held out his hand, studying the lines. "At birth, all Stiyaha males receive a mark that represents their core values."

"What are yours?"

Slow and deliberate, he touched each knuckle in his right hand starting with his index finger and ending with his pinkie. "Responsibility, benevolence, empathy, and patience."

She took a tentative step toward him. "Why did the line fade just now?"

A tic pulsed to life in his jaw, tightening his handsome face. "If the male doesn't honor the values, his mark will fade until it disappears, and..."

"What happens then?" she whispered.

"You don't want to know—" He inhaled and leaned on his cane.

A wave of empathy had her moving to him in an instant. She trailed her hand down his arm and over the thick, black line. The mark was smooth, soft, and tickled her fingers. "What's wrong?"

Anguish and torment radiated in his pale blue eyes. "I'm fine. I just need...my medicine."

She released her hold on him, despite the ache growing in her chest.

With his free hand, he reached into his pocket and retrieved a beautiful blue stone. The sunstones lining her bedroom walls flared to life, reflecting off the crystal in his palm.

"*Craya.*" He shoved the gem back where it came from and withdrew a small satchel. Fingers shaking, he popped a pill into his mouth and swallowed. The tension in his shoulders eased. "Forgive me. I'm not..." He exhaled and pinched the bridge of his nose. "Perhaps another male would better suit your needs."

A chill swept along her arms. The last thing she wanted was another male. "But I thought you came here to..."

He strode toward the door, the tapping of his cane loud in the small room. "I'll ask Saar to find—"

She gripped his arm, stopping him. "Please, I don't want another male. I want you."

He peered over his shoulder, studying her. "Why would you want an old, broken-down male like me? You should feed from a strong warrior."

"Because you saved me." Her lip quivered, so she bit it.

His gaze riveted there, and the beautiful gold flecks in his eyes swirled in the aquamarine once again. "You have no idea what you're dealing with."

The tension between them turned dark and sensual. Beneath her blouse, her nipples peaked. "I trust you."

A low growl emerged from him, deep and possessive. He gripped her arm, flipped her around, and pinned her against the door.

She squealed at the sudden movement, but he hadn't hurt her. On the contrary, he cradled her in his arm, sequestered between the door and his large body. Her breasts pressed against the firm muscles of his chest, each panting breath teasing her already puckered nipples.

He leaned his cane against the door and drew his hand to her face. With a tenderness that contradicted his rough behavior, he trailed a finger down her cheek. "Perhaps you shouldn't."

His minty breath mixed with his unique tarragon scent, weaseled inside, and stroked her in places she never knew existed. Her mind fogged. "Shouldn't what?"

He smiled. "Trust me."

"Why not?" She squirmed, but that only stoked the heat building between them, the liquid fire racing through her veins.

He held her still. "You want to know what happens when I lose my mark?"

She nodded. He lit up her nerves everywhere he touched. Her heart pounded loud in her ears, each rapid breath feeding the frenzy building inside.

"I'll lose control of my beast. You...you..." He cradled her head in his palm. His rough, callused thumb skimmed over her bottom lip. "You...tempt...me..."

Caught off guard by his words, she inhaled. An ache built along her gums, and she moistened her lips.

He kissed her, his mouth hard and firm against hers, bruising her in its intensity. Thrilling warmth flooded all the way to her core, dampening her panties. He slid his tongue along the seam of her lips, the smooth, silkiness of his stroke teasing her. She let him in despite the awareness that doing so made her emotionally vulnerable to him, but she couldn't seem to stop herself.

Taking advantage of her acquiescence he deepened the kiss, exploring her, owning her, possessiveness radiating from him in waves.

A craving she couldn't quite identify zipped along her nerves. Sharp pain erupted from her gums as her canines elongated. She broke the kiss, gripped his shirt collar, and yanked.

The loud rip of material echoed through the room.

Before she could think about her actions, she sank her teeth into the sensitive spot at the base of his neck. Blood slipped down her throat.

She really wasn't human anymore. Unwilling to face the truth, she forced the thought away and gave herself to the pure, erotic pleasure coursing through her veins.

As she drank, he cradled her against him. Soft and soothing, Gaetan's murmured words pierced the fog invading her brain. The urge to rip off his clothes, push him to the bed and have him right here, right now, rippled through her. She tugged on his shirt, the cloth bunching between her fingers.

A low, predatory growl burst from him. He tightened his grip on her arms. "Stop, Nicole."

If only she could.

～

Nicole's soft, sensual lips on Gaetan's neck, and the gentle tugs as she drank from him sent a rush of blood south, lengthening him, fueling his desire for her. Feeding her, giving her what she needed to survive was more erotic than he'd imagined. Constrained like his beast, his shaft pulsed painful and hard against his pants. What he wouldn't do to have more time with this female.

His bonding sac hardened under his tongue to the point of pain. The ink that would bond him to a female had never surfaced before, not once in his long life. To have it do so now sent a frantic chill over his shoulders and down his back. He'd avoided females, afraid of tying one to him with his deformed leg and his commitment to his sister. After what he'd done to Ginnia, he could never walk away from her. They were a package deal. No female wanted that.

With more force than he'd intended, he barked at her. "Stop, Nicole."

She withdrew her fangs, and with tender strokes licked his skin, sealing the wound with her saliva. Not long ago, he'd done the same to her, saving her life in the process. He was bound to her, responsible for her. An odd satisfaction warmed his chest. His inner beast, silent for centuries, growled his assent. Had his beast woken because of this female, the one he couldn't get out of his mind, or was the beast here because he was so close to losing his sanity?

"Umm, you taste so good." She peered at him through sleepy eyes, gratification and bliss evident in her gaze. With a quick slip of her tongue, she licked her plump, reddened lips.

His attention pinpointed on the soft flesh. He couldn't stop himself. After sliding his hand to the back of her neck, he angled her head, preparing her for his kiss once again. Drawing her to him, he pressed his mouth against hers, enjoying how she molded to him, matching his intensity.

She trailed her fingers into his hair, holding him in place, and slid her tongue between his lips. Her fangs elongated, scraping against his tongue, igniting his need and want of her. Blood pounded at his temple. His mind clouded to all thoughts except the physical sensations of her touch, her taste, and her scent searing into him.

Nicole moaned. The vibration travelled from her mouth to his, and his bonding sac pulsed, the membrane stretching taut beneath his tongue. A tendril of fear drifted into his mind, bringing him out of his aroused state and freezing him in place. To bond to her would be a mistake, and he stiffened.

She jerked in response. One of her fangs sliced under his tongue, puncturing his bonding sac. The pungent taste of tarragon filled his mouth. With more force than necessary, he broke the kiss, his hands pinning her shoulders against the door's fine wooden grain.

She stared at him, her green eyes wide. "What was that?"

Dread skittered over his back and down his leg, seeking the weak point in his knee. Pain bloomed from the joint, but couldn't match the fear twisting his insides, squeezing the breath from him.

Half blind with fear, he pushed away from the door, away from her, this female that he'd just committed his life. *I'm a bonded male.* Usually, bondings happened during lovemaking. The sex, combined with the bonding ink, produced the mirror image of the male's mark onto the female's skin, tying the female to the male as well. That hadn't happened here. She wasn't as bound to him as he was to her.

He stumbled, his leg, as well as his heart, unable to bear the weight. His knee hit the ground with a hard thunk. Pain travelled along his nerves until white spots formed in his vision.

"Are you okay? Did I...hurt you?" Nicole's soft words cascaded over him, her voice filled with anguish.

His beast growled, the need to take her, complete the mating portion of the bonding, rippling over him with an intensity he'd never known before. The hair on his arms elongated.

"No!" His scream echoed off the chamber walls.

She flinched and recoiled from him, easing toward the table, as if the furniture could be an effective barrier between them. If he changed, there was no protection, not here, not anywhere.

His breaths heaved in and out of his lungs. In his crouched position, he couldn't move, the pain riveting him in place. Pulling on the inner strength he'd honed over many centuries, he clamped down on his beast, trapping it in his mind. The hair on his arm receded to its normal length.

Nicole approached, one tentative step at a time, her soft-soled shoes swishing across the stone floor. She placed her hand on his shoulder and knelt next to him. The warmth of her skin, even through his shirt, was welcome and comforting. "I'm sorry. I didn't mean to hurt you."

She thought herself responsible. His heart clenched. He breathed in deep, forcing himself to calm, yet he couldn't bring himself to look at her. "No, it is I that should apologize to you."

She brushed her finger over his forehead, down his cheek and under his chin. With a soft tug, she encouraged him to look at her. "I don't understand. What happened?"

A crease formed between her brow, marring her beautiful features. He couldn't allow that. He pointed to his cane. "Would you..."

Before he could finish his request, she rose to her feet and padded to retrieve his crutch, at least the physical one. In the back of his mind, he understood all too well that the pills in his pocket could be a bigger crutch and much more dangerous.

He glanced at his hand. The marking for patience was gone, and the others, the ones for responsibility, benevolence, and empathy were almost invisible. Sweat beaded his brow. He couldn't lose the other three. His leg shook, the tremble wracking his entire body.

Nicole's warm palm brushed down his arm, calming him and electrifying him at the same time. "Here."

She drew his hand to the orange sunstone in the handle. The crack in the stone reflected the light, sending a brilliant cascade over her features, turning her into his own private jewel.

He gripped his cane and forced himself to a standing position. Blood fled from his brain. He concentrated on her pursed lips and the determined glint in her eye.

"Do you want to lie down?" She motioned to her bed.

No. Not in a million years. For a male to touch a female's bed was a sign of commitment. He'd just done the ultimate in that one department, but he wouldn't cross that other line, not now, not ever. Despite the bonding ink flowing through his veins, he wouldn't force her to be with him. If he lay on her bed, he had no doubt they'd end up naked and between the sheets.

He met her gaze. "I'm fine now."

She blinked, and her brows drew together.

He pinched the bridge of his nose. What a mess he'd created. This was a colossal cluster of enormous proportions and all his fault. He should've never kissed her in the first place. Maybe she hadn't drunk any of his bonding ink. The thought sent a jolt of adrenaline into his bloodstream. "Did you taste anything unusual?"

She tilted her head, and a few strands of her golden-blonde hair cascaded over her shoulder. He wanted to reach out and touch the fine tresses, feel the silkiness between his fingers.

"I'm not sure. When you're near, I smell tarragon, and after we kissed, I tasted it as well. Is that what you mean?"

Heaviness settled onto his shoulders. She'd indeed taken some of his bonding ink. He touched the skin on his throat. In a matter of hours, his bonding bands would appear. How many would he receive? He didn't dare hope for three, but he prayed he received more than one. A single band was the sign of a bad relationship.

He shuffled closer to her, each step sending a jolt of agony up his leg. As he approached, her unique scent of ripe melons washed over him, reigniting his desire for her. "I'm afraid I have some bad news."

She closed the distance between them. "Tell me."

It took all his willpower not to pull her to him, kiss her until she begged for more. Instead, he wrapped his fingers around her elbow and rubbed his thumb over the tender skin on the inside of her forearm. "What you tasted was my bonding ink."

"Bonding ink? What does that mean?" She narrowed her eyes.

The urge to kiss her overwhelmed him. He clamped his jaw so hard his teeth rattled. "It means I am your mate...bonded to you."

Her eyes widened. "What?"

He continued to stroke her arm, as much for his need to touch her as for his desire to give her some measure of comfort.

"Your mate? No, I belong to no man...er, male, ever." She jutted her jaw.

"I can't, no shouldn't, be bonded to anyone either. However, because I released my bonding ink, I am bound to you, but you won't be mine until we complete the physical bonding..." She'd come from another world. Had she left behind a male, someone she cared about? The burning desire to know crested over him, and he tugged her close, his need to feel her next to him overriding his common sense. He blurted the question before he could stop himself. "Was there a male in your life?"

She swallowed and licked her lips.

He growled, his beast eager to claim her.

She raised her chin. "No. I had a boyfriend a while back, but he's no longer in the picture."

Relief skittered over his nerves, and the tension in his shoulders eased.

She pushed away from him, and he let her go, sensing she needed some space. Not that he blamed her. This was his fault. His mark for responsibility burned on his hand, the line barely visible. There was no way he could keep up his commitment to her. He had a mission to complete, to find Anlon, one he likely wouldn't survive due to his weak leg, but first, he had to see Ginnia, if for no other reason than to say goodbye.

"I have to visit my sister, Ginnia, before the evening repast. Would you like to meet her?" He blinked. He hadn't intended ask to Nicole to go with him, but he couldn't stand the thought of leaving her alone. Deep inside, he wanted to keep her next to him.

She studied him for a long moment, assessing him. At last, she exhaled. "Is she stoic and demanding like you or different?"

"Different, very different." Shame heated his back and raced over his ears.

Nicole crossed her arms. "Then I'd love to meet her."

CHAPTER 13

*N*ikki skimmed her fingers over the sunstones lining the corridor walls. Their warmth filtered into her skin, easing some of the tension flowing through her veins, but not enough, no, not nearly enough.

Gaetan is bonded to me. A mixture of trepidation and excitement skittered over her shoulders. Her gaze drew to Gaetan, her mate.

Shoulders stiff, jaw tense, he proceeded along the corridor, his pace quick despite the limp in his gait. The rhythmic ping of his cane echoed off the walls. Unbidden, memories of his kiss, so demanding and possessive, raced through her mind.

Everything had happened so fast. One moment they were in a conversation, the next he'd pinned her against the door, his large body holding her in place. She'd wanted him to kiss her with a fevered intensity, and he'd done exactly that, giving her more than she'd bargained for.

Gaetan halted.

Nikki plowed into him, her front molding to his backside. Her hands landed on his shoulders, and he tensed beneath her fingertips. He gripped her thigh, steadying her. Through the thin material, the warmth of his hand burned, igniting a shiver of desire that travelled all the way to her core.

"I didn't mean to startle you." He turned to face her, gliding his hand up her thigh to rest at her hip, the movement sensual, possessive. Lines formed around his concerned eyes. "You okay?"

His careful attention to her wellbeing touched her, more than she cared to admit. "I'm fine."

"Good." He withdrew his hand from her hip and ran his palm over his face. "I have to tell you about Ginnia before we arrive."

The hair along Nikki's nape rose. "What is it?"

"My sister," Gaetan shook his head, "she's in our strong room, the dungeon, for treason."

Nikki inhaled. "What did she do?"

"She released a prisoner, a traitor...Mauree, the one you saw kill Noeh." Gaetan clamped his mouth shut, his lips drawing into a thin line. Pain and torment reflected in his eyes.

Nikki's chest ached, and she placed her hand on his arm. "That was Mauree's doing, not Ginnia's or yours."

He flinched, his muscles tensing beneath her fingers. "Come, we are almost there." With determined strides, he continued down the corridor, his cane tapping in counterpoint to his steps.

This is what Bet had alluded to during their conversation. Gaetan blamed himself for the loss of his friends. Nikki wanted to wipe away his guilt and pain, but she didn't know how. A headache pounded at her temple, and she had to run to catch up.

Gaetan peered at her over his shoulder. "There's something else you need to know about my sister. Although she's an adult, her mind isn't..." His jaw tightened. "There was an accident when she was a child. Please understand she may not take to you right away or may say odd things. She has visions and is a seer, of sorts."

A swell of empathy filled Nikki's chest. There was more to the story, she could tell, but he didn't seem willing to share, not yet, anyway. She placed her hand on Gaetan's shoulder, stopping him. "My brother, Toby, had Down Syndrome. He was the same way, forever young at heart, but he's no longer around. I loved him dearly." Hot tears welled in her eyes.

Gaetan clasped her hands, his warmth seeping into her, easing some of the anguish. "Then we have something in common."

Her heart ached for them both. "I look forward to meeting her."

His mouth curled into an adorable smile, accentuating his handsome features. He gripped her hand, squeezing gently. "She's just around the corner. Let's go."

Nikki nodded and let him lead her down the corridor. In this part of the Keep, there wasn't much traffic, and they didn't encounter a soul. As they rounded a bend, light emitted from a small room, casting the hallway in a soft glow. Bars covered the entrance, and a large padlock secured the latch.

Gaetan cleared his throat. "Ginnia, I've come for a visit."

The rustling of sheets and soft padded footsteps echoed down the corridor. A tall female wrapped her fingers around the bars and pressed her forehead to the rods. Strands of her brown hair protruded between the iron as if eager to escape.

Gaetan smiled. "Ginnia, this is Nicole, my—"

"Mate." Ginnia's pale blue eyes, a perfect match to Gaetan's, locked onto Nikki.

Confusion fluttered in Nikki's mind. "How did you—"

The innocent-looking female smiled, her eyes twinkling with mirth. "I just know."

Nikki held her breath.

"It's okay. You're good for Gaetan, I can tell. I like you already." Ginnia giggled. "Ooh, want to play a game? You like games and puzzles, don't you?"

Nikki furrowed her brow and glanced at Gaetan. "What..."

Gaetan's handsome smile grew, yet the lines around his eyes remained, lending him a haunted appearance. "Like I mentioned, Ginnia is our seer."

Nikki studied Gaetan for a moment then approached his sister and held out her hand. "It's nice to meet you, Ginnia."

Ginnia gripped her palm, drawing Nikki's hand through the bars.

Nikki gasped. "What are you doing?" She tugged, trying to free herself, but the tall female's grip was too strong.

Gaetan stepped forward. "Ginnia, release her!"

Ginnia grabbed Nikki's wrist and forced open her palm. The seer traced her finger over the mark in Nikki's hand. The blemish, pink and raw, burned from the seer's touch. Nikki jerked her arm and, this time, Ginnia released her.

Gaetan wrapped his arms around Nikki and drew her away from his sister. His welcome touch eased the anxiety running through her.

"It's you! It's you!" Ginnia jumped up and down, her hair bouncing to and fro. "You're the one!"

Gaetan squeezed Nikki's arm, released her, and approached his sister.

"What do you mean, Angel?" Gaetan's low, soothing voice rumbled in his chest.

Ginnia smiled, her innocence reflecting in her wide-eyed gaze. "She's the final piece needed for the catalyst."

Catalyst? Nikki's stomach hardened. Fear crept deep inside, draping around every cell in her body. "Me? I'm no one special."

Ginnia blinked. "Of course you are. You and Gaetan, together, will save us all."

Nikki glanced at Gaetan, a sense of foreboding cresting over her shoulders.

"That sounds pretty ominous. Can you tell us more?" Gaetan brushed a few strands of stray hair behind Ginnia's ear.

The seer tilted her head. "About what?"

Gaetan exhaled and kissed his sister on the forehead. "Angel, that's enough for now. I want you to know that I love you, no matter what. Okay?"

Ginnia's expectant gaze roamed over Gaetan. "Did you bring me one? Did you? Did you?"

Gaetan's eyes narrowed. "Bring...what?"

The enthusiasm in the air deflated in an instant. Ginnia's brows furrowed. "You forgot my favorite treat."

Gaetan's shoulders slumped. He yanked the small pouch from his pocket once again. His fingers trembled as he withdrew a small, round pill. With a quick pop, he shoved the medicine into his mouth and swallowed. Dry, without water, no less. A shiver wracked his shoulders and relief flickered over his features.

He's addicted. Nikki's vision pinpointed, white spots forming before her eyes. She placed her hand against the stone wall, but the cool surface did nothing to ease her anxiety. He'd taken a pill a few minutes ago and now he'd taken another. The shakes…the shiver…the look of immediate relief on his face were all signs of addiction. *…and he's my mate.* Dread slid down her back like ice.

A forced smile bloomed on Gaetan's face. "Nicole and I are on our way to the Grand Hall right now. We'll bring you back the largest blueberry muffin in the entire Keep. How about that?"

Ginnia's excitement returned with childlike fervor. She clapped her hands. "Yeah! Yeah!"

The guilt in Gaetan's pale blue eyes burned its way into Nikki, tugging on the threads that bound her heart, searching for a way to unravel the protective barrier. Although she hadn't known him long, she'd already begun to care for him, but she couldn't afford to let him inside and allow herself to love him.

With his addiction problem, he was too much like her father. He could never love her. The pills would always be more important to him than her. Yet, he was her mate and bound to her. A scream bottled up in her throat. It took all her will power not to let it out.

CHAPTER 14

$\mathcal{M}$auree tapped one long, red, polished nail against the wood rail. The small ping beat against her nerves, and her pulse quickened. From her vantage point on the deck balcony, she had a good view of the troops on the lawn below. Gossum and Ursus sparred, the grunts and shouts melding together into a dull buzz. The air reeked of sweat and the bitter tang of Gossum, but even the stench couldn't bring down her elation.

They were so close to winning this war, she could taste it. Soon, she would enslave and rule over the humans, forcing them to aid in the transport of water to Lemuria.

"My lady." Eldon's scratchy voice broke through her thoughts.

She whirled to face him.

He wiped his palms over his dirty jeans. A slow smile curled his lips and creases formed around his dark eyes.

"Eldon, you've done well. The new recruits learned quickly." She quirked her finger, motioning for him to join her.

"I aim to please." He strode across the deck and leaned against the wooden rail. His gaze tracked to the sun low in the sky. "Nightfall isn't far off. When do you anticipate our enemy will arrive?"

Mauree raised her chin and evaluated her first lieutenant. His confidence and determination were evident in the set of his jaw. She'd done well in selecting him. The memory of Theron, her prior first lieutenant and lover, along with his betrayal, slid through her mind. He'd helped his niece, Kaelyn, and her beloved Saar. Mauree tracked her fingers to the patch over her eye, and she curled her hand into a fist. "They will come soon after sundown. When they do, I want Kaelyn."

Eldon placed one of his boots between a couple of slats, resting the sole against the rail's wooden frame. A light chuckle eased from him. "Your desire for revenge goes far deeper than I ever imagined."

"You have no idea." Bitterness swept across her shoulders like a bad chill, wracking her body. She rubbed her arms and longed for the sweater she'd left inside. "The warriors' anger and need for retribution will make them distraught and disorganized. They will fall like trees in the aftermath of a volcanic eruption."

"Now there's a vision I hadn't imagined before. Interesting word choice." Eldon studied her, his dark eyes glinting in the sunlight. He tapped his finger against his chin. "I expected you to be a bit more elated since you killed Noeh. That's been your main goal as long as I've known you."

Adrenaline surged through her veins. Without warning, she unsheathed her dagger from the strap on her thigh and pressed the pointed tip under his chin.

He stilled, the muscles in his arms rigid. His pulse throbbed at his throat.

"Your job is not to question my motives, only to do as I say. Is that in any way unclear?" She increased the pressure on the blade. The tip pierced his skin. A drop of blood welled from the cut.

He swallowed, and his Adam's apple bobbed. "Yes, I mean no. Your message is very clear."

She withdrew the knife then wiped the blade on his shirt sleeve. A black stain darkened the material.

He stepped away, giving her some space.

The adrenaline rush had her head spinning, but his words had hit their mark. *Noeh...* An ache built in her chest. "Prepare the troops. I'll join you in a few minutes." Before he could respond, she turned her back on him and stared at her troops sparring on the lawn.

"As you command." He marched off, and his booted feet echoed across the deck until he reached her bedroom. The sliding glass door closed with a soft click.

Alone at last, she released a long exhale. The sound turned into a moan, and she brought her fist to her mouth, trapping the wail. Confusion swirled in her mind, and a fine sheen of sweat broke over her arms.

Noeh...

She should be happy, glad that she'd killed him and earned her retribution. Yet, instead, there was a dark place in her soul.

"All I ever wanted was to be your queen." She choked on the words.

No! Stop it! She fisted her hand and rammed it against the rail, again, again, and again. He'd rejected her, tossed her aside like yesterday's trash. All for that twit of a female—Melissa. Noeh had deserved death, and Mauree had come too far down this road to have any regrets.

Males have a habit of betraying you, don't they?

"Never again!" Mauree ground her teeth together so hard, a jolt of pain raced up her cheek. "There isn't a male on this planet I trust, not a one, and I will bring down the Stiyaha if it's the last thing I do. I swear it."

The commitment wound around Mauree's soul, tightening like a ball and chain. Deep inside, buried in the far reaches of her heart, a little girl cried.

CHAPTER 15

*G*aetan hobbled down the hall, using his cane to take some of the pressure off his leg. Nicole hadn't said much after their encounter with Ginnia. She'd been through so much over the past day, he hadn't pushed her, giving her time to process all the changes in her life. As they rounded the corner into the Grand Hall, the scent of fresh baked bread, eggs, and hash browns permeated the air. His stomach rumbled.

Nicole tugged on his arm. Her eyes widened, and a look of sheer wonder crossed her features. "What is this place?"

Mesmerized by her fascination, he peered around as if seeing the place through her eyes. Rows of banquet tables filled the center of the large room. Along the walls, platters of meats and cheeses sat alongside those with fresh cut melons and grapes. Bowls crammed with scrambled eggs, glasses brimming with juice, and baskets overflowing with rolls completed the spread.

Warriors, merchants, and council members sat on benches alongside the tables, eating their meal. Several glanced his way. Skylar met Gaetan's gaze. The council member curled his lip, leaned next to his comrade and whispered into his ear.

Heat raced up Gaetan's back and over his ears. He cleared his throat and focused on Nicole. "This is the Grand Hall. It's where most residents choose to eat their meals."

She placed her palm over her chest. "I didn't realize there were so many others here."

Gaetan's appetite waned. Now that Noeh and Melissa were gone and Anlon was out there, somewhere, their chance of survival and winning this war were slim. How he longed to go back in time, prevent Anlon from crawling through the portal.

"Come, let's get you some food." He clutched her hand and guided her toward the serving tables. Silverware clinking on plates mixed with the loud murmurs of the crowd intensified the headache building behind his eyes.

He handed her a plate, and she held on to his fingers. His attention flicked to her beautiful sea-green eyes. She studied him, her gaze roaming from his face to his neck.

A spiral of fear tightened inside him. "What is it?" He had an idea, but he couldn't bring himself to voice it.

"You have a mark around your neck." Her brow furrowed, and she reached toward him.

He stepped out of her way, and the plate slipped from his fingers. The dish flipped end over end on its descent then crashed against the stone tile. Ceramic shards skittered over the floor.

The room quieted for a brief moment before the murmurs resumed once again.

"How many do I have?" He rubbed his fingers over his neck as if he could tell by touch, but his skin was no different.

She blinked. "One. What is it? Is that bad?"

His head reeled, thoughts spinning in his mind faster than he could track. Pain flared in his knee, sharp and biting, bringing him to the floor.

"Gaetan!" Nicole placed her hands on his shoulders and knelt next to him. Her warm touch penetrated through his shirt and lit up his nerves. *Mine...*

A low growl erupted from his throat. *The mating bond. One band. No!* That was a bad sign, a very bad sign indeed, yet he couldn't ignore the beast's desire to finish the bonding and claim his mate. Even if he did, because of the one band, she'd be free to seek the bed of another male.

"Haelen. Do you need assistance?" Quentin's voice broke through Gaetan's thoughts.

The other male stood close by, too close to Nicole. A flare of energy pulsed through Gaetan, and he rose from the ground with a start, pushing Quentin away. "Keep back."

Caught in the undertow of his actions, Nicole fell. Her hip cracked against the nearby table. She cried out.

Blood pulsed in his ears, drowning out all sounds. He took a step back, but without the aid of his cane, his leg couldn't support the weight. He crashed to the floor once again. A tormented scream tore from his throat.

He was responsible for Anlon's disappearance.

He was responsible for Noeh's and Melissa's deaths.

He was responsible for Ginnia's condition.

He'd hurt his female and doomed her to a dismal life...with him.

The lines on his hand burned, the pain so intense he couldn't breathe. He glanced at them and watched as they faded from view.

He looked up. Quentin had his arm around Nicole's waist, pulling her away from him. Lines creased her forehead, and her mouth moved as if she'd spoken, but Gaetan couldn't hear anything above the ringing in his ears.

Adrenaline pumped through his veins, fast and furious, fueling his muscles, lengthening his bones. The hair on his arms grew, covering his skin in an instant, his clothes disappearing beneath the fur. Tusks erupted from his mouth. Pain rippled along his nerves. A roar burst from his lips.

Stunned silence filled the Grand Hall.

His panting breaths were quick, filling his lungs with oxygen and the energy his muscles so desperately needed.

Others in the room circled him, but no one approached.

He searched for his female.

Quentin held her in his embrace. Her wide eyes were full of fear.

The rejection stung, penetrating into his heart like a blade. He couldn't handle the rebuke, and the beast's need to flee had him bolting for the doorway.

Three warriors blocked the entrance. He plowed into the trio, carrying them into the corridor.

One hit his head against the stone wall and slipped to the ground. Another wrapped his hands around Gaetan's neck. Gaetan gripped him by the back of the collar and tossed him down the hallway. The third unsheathed his sword.

Gaetan slammed his fist against the blade. The metal broke in two.

He fled down the hall. Gaetan had an awareness he didn't limp, but then the thought was gone as quickly as it came. In the back of his mind, he understood he was a lost cause, but the beast ruled, and he couldn't stop himself.

"Gaetan!" Nicole's distressed scream chased him all the way down the corridor.

~

"Let me go, you brute!" Nikki kicked, punched, and scratched at the male trapping her in his arms, but she couldn't break his hold. "I have to help Gaetan."

The male flipped her around to face him. His nostrils flared. "My name is Quentin, and there's nothing you can do for him."

Nikki gasped. "How can you say that?"

Quentin shook her. "Are you blind, female? Did you not see his beast? Unless he can bring himself back, which is unlikely, he's a danger to us all."

Another warrior, one with a gold stud in his ear, clasped Quentin's shoulder. "Quentin, you coming? We need to track Gaetan before he makes it out of the Keep. I've alerted Kaelyn and Saar through the sunstones."

Quentin paused. "Yeah, on my way."

Nikki pushed away from him, putting all her strength into her shove. Not that it did any good, he was as immovable as a stone. "I'm going with you."

He shook his head. "I can't allow that. He'll try to claim you, inciting his beast into a frenzy. Stay here for his benefit as well as your own. Besides, he had one band around his throat. Your relationship isn't a good one. Why would you want to be with him, anyway?"

An ache built at the back of her throat. Despite her initial unease, she'd enjoyed Gaetan's company. To think their relationship didn't have a chance was something she couldn't accept. Even if he wasn't perfect for her, she wanted to help him. She glared at Quentin then crossed her arms. "I don't agree with you, but it seems you've decided for me. Fine, for now, I'll stay here."

"Good choice." Quentin turned and followed his friend to join the other warriors not injured by Gaetan.

Nikki glanced around the Grand Hall. Merchants, council members, and Jixies huddled in small groups. The din of excited voices rose in volume.

"What do I do?" Nikki wrung her hands, her fingers trailing over her rhinestone bracelet. Her jewelry reminded her of Gaetan's marking. As he'd fallen to his knees, the lines on the back of his hand had disappeared. Fear sent a ripple of goosebumps up her arm. "I need to talk to Sheri."

She headed toward the corridor and, through the doorway, saw her friend kneeling next to one of the injured warriors.

"Taron, Nico, transport the wounded males to the infirmary. Without Gaetan, I'll need the two of you to assist me." Sheri wiped her brow with her palm.

Nikki stopped. Sheri had her hands full attending to the injured warriors. She didn't have time to deal with Nikki's insecurities and fears. *Now what?*

Nikki stepped back, and her tennis shoe crunched on something hard. Shards of the broken plate littered the area. She stared at the spot where Gaetan had fallen to his knees. His cane lay on the floor a few inches away.

Tears pricked behind her eyes. She walked to the spot, bent down,

86

and wrapped her fingers around his staff. The exquisite wood grain, smooth to the touch, warmed her palm. At the tip, the orange sunstone glittered in the light, reminding her of the gold flecks that swirled in his beautiful aquamarine eyes. A lump formed in the back of her throat, and she forced it down with a hard swallow. "I'll find a way to help you, Gaetan. I promise."

He'd saved her, and despite her fears over his addiction and what it meant for their relationship, she vowed to do the same. She glanced at the others in the Grand Hall. Still huddled in their groups, they didn't seem to notice her, nor care. Her chin trembled.

Who can I talk to? She didn't know any of them and certainly not well enough to share her thoughts or her fears. Her gaze tracked to the tables filled with an assortment of fruits, vegetables, and pastries. A sugary treat caught her attention. Blueberry muffins.

Ginnia...

A flutter of hope tickled Nikki's insides. With Gaetan's staff in one hand, she dashed to the tables, placed two blueberry muffins on a plate, and headed for the corridor.

CHAPTER 16

The fresh scent of pine and cool rain urged Gaetan down the corridor. He stumbled over the uneven floor, and his toe crashed against a stone protruding from the ground. A howl of rage burst from him, reverberating off the walls. As if the Keep shared his pain, sunstones lining the wall flared to life.

His jumbled thoughts were like fireflies, flitting around his mind without rhyme or reason. He continued onward, one foot in front of the other. His goal, to escape these walls, this prison that bound him. Only the fresh air and his need to run free kept him moving.

"He went this way!"

"Hurry, we have to stop him before he gets outside."

Shouts, distant, but recognizable, filtered down the ancient passageway.

Gaetan growled and picked up his pace, distancing himself from the shouts filtering toward him in the ancient passageway.

Anlon... Nicole... Anlon... Nicole...

Unsure of the meaning, he focused on the mantra for it helped ease the swirl in his mind.

Heavy footsteps echoed down the passage, urgent and rushed.

A soft glow at the far end of the row beckoned him. With each step, the small light grew. An explosion of energy propelled him forward. He ran for the first time since he was eight, the first time since the devastating accident that had injured Ginnia as well as himself, the one he'd caused.

"I see him! Hurry!" a warrior shouted.

Anlon... Nicole... Anlon... Nicole...

Gaetan focused on the words, the light, the words, the light, the words.

The spicy scent of pine thickened. Rain pelted the trees, the brush, and the rocks at the Keep's hidden entrance.

He burst into the forest. Between the treetops, the setting sun's rays lit up the clouds in brilliant shades of pink and red. The exposed skin on his face and hands burned. Agony rippled along his nerve endings. He screamed.

Behind him, a warrior shouted, "Craya! The sun's not down yet."

"We'll have to wait until it is. At least in his beast form, if Gaetan stays in the shadows, he'll be all right. Ten more minutes and we'll be safe."

The warrior's words penetrated into Gaetan's thick skull. He covered his face with his hands. Leaving space between his fingers so he could see, he bolted deeper into the forest.

Water from the passing rain shower dripped from tree branches, coating his fur and dribbling over his fingers. The coolness was a welcome relief to his burned knuckles.

He ran and ran and ran. How long, how far, to what purpose, only his battered beast knew, but the mantra continued.

Anlon... Nicole... Anlon... Nicole...

Kaelyn checked the strap at her belt. Her trusty mace rested in its leather pouch, ready for action. The rumble of voices, heated and intense, reverberated off the Portal Navigation Center's walls. She peered around the large room at the warriors under her command.

Strong, loyal, and devoted to their former king, their goal to find the prince was their number one priority. She glanced at the numerous sunstones lining the ceiling. "Alora, please keep the little tyke safe and help us find him."

"The sun is down." Saar's deep voice rumbled between them.

"It's time to go." She stepped onto the portal's platform and blew her whistle. The high-pitched tone echoed through the room.

The warriors quieted. Only the sound of their feet shuffling over the stone floor filled the air.

Kaelyn scanned the soldiers. "Our main goal is to find and retrieve Anlon. Mauree is searching for him and, for all we know, may have him. Three-quarters of the team will proceed with Saar and myself to the lake house. The rest of you will search for Gaetan. Don't kill him unless you have no other choice."

Several warriors nodded in agreement, their sullen faces representative of the task at hand. The chances of success for either group didn't look good, but they'd battle the odds and win anyway.

As she stepped away from the platform, she glanced at the Portal Navigator. "Rin, do your magic."

"Ya don't have ta ask me twice." Resolve glinted in his blues eyes.

He turned and swirled his gnarled fingers over the concentric circle of sunstones lining the giant portal stone. The gems in the outer circle ignited, brightening to a soft glow. He moved with grace and power, churning his hands over the precious crystals. One by one, the concentric rings ignited until the solitary red sunstone in the center filled the room with a faint red glow.

A mist appeared over the platform, opening to a forest bathed in soft moonlight. The eerie hoot of an owl filtered into the room, along with the scent of pine and cedar.

"Squad one, let's go." Kaelyn's muscles tightened in readiness. If Mauree found the prince, she'd better not have hurt him. The thought of meeting up with her nemesis sent a tingle of excitement over Kaelyn's shoulders. This time, Mauree would get her due. One way or another, the evil bitch wouldn't last another night.

CHAPTER 17

*N*ikki sped along the corridor, holding tight to the plate of muffins. She scrunched her brow. All the passages had the same cut stone, the same polished floor, and the same mixture of sunstones embedded in the walls. She couldn't quite remember if the strong room was down the hall to her right or around the following corner. Frustration beat at her temple.

"Gaetan? Is that you?" Ginnia's quiet voice echoed down the corridor.

Relief fluttered over Nikki's shoulders. She picked up her pace, rounded the bend, and the light from Ginnia's cell flooded into the hallway.

"Ginnia, it's Nikki," she blurted out, eager to see Gaetan's sister.

The seer gripped the bars and pressed her forehead against the metal. Her blue eyes glowed with an eerie luminescence, reflecting the light from the sunstones embedded in the wall. "Hi, Nikki."

As Nikki approached the cell, Ginnia focused on the sweet treats on the plate. She clapped her hands and squealed. "You brought me a muffin!"

Ginnia's infectious enthusiasm warmed Nikki, reminding her of Toby and his love for pizza. He'd reacted the same way every time she brought home a box after her shift at the pizza parlor. That was many years ago, during high school, and long before the accident that had taken him from her.

"I sure did. Here." Nikki slid a muffin through the bars.

Ginnia bit into the dough. A piece of frosted sugar clung to her lip. She smiled as she chewed, and Nikki had to fight the urge to ask her to hurry. Gaetan could be anywhere by now, maybe even caught or killed. No, she couldn't go there.

"You gonna eat yours?" Ginnia pointed to the lone remaining muffin on the plate.

Not wanting to scare Ginnia, Nikki decided to play along for a moment before she brought up Gaetan. With a quick smile, she forced a wink. "I guess I better."

Ginnia giggled and took another bite of her muffin.

Nikki propped Gaetan's staff against the wall and bit into the pastry. Although the berries' juices filled her mouth, the muffin tasted like sawdust. She swallowed, and the dough scratched her dry throat.

Ginnia finished her treat and licked her fingers then leaned against the bars. She glanced at her brother's cane. "Don't be sad. Gaetan wouldn't want that."

The hair on Nikki's nape rose. She placed her half-eaten muffin back on the plate and set it on the ground. "There's something I need to tell you."

"No, you don't. I already know." She blinked and innocence shone from the depths of her eyes. "His beastie took over. He's in the forest, but lost. You need to help him."

Nikki clamped her jaw so tight pain flared at the joint. She banged her palms against the bars. "How do I help him?"

Ginnia recoiled from the rails, turned her back, and shrugged.

Nikki's heart twisted for the little seer. "I'm sorry if I scared you. I'm not mad."

Ginnia peered over her shoulder. "You promise?"

"Yes, I promise. Please tell me, what can I do?"

"You have some of his blood. Focus on it. Follow your instincts, your heart." A warm smile broke across her face, and she ran to the bars once again. "Say, you want to play a game?"

"Oh, Ginnia. I don't have time for—"

Ginnia pouted, her bottom lip quivering. "But you have to play. It's the only way to get you out of the Keep so you can find my brother."

Nikki wrung her fingers over her bracelet and stepped closer. "You can help me get out of the Keep? Show me how to find Gaetan?"

Ginnia nodded, a small smile tugging at her lips. "I already told you how to find Gaetan, silly."

A little root of hope sprouted in Nikki's chest. "What do I need to do?"

The little seer pointed to Gaetan's staff, her fingers curling. "Gimme."

Nikki gripped the worn wood and placed the staff against the bars.

Ginnia's eyes gleamed. She wrapped her fingers around Gaetan's cane and touched the sunstone embedded in the handle to the lock. A bright flash of light emitted from the gem.

Nikki cried out and covered her eyes.

Thunk. Something heavy and metal hit the stone floor.

The brightness from the sunstone receded.

Nikki opened her eyes. The open padlock lay on the ground next to Gaetan's staff.

Ginnia pushed against the bars. A loud squeak echoed down the hall.

She gripped Nikki's hand. A soothing warmth spread up Nikki's arm, calming her. "Come. Let's go."

"Where are we going?" Nikki picked up Gaetan's cane.

Ginnia giggled. "To visit Rin."

As Nikki crossed the threshold into the Portal Navigation Center, memories flooded her mind. The Gossum attack, Gaetan cradling her in his arms, the jump through the portal. Her heart skipped a beat.

Gaetan had saved her life. Even though she had this overwhelming desire to be with him, his addiction to his medication scared her. With the single band around his throat, she wasn't sure if their relationship could survive, but she'd do everything in her power to help him. She owed him that much, at least.

Ginnia crossed her arms and huffed. "Rin's not here."

Indeed, the Portal Navigation Center was empty except for the giant central stone, a desk along the side of one wall, and a couple of wooden stools. A small stream encircled the stone and disappeared down a small hole nearby.

Ginnia darted to a dark place in the room and disappeared.

Nikki inhaled and ran after her. "Ginnia?"

The little seer emerged from behind a rock outcropping. An assortment of wheeled beds, wheelchairs, and other medical transportation equipment lined the walls. "I thought Rin played hide and seek with me, but he's not here."

"Where do you think he is?"

Ginnia placed her finger against her mouth and stared at the ceiling. "He only leaves here at night if all the warriors are away, but he won't be gone long. That's okay. I can do this on my own."

Nikki furrowed her brow. She didn't want the other female to do anything dangerous and injure herself. "Do what?"

"Start the portal, silly. That's the game, but you have to help me."

Restlessness darted along Nikki's nerves. "Help you? What can I do?"

Ginnia skipped to the large portal stone and peered at the collection of sunstones lining the top. She scrunched her nose then smiled. "I'll use my powers. You use yours. Together, we'll open the portal. Wanna play?"

Nikki narrowed her eyes at the seer. "I don't know if I can control my powers. What do I—"

Ginnia placed her hands on her hips. "I swirl my hands over the stones on the porte stanen. You swirl the mist, you know, the water, like you did in the bathtub."

A chill scurried over Nikki's back. "How do you know about that?"

94

A chagrinned look crossed Ginnia's features. "Don't worry. I closed my eyes when you got in and out of the tub. Let's start."

Ginnia spun her hands over the stones, faster and faster. A soft glow emitted from the gems lining the outermost ring. "Hurry, get into place by the platform."

Nikki sprinted across the room and stood on the platform's bottom step. Mist formed over the large flat stone. She swirled her hands, trying to imitate Ginnia's movements. Nothing happened. Panic welled inside. "It's not working."

"You're trying too hard, silly. You have to play with it. Like this." Ginnia launched her hands in the air then brought them back down, her fingers skating over the stones as if they were a baby grand's keyboard. "Have fun!"

Nikki swooshed her hands through the air. Nothing happened, but she focused her attention on the mist and pretended she was a great musician, playing Mozart for a grand audience. Her chest expanded, and she let her emotions flow. The vapor coalesced into a ball, swirling faster and faster. "It's working!"

"We're...almost...there!" Ginnia squeaked.

"Where am I going?"

"I thought we talked about this." Ginnia pursed her lips. "To save Gaetan, silly. Oh, and tell him I don't blame him, never did."

"What?" Distracted by the seer's comment, Nikki lost her focus. The swirling mist slowed.

"Don't stop!" Ginnia's wail echoed around the room.

Nikki concentrated on the mist again, pulling water from the stream that ran along the edge of the porte stanen. As the mist solidified, a grove of trees came into view. A cool breeze carried the scent of fresh rain and cedar.

The red sunstone in the central portal brightened.

Ginnia jumped up and down. "Go, go!"

Nikki took a deep breath, grabbed Gaetan's staff, and sprinted through the opening. The last thing she heard was Ginnia's voice. "Don't let Gaetan lose the blue sunstone..."

CHAPTER 18

*A*lora slapped her palm against the table. The wood shook from the force, rattling the vase of Coletta flowers against the polished grain. A single petal slipped from one of the flowers and landed gracefully on the table top. The delicate frond was a symbol of what could happen if she gave in to Zedron's demands—her life would slip away.

Perhaps the war over Earth wasn't worth the price.

Anlon's giggles filled the room, along with Carine's soft, encouraging murmurs. Her new friend gripped Anlon's small hand, helping him toddle past the couch and into an open area of the room. His smile lit up his features, triumph gleaming in his eyes.

Alora's jaw tightened. No, she couldn't give up on Earth. Anlon's fate, as well as all her characters on the planet, including the humans, depended on her to win the war. Otherwise, the humans would be enslaved and her characters would be marked as failures.

"He's learning so fast." Carine's smile faded as she met Alora's gaze. "What is it?"

Alora strode to her visus bacin and leaned over the still water. Her reflection stared back at her, and she couldn't stand to look at the lines etched around her eyes, so she turned around. With a loud exhale, she leaned against the hard rim. "This war needs to end, soon. I miss Veromé."

Anlon squealed. He raised his hands and smiled.

In mid-air, his red sunstone floated toward the character board. With a hard smack, the gem hit the display. The screen lit up.

"Anlon, no, honey, don't do that." Carine ran to the little boy and scooped him into her arms.

A loud, protesting wail rose from him.

The sunstone dropped to the ground with a loud thunk.

Alora rushed to her character board. The last thing she needed was a broken screen. She studied the display. Smooth and unblemished, the surface was as perfect as always. Red and green dots, representative of the characters in the game, congregated on the board. A quick shiver of relief traced down her arms.

"Anlon, stop." Carine tried to contain the babe, but he stretched his arms and legs as he squirmed and slipped from her grasp.

He toddled to the couch and raised his hands. The sunstone rose in the air and smacked against the character board once again. This time, the display darkened, all the characters disappearing from view.

"No, oh, no!" Panic welled in Alora's chest. "I need to see the character board!"

The board flickered, once, twice, three times. Words appeared on the screen. Alora inhaled.

"What does it say?" Carine whispered.

Alora took a deep breath. "Congratulations! If you can read this, you have unlocked a hidden level within the character board. As your reward, you may return one player from the deceased to the active section of play. Good luck!"

The words disappeared from view, and the display returned to its normal state, the red and green dots filling the screen.

Alora turned her attention to Anlon. He crawled to the sunstone and retrieved it from behind the couch. "I always knew you would be important in the game, but I had no idea you would help me in this way."

She scooped him into her arms and hugged him. He squirmed, his

97

arms and legs flailing like an octopus. Alora set him on the wooden floor. As if with a purpose, he crawled to the couch and drew himself to a standing position. His pure smile beamed from ear to ear.

Carine cleared her throat. "I'm not sure I understand. You get to bring back one of your characters?"

Alora's chest swelled. "Sure seems that way. This could be a game-changer for me." She tapped her finger against her mouth. "Who should I choose? There are so many fine warriors and kings that have come and gone during this war."

Anlon cooed and slapped his hands against the couch. The innocence in his eyes broke through Alora's glee, dampening it. Anlon had lost both his father and mother.

"I should bring back Noeh. He would help win this war..."

Carine's brow furrowed.

"You don't like that idea?"

Carine licked her lips and glanced between Anlon and Alora. "I'm sorry, but in my humble opinion, a babe needs his mother."

"Melissa..." Alora whispered.

A soft cry filled the air. Anlon wobbled on his feet, then plopped to the ground. A mixture of pride and frustration crossed his features.

Alora's mind raced through the possibilities—Noeh or Melissa. Before she could decide, a soft hum resonated in the air. Light shimmered as particles of energy coalesced in the middle of the room.

Alora glanced through the window. Clouds in shades of orange and pink dotted the Lemurian sky. Morning had come so quickly.

The molecules fused together and Veromé appeared. His shoulder-length brown hair needed a trim, along with his goatee, but that made him all the more manly and handsome in her eyes.

Alora ran to her mate, eager to touch him, hold him.

He wrapped his arms around her, tugging her close. "My love."

Burying her nose against his neck, his cool, fresh scent washed over her. "Veromé, so much has happened. I have to tell you about—"

Waahhh...

Veromé flinched, his arms tightening around her waist. "What is—"

Alora pulled back to look at him. "That's Anlon. Noeh and Melissa's son."

Carine picked up the babe, and he rested his head against her chest. "The little guy needs a nap. I'll take him upstairs and leave you two alone for a few minutes."

"Thank you, Carine." Alora toyed with a lock of Veromé's hair, enjoying how the silky strands tickled her finger.

Carine's soft, retreating footfalls were the only sounds in the quiet room.

Veromé cleared his throat. "You ready to tell me about this?"

Alora drew away from him, her anxiety fueling her anger. "You assume I've done something, don't you?"

He crossed his arms, and the muscles in his biceps bulged. "It bothers me that I'm unable to help you in this war other than to provide support. I love you dearly, but I don't trust Zedron in this game."

Irritation flared along her nerves. He'd reminded her of Zedron's requirements. How could she tell her mate of her decision? She couldn't, so she concentrated on the child. "Anlon fell through a portal. Carine found him and rescued him from a rhondo beast. We brought the babe here. What was I to do?"

He blinked. "A rhondo beast?"

She nodded, biting back the tears that welled behind her eyes. Her frustration, anger, and fear boiled over, and one slipped over her lash. Time was not her ally.

Veromé opened his arms. "Forgive me, my love. Come here."

She melded into him, thankful for his acceptance and his loving care. "I don't want to lose you."

He stroked his fingers through her hair, petting her. "Sh...sh...I'm not going anywhere."

...But I am... As much as she loved her mate, she couldn't let Zedron win and enslave the Earthlings. She'd go to her nemesis come nightfall.

"Kiss me," she said, tears streaking down her cheeks.

Veromé cradled her head in his palm and pressed his lips to hers.

She gripped the edge of his shirt, her fingers curling around the material. The familiar tug started in her gut, and she disappeared to her dark place.

CHAPTER 19

*G*aetan ran, faster than he ever dreamed possible. Muscles in his leg stretched and flexed, propelling him forward. He leapt over a tree snag. The roots protruded into the air like fingers trying to stop him, but the beast ruled, elated to be free.

Landing on the soft ferns, one whipped against his arm, spraying droplets of water across his cheek. He crouched for a moment to listen, assess, learn. The forest was eerily silent. No creature dared make a sound in his presence. A low growl burned at the back of his throat.

The breeze picked up, rippling the fur on his arms. He flared his nostrils and sniffed the air. The scents of the forest filled his senses—pine, damp foliage, the droppings of a nearby fox. No scent of his enemy or his kind. He'd evaded his pursuers, and tension in his shoulders eased.

Small feet scurried over the bark. He turned his head toward the sound. In the moon's soft glow, a mouse quivered on an adjacent branch. It stared at Gaetan, fear reflected in the tiny creature's dark round eyes.

Gaetan chuffed. The creature had nothing to fear from him. A desire to touch the small rodent flitted over his mind. He extended his index finger toward the animal.

The mouse fled, its feet scuttling over the fallen log's deteriorating bark.

A sadness he didn't understand built inside. Low and forlorn, a moan eased from his mouth. He shoved away from the snag and continued on. Something tickled the back of his mind, his destination or his goal perhaps.

Anl... Nico... but he couldn't quite grasp the images. His goal faded from his consciousness. Grief. Anguish. Guilt so heavy, each step was an act of stubborn will.

The moon slid across the sky and, still, he wandered. Exhaustion took hold of his muscles long before his mind. The beast needed to sleep.

He placed his hand against a cedar. The bark's sweet scent filled his lungs. Not far away, rushing water echoed between the trees. His pulse sped, but he knew not why.

With an urgency he didn't understand, he bolted toward the sound. Tree branches snapped in his wake. Moist from the recent rain, soft loam squished beneath his feet.

He came to a small bluff. In the chasm below, a great waterfall roared into the most magnificent blue pool he'd ever seen. A wistful tightness formed around his chest.

Blue Pool...

He didn't know what the words meant, but they continued to echo in his head.

Blue Pool...

Blue Pool...

Blue Pool...

I found it.

He growled. In the back of his mind, something pushed against his subconscious, as if trying to take control. He lashed out, his large hands fighting an invisible enemy. His fingers snagged on a large tree branch. A loud crack rent the air.

The bough careened over the cliff and landed in the pool below.

The sheer force from the waterfall smashed the limb against the rocks. Bits and pieces floated downstream.

"Gaetan." A soft, feminine voice slid by on the breeze.

He stilled. He flared his nostrils and inhaled. The scent of sweet, ripe melons trickled into his senses, familiar and enticing. With a quick turn, he searched the forest.

There was nothing, no one.

A low moan, filled with frustration, ripped from him.

"Gaetan, I'm here to help you." The female's voice came again, this time from his right. He turned in time to see her supple, curvy figure emerge from behind a tree. She held a long staff.

A mixture of desire, fear, and longing warred within, confusing him. He took a step back, toward the cliff's edge.

She approached him, this beautiful, thoughtful female with her light hair and compassionate eyes. He had the sudden desire to touch her, but the memory of the fleeing mouse whipped through his mind. A low, keening wail filled the air and it took him a moment to understand the ragged cry came from him.

She placed the cane against a cedar, held out her palms, and edged toward him. "Gaetan. It's Nikki...er...Nicole."

Nicole... A loud ping resounded in his ears. His legs shook.

"I know you won't hurt me. I'm your mate. Let me help you." Close enough to touch him, she reached forward and placed her hand on his forearm.

Her electric touch sent a shockwave of desire through him. Operating under pure instinct, the beast wrapped his arm around her waist and tugged her close.

"Mmmmmine," he snarled, unable to soften his tone.

Wrapped in Gaetan's arms, Nikki's cheek pressed against his chest. Smothered by all his fur, she struggled to breathe. He rubbed his palm over her backside, and despite the utter strength he emitted, his touch was gentle.

She squirmed against him. He growled, the sound low, predatory, and filled with sexual need. Her nipples peaked in response, hardening against his chest.

His erection grew hard and firm, pressing along her abdomen and between her breasts. She inhaled at his sheer size. Holy hell, in his beast form he was more than she could handle. "Gaetan, let me go."

"Mmmmmine."

With as much force as she could manage, she pushed against his chest, putting enough distance between them to look at him.

His aquamarine eyes focused on her from behind a low brow ridge. Tusks protruded from under his bottom lip, pointy sharp and glinting in the moonlight. Labored and rough, his breaths wheezed from his lungs.

"Yes, I'm yours, and you need to come back to me." This strong, proud male, seemed to have endured so much, but he didn't deserve to be hunted down and killed by his own kind. Thank goodness she'd tracked him through their blood connection. The portal had opened not far away, and between the blood bond they shared and his howls, he was easy to find.

He blinked, and weariness formed in the creases around his eyes. A grunt eased from him.

Wishing she could take away his pain, she stroked a finger down the side of his face. "Relax, Gaetan, relax."

She didn't know what to do to help him change back, and a tendril of doubt crept inside. On impulse, she bit her lip.

His attention riveted there. The muscles in his arms tensed.

"C'mon. Let's step away from the ledge, okay?" She drew back, but he wouldn't let her go. "It's all right. I won't leave you."

He chuffed, and his eyes flicked back and forth as he studied her.

"You saved me. Now, it's my turn to save you. We can tackle your problems together, but you must return to human form." She tugged on him again.

Slowly, he followed her. She stopped a few feet away, underneath the large cedar where she'd left his cane resting against the trunk. The boughs whispered in the wind, as if encouraging her.

Instinctually, she understood he needed to trust her, believe in her, believe in them.

She turned to face him and took one of his large, calloused hands in hers. With purpose, she drew his hand to her chest, right over her heart. "I believe in you, Gaetan. You are a good, caring soul, and I...I need you."

His grip tightened around her fingers, and he lowered himself to his knees. At eye level, he studied her with his stunning aquamarine eyes. A flicker of something, recognition perhaps, flashed across his beastly features.

Encouraged, Nikki brought his hand to her face, and she rubbed her cheek against his knuckles. "I believe in you, Gaetan. I. Believe. In. You."

A low moan escaped his lips. He swayed, his body rocking from side to side.

She held on, rubbing her thumb over his knuckles, encouraging him with soft murmurs.

He remained that way for several long moments. The hair on his arms started to recede, slow at first then faster. Before she could stop him, he crumpled to the ground at her feet. Clothing reformed on his human-like body.

His right hand lay exposed across his chest. A single black mark darkened the back of his hand across his second metacarpal. She remembered this one represented benevolence.

Her heart swelled. They had a chance.

She knelt beside him and shook his shoulder. "Gaetan. Gaetan."

His eyes fluttered.

"Wake up, medicine man." An uncontrollable giggle, born of relief, reverberated in her chest.

His eyelids popped open, and he focused on her. "Nicole..."

The deep timbre of his voice slid over her nerves, warming her, making her feel wanted, needed. She could get used to that sound all too easily, but sooner or later, if he didn't get over his addiction, she'd have to leave him. Besides, he had other priorities, like his sister, his job, Anlon.

Anlon...

She'd forgotten about the babe. As far as she knew, he was still lost out here. Her face heated at her selfishness.

"Nicole, you helped me return from my beast. We're at Blue Pool, the sacred site. I couldn't have found this place if I'd tried." He placed his palm against the cedar's trunk and stood. His gaze drew to the back of his hand. Creases formed around his eyes. "Why did you come after me? I could've killed you."

...because I care. Her mouth went dry, and the words wouldn't come.

He took a step toward her, his limp pronounced once again. With rapt attention, he tucked a few strands of hair behind her ear. "You shouldn't have taken the chance on me. I'm not worth it."

Tears welled in her eyes. "How can you say that? You're kind, gentle, and so many care for you."

A sarcastic snigger eased from him. "It's my fault Anlon is missing, my fault the king and queen are dead."

She inhaled. How could he think himself responsible? "That's terrible."

He flinched, as if she'd slapped him. Remorse reflected in his eyes. "Even you blame me."

"No! That's not what I meant—"

"Enough!" He slammed his fingers against his thigh. His eyes widened, and he shoved his hand into his pocket. As he withdrew his fist, a blue glow emanated from the stone in his hand.

"This, this thing. As much as I blame myself, I blame the sacred blue sunstone for starting it all." He drew back his arm and before she could stop him, he launched the stone over the cliff's edge. "Go back from where you came."

"No!" Nikki screamed, and it was Ginnia's words that echoed in her ears.

"Don't let Gaetan lose the blue sunstone..."

CHAPTER 20

*K*aelyn set her palm against the cool stone and peered over the boulder. Through the trees, moonlight reflected off the small lake, glimmering on the water's still surface. Not far beyond the meadow, Mauree's lake house and the small cottages contained numerous soldiers ready for battle. Along with the Gossum she so despised, Kaelyn recognized many of her kin. A bead of frustration ran down the side of her face, and she tightened her grip on her mace.

"They've built up their ranks." Saar's rough whisper tickled her ear.

"They're expecting us." She peered at him. "Are you surprised?"

The soft moonlight cast shadows onto his features, accentuating the scar across his face. "Not at all. Actually, I look forward to the challenge."

Kaelyn ran her hand down his arm, enjoying his taut muscles beneath her fingertips. "Remember, our goal is to find Anlon. This isn't a suicide mission."

A low growl eased from his lips. "I want revenge for Noeh's death."

"As do I, but with some of our troops searching for Gaetan, we're not full strength. Our number of warriors was small to begin with."

A flicker of worry crossed his eyes. "This war can't go on much longer."

"I agree, but if we don't find Anlon, I fear the warriors will give up hope. We must find him. In some ways, I pray he's not here, in the midst of our enemy, in other ways, I pray he is, so we can bring him home." Kaelyn let loose a long breath. "We've stalled long enough. Let's go."

Saar tugged her against him and gave her a quick, passionate kiss. "Whistle if you need me."

She brought her bear's head whistle to her lips and blew a single soft note.

A moment later he was gone. Noiseless and swift, his shadowed form sped between the trees, other warriors following close behind. According to plan, each would approach from a different angle, searching for any signs of the little prince.

Alone, she slipped between the trees, her boots squishing in the mud along the path. Closer and closer, she skirted the edge of the lawn, staying under the forest's dark cover.

The distinct astringent smell of Gossum assailed her nose. She clamped down on a growl. From her vantage point, Kaelyn had a good view of the second-story deck, Mauree's favorite resting spot. Only the deck's railing graced the scene, resembling a row of bad teeth.

Not far away, along the back edge of the garden shed, a Gossum gripped a loose piece of skin from his arm. He tugged at it. A soft rip, like a Band-Aid from flesh, filled the space between them. He held up his grisly prize, studying the thin film captured between his fingers.

Prickles travelled down Kaelyn's back, and an uncontrolled shiver racked her body. She unhooked her mace from her belt.

The Gossum stilled. His attention whipped toward her.

Damn...discovered.

She stepped from her hiding spot, twirled her mace, and sprinted toward her enemy. Adrenaline, fueled by hatred, pumped through her veins.

The Gossum met her half-way. His tongue snaked from his mouth, the barbed end snapping near her ear. Warm spittle landed on her cheek.

She swung her mace. The spiked tips embedded into the creature's shoulder. A loud scream tore from him, and he clawed at her arm. Pain flared from the wound.

He staggered, but regained his composure. Crouching, the muscles in his shoulders and legs bunched beneath his dark clothes.

She switched her mace to her other hand and raised it into the air. With a quick thrust, she twirled her weapon. The rhythmic rush of air resounded in the night.

As her enemy leapt toward her, she crashed the spiked ball, nailing him in the head. He fell to the ground, panting.

Heart pounding, she tugged her weapon free. His dark blood oozed onto the lawn.

Stepping on his neck, she dug the toe of her boot into his flesh. The urge to shove the tip until it embedded in his brain raced through her, but she needed him alive, at least for the moment. "Where is the babe?"

His breathing became irregular.

She had to hurry. "Where. Is. The. Babe?"

"W…what babe?" he rasped.

She increased the pressure, and a gargled sound emerged from his lips. "Anlon, the Stiyaha prince."

His brow furrowed. "Don't know."

"Are you telling me he's not here?" She leaned forward, studying his expression.

"No child, no child—" Before he could say another word, he disintegrated into a pile of black goo.

A mixture of relief and frustration rippled along her nerves. If Mauree didn't have him, where was he?

Screeeee!

The cry of a warrior's sword pierced the air.

Kaelyn's heart leapt into her throat. The battle was on. She raced around the shed.

On the large lawn, warriors fought against Gossum and the Ursus.

Rage, frustration, and fear erupted from her like a cork from a bottle. She let loose a war cry and headed toward the melee.

Movement out of the corner of her eye shifted her focus from the battle. Mauree, wearing her signature short skirt and a sheer blouse, approached the home's second story deck. Her blonde hair cascaded around her shoulders, but couldn't hide the dark patch over her eye.

A twinge of retribution flared in Kaelyn's chest. She'd caused that damage, and she'd do a whole lot more given the chance.

A shout.

A groan of pain.

A tormented scream.

Kaelyn drew her attention back to the battle. Her warriors fought, wrestling with their enemies, but there were too many. If her kind stayed, they'd die.

Hatred burned in Kaelyn's soul. She gripped her whistle and brought it to her lips. After taking a large breath, she blew through the hole. A loud piercing tone rang through the air.

"Retreat!" The word tasted bitter on Kaelyn's tongue.

Mauree's high-pitched titter echoed from the balcony. "Oh, please stay. We were having so much fun."

"Have no fear, Mauree. You and I will see each other again, soon." Kaelyn spat on the ground and bolted for the trees, hot on the heels of her warriors. This wasn't the end, not if she had anything to say about it.

CHAPTER 21

"*N*o!" Nikki screamed. Gaetan had thrown the blue sunstone over the cliff. She bolted for the edge, her feet skittering over twigs and loose pine needles. Descending toward a beautiful blue pool at the base of a magnificent waterfall, the gem caught the moon's light.

"Don't let Gaetan lose the blue sunstone..." Nikki didn't understand the reason, but Ginnia had been adamant.

Fear for Gaetan bubbled up inside her, and a jolt of energy surged from her fingers. She concentrated on the stone. As if by magic, the pool's water swirled around and around into a funnel. The blue sunstone skittered across the surface, travelling down the cylinder. At the end of the tunnel, a small cave emerged.

Gaetan inhaled, the sound snaking between his teeth. "What did you do?"

"I...I don't know, but my power has something to do with water." She focused her attention, concentrating on maintaining the opening.

"I'd say that's an understatement."

She didn't dare look at him for fear she'd lose control. "We have to get that stone back."

"What are you talking about? That stone is nothing but trouble. I threw it into Blue Pool to get rid of it." His words came out rough, but she sensed his commitment, his desire to do the right thing. That warmed her heart.

"Ginnia said not to let you lose it." She held out her arms, the muscles trembling under the strain.

He placed his hand on her shoulder. "What else did she say?"

The warmth of his skin seeped into her, sparking her energy level. "Nothing. That's when I jumped through the portal to search for you."

"I'm glad you did. *Craya*. We need to retrieve that stone and find out what Ginnia meant."

Sweat beaded on her brow. "I...I can't hold this much longer." As she said the words, the strength in her arms gave out. The water in the pool rushed over the tube, burying the stone in its watery grave.

Gaetan's fingers tightened on her shoulder. "I'm sorry, Nicole. This is my fault—"

She whirled on him, knocking his hand away. "Stop it, Gaetan. This is not your fault, none of it is. This is a war. Bad things happen. You aren't to blame."

His mouth drew into a thin line, and a tic started in his jaw. He shoved his hand into his pocket and withdrew his satchel. Fingers shaking, he opened the twine and shook a single pill into his palm. Staring Nicole in the eyes, he popped the pill into his mouth, swallowing it dry. "You have no idea of the things I've done..."

"The male I know is a sensitive, caring soul. Others in the Keep respect you, love you..." *As do I.*

She couldn't say the words, wouldn't allow herself to open up to him. As much as she wanted to, she had to protect her heart. She'd do everything she could to help him, but in the end, his addiction would win. Quentin had said the single band around his throat was the sign of a bad match. They were doomed no matter what. She'd have to leave him.

He studied her, his eyes flicking back and forth. The desire to believe her radiated from him, but she wasn't sure he would. He cleared his throat and broke eye contact. "Maybe Ginnia believes the blue sunstone will help me find Anlon. I must retrieve that stone. If you're willing, I could use your help."

She sighed. The young prince should be their priority. They could focus on their relationship later.

Determination built in her chest. She'd help him no matter what. If, at the end of the day, he didn't love her, then she'd just deal with it. "What can I do?"

"Can you part the water again?" A smile tugged at his mouth, lighting up his gorgeous eyes.

She couldn't resist his charm and nodded. "I can try."

"Let's go to the shore. You can try from there." He gripped her hand, and his calming warmth spread up her arm. With a soft tug, he led her to the pine, where his cane leaned against the bark. He wrapped his fingers around the sunstone handle then peered at her. His eyes sparkled, more beautiful than anything she'd ever seen. "Thank you for helping me."

She blushed, heat racing to her cheeks.

Gaetan glanced skyward. Through the trees, the first hint of dawn turned the dark sky into a deep purple. "There's not much time. We need to retrieve the sunstone and return to the Keep before sunrise."

She nodded in agreement then followed him along the trail to the shoreline. Even with a path, Gaetan's progress was slow. His cane caught on bits of grass and small rocks that littered the trail. The muscles in his back bunched with each step, pulling his shirt tight across his shoulders. He was strong, proud, and defiant, and her heart ached for him.

At last, they arrived at the shore. Water lapped against small, round rocks. Gaetan pointed to the deep pool, and his lips moved, but the waterfalls deafening roar was too loud and drowned out his words.

He stepped closer and brought his lips to her ear. His breath tickled the skin at her nape. A pleasant shiver raced down her spine. "Use your power."

She gnawed at her lip. Could she? Closing her eyes, she concentrated on the water and tried to force the energy from her hands.

She peeked through her lashes. Nothing happened.

He gripped her arm, his calloused fingers tickling her skin. "What's wrong?"

"I...I'm not sure, but both times it happened before, I had an intense emotional reaction, and—"

Gaetan's cane slipped from his grasp. He wrapped one hand around her waist and cradled her head with the other. "Perhaps this will help."

She parted her lips and inhaled. "Gaetan, what..."

He silenced her with a rough, demanding kiss. A low moan eased from him, reverberating deep in his chest. Her pulse spiked as a rush of desire slid all the way to her core. She thrust her hands into his hair and scraped her nails against his scalp, claiming him. He tightened his grip around her waist, crushing her breasts and her hardening nipples against his chest.

"Nicole..." She loved how he said her name, drawing it out.

His arousal grew, but she forced herself to focus. "I...I think I can try now."

"Good, very good." He released his hold on her, but he kept his hands on her hips.

She turned and leaned into him, her back pressing against his chest. Using the desire he'd ignited in her, she concentrated on the water.

Bubbles formed on the surface. The water funnel reappeared. Rocks became visible on the ground, and the path led into the small cave. Water encircled the opening, swirling and churning, but not a single drop fell.

Nikki's chest swelled, a feeling of accomplishment lightening her heart.

"Let's go." Gaetan picked up his cane, gripped her hand, and headed into the water tunnel.

She sucked in a deep, shuddering breath. What awaited them?

CHAPTER 22

*T*he tip of Gaetan's cane slipped between two rocks, sticking in the soft mud. He yanked on the wood and the mud gave way, a loud sucking noise issuing from the gap. Tightening his grip on Nicole's hand, he drew her into the small cave.

A cool, damp breeze caressed his cheek, the source unknown.

"This is it?" Nicole's soft voice echoed around the chamber.

Water rushed over the tunnel, filling in the space. Darkness closed in around them. Gaetan's pulse rose, a sense of entrapment slithering along his nerves.

Nicole gripped his arm, her fingers digging into his muscle. "I can't see."

She fears the dark.

Empathy for her crept from a tiny place in his heart. The back of his hand burned, the line reappearing. His chest swelled. He placed his hand over hers and gave her a gentle squeeze. "Don't worry, my little water lily. I can take care of that."

He rubbed his thumb over the sunstone embedded in his cane. A soft glow emitted from the gem, lighting up the cave walls.

A gentle sigh eased from Nicole's lips. "Thank you. That's much better."

The relieved smile that graced her features accentuated her rosy cheeks and the sea-green hue of her eyes. He held his breath, mesmerized not only by her beauty, but by the zest for life that reflected in those deep green depths. How he longed to feel the same way, but after so many years, the pain had dulled his senses.

Pain... The constant agony in his knee was blessedly gone.

A brief memory of running through the woods in his beast form skimmed across his mind. The beast hadn't experienced any pain. Was he healed?

A sudden rush of blood zipped through his veins. He took a tentative step without his cane, putting pressure on his bad knee. The leg started to buckle, and he leaned on his cane once again. No...he wasn't healed. The urge to pop a pill made his mouth water. His fingers twitched, and he fought the impulse to reach for his satchel. "At least the pain is gone."

"There are so many rocks here. Do you see the blue sunstone?" Nicole's voice brought him from his reverie.

Light from the sunstone in his staff reflected off a small pool of water near the cave entrance. Rocks in all shapes and sizes lined the shore. He raised his cane, illuminating more of their surroundings, and scanned the area, eager to find the blue sunstone. "It's here somewhere. It has to be."

He wouldn't entertain the idea that they were wrong. They'd seen the gem through the water tunnel, but what if that had been an illusion? No, he wouldn't go there. He had to retrieve the stone and find Anlon. The guilt he'd become so familiar with resurfaced, heavy and burdensome.

Nicole searched near a pile of small boulders, her brow scrunched in focused determination. Soothing warmth started deep inside, easing up his chest and across his arms. Her willingness to help him stripped away one of the chains around his heart, easing the weight.

A sense of urgency pushed him in the opposite direction. If they didn't hurry, they'd be stuck here all day. He scanned the rocks, searching...searching...

"Oh! I found it!" Nicole held the blue sunstone between her

fingers. It caught the light from the gem in his cane, reflecting in a brilliant cascade. She scrambled over the small pile of rocks and handed him the sacred stone.

"Seems I can't get rid of you. Not yet anyway." He shoved the stone into his pocket. "We should leave while we still can to find Anlon and—"

A shudder rippled over his skin. "No, no, no!"

"I felt it, too. We're too late. The sun is up." Nicole trailed her fingers over the back of his hand, caressing his mark.

The desire to pull her to him, kiss her until she cried out his name, flared along his nerves. But, he didn't deserve her. He was too broken and too scarred. With enough force to kill his enemy, he slammed the tip of his cane against the ground. The light on the end flared.

"Look!" Nicole's soft voice echoed around the chamber.

In the far corner, cut into the very rock itself, a small passageway became visible.

"Let's check it out." Nicole tugged on his arm.

"Since we're stuck here, we might as well." He gripped her hand, and she clasped her fingers around his.

A smile curled her mouth, tugging at her plump lips. The urge to kiss her rippled over him once again, but she drew him forward. All he could do was follow.

As they approached the small entrance, the breeze picked up, flipping Nicole's tresses over her shoulder. He couldn't stop himself, and he caught a few tips between his fingers. She glanced at him, her brow furrowing around her inquisitive eyes.

He returned her smile, his chest expanding from the brief exchange.

Closer now, the dark outline of objects in the room took shape—a desk, a chair, a bed, and the scent of ageless time carried by on the breeze.

After crossing the threshold, sunstones embedded in the walls flared to life and brightened the room. Scattered over the desk were several old tomes, some open, others stacked on top of one another. Next to a table sat an old, rickety wooden chair with a slat missing from the back. A large green comforter covered the massive bed. In the corner was an odd looking sink, water filling the bowl to the rim. Despite the sense of age, everything appeared clean and untouched.

"It looks like someone lived here." Nicole picked up an odd stylus from the desk. She studied the tipped end.

"Indeed, but who?" He trailed a finger over one of the ancient tomes. Cuneiform characters graced the cover. "Hey, I recognize this language. It's Lemurian."

He read the titles of the closest books. "Research... Portal transportation..." His gaze landed on one with the distinct symbol of the letter 'M.' "Lemuria."

"I wonder what they say?" Nicole pulled close, and her arm rubbed against his.

Heat ignited between them. He fisted his hand and swallowed, unwilling to give in to his desires. "Let's find out." He cracked open the first one and began to read.

~

Nikki had seen the gleam of desire in Gaetan's eyes when she'd brushed her arm against his. A part of her had wanted him to kiss her like he had before, to take her and finish claiming her as his mate. For a moment, she thought he'd do exactly that, but he hadn't. Instead, he'd buried himself in the old tome.

While he read, she explored the small room. In a cabinet over the table, she found canisters with dried herbs and a few jars with some peaches. She unscrewed one and sniffed the contents. The peaches' sweet scent tickled her nose. There must be some unique magic in this place to keep the food so fresh.

She approached the basin against the far wall. Smooth as glass, the water filled the bowl to the rim. She peered into the dark depths. Her fingers twitched. A small ripple danced over the surface.

"This is fascinating. Someone named Mitan lived in this small cave. From what I can tell, he was a Lemurian god, like Alora."

Gaetan's voice floated across the room, but Nikki's attention was on the water as it started to bubble.

"His notes indicate he had characters here, a long time ago. He marked them all with an...an... 'M' in their palm for 'Mitan.' Do you know what that means?" The scrape of the chair leg against the floor resounded in the room. "It also mentions that even though they are gods to us, we as characters, have free will. That's life altering."

"Gaetan, come quickly." The water in the bowl churned, swirling, splashing droplets down the basin's side and onto the rocks lining the floor. She couldn't control her power. Fear sent her pulse tripping through her veins.

He approached her from behind and brushed his hands down her arms, sending a calming warmth under her skin. With a quick tug, he pulled her against him, his breath tickling the back of her neck and causing a shiver of need to tickle her bottom. The water in the bowl calmed along with her racing heart. She relaxed into him, letting him catch her, bear her weight.

Images flashed across the water. A green planet, red patches marring its surface. Two moons. Tall trees, branches intertwining above a sea of houses and platforms embedded into their massive trunks. The vision pinpointed on a single home in a large tree, a deck surrounding three sides. A man dressed in a pair of silky white pants and a matching shirt placed his elbows on the deck railing. His brow furrowed over a pair of intense brown eyes.

"Who is he?" This was unlike anything Nikki had ever seen before, and her voice trembled.

Gaetan planted a warm kiss along her earlobe. "I don't know. Perhaps—"

Heated voices burst from the image.

"Let's watch," Gaetan whispered.

Nikki relaxed into him, eager for his comfort and his tender touch.

Another man, this one dressed in a tailored suit strode onto the deck. He had shoulder-length brown hair, piercing blue eyes, and a tiny jewel glittered in his nose. Arrogance and menace radiated from him, permeating the air with tension.

The first man turned around and crossed his arms. "Zedron. I told you never to come here."

Zedron... Zedron... Nikki recognized that name but couldn't place him. *Wait! Sheri mentioned this to me. That's Alora's nemesis. The god we're fighting against.* Nikki held her breath and focused on the picture.

"Oh, Mitan. You'll come around, you always do." Zedron smiled, revealing a perfect set of white teeth.

"I won't be a party to your plan to win Alora's hand. She's my best friend from childhood. Once she finds out you intend to tarnish Veromé's reputation, she'll never bond to you." Mitan's eyes flashed.

Zedron trailed his finger over the back of a deck chair, toying with the cushion's ribbon. "Perhaps I should tell the council that a member of the neutral faction colonized a planet, a little blue planet with a single sun."

Mitan pushed away from the railing. The wood creaked from the pressure. "You wouldn't dare."

"Oh, I would." Zedron tsked. "Neutral faction families don't support free or slave parties, so your actions are scandalous. I know how much pain that would bring your council member father. He'd lose his seat in disgrace."

Mitan's nostrils flared, and his fingers curled into a fist. "Alora won't love you, not like she does Veromé. That's something your money and power could never buy."

"So, you're telling me you won't cooperate?" Zedron took a step forward, his blue eyes flashing.

Mitan closed the distance, the males mere inches apart. "No, and better yet, maybe I should turn you in. I'm sure the council would be very interested in how you acquired this information. Spying is a capital offense."

The muscles in Zedron's shoulders tensed, his arms shaking with fury. A roar of pure rage rushed from his throat. He gripped Mitan's shirt and shoved him.

Mitan stumbled across the deck. He collided with the wooden rail.

A loud crack echoed between the trees.

Mitan ran toward Zedron, but the evil god was ready. His fist connected with Mitan's chin. Mitan crashed against the railing once again. Wood splintered and slipped over the edge.

"Goodbye, Mitan." Zedron's lip curled, and he kicked Mitan in the gut.

The railing gave way with a loud, sickening crack.

Mitan yelled and disappeared over the edge.

Low, predatory growls rose from below.

Nikki screamed, her heart racing. As she pushed away from the strange basin, her fingers scraped against the rough stone edge. Pain rippled up her arm, and blood dripped into the water, mirroring her sympathy to Mitan's plight.

CHAPTER 23

Gaetan wrapped his arms around Nicole, tugging her close. She trembled against him, her soft skin making contact with his fingers, the pleasant sensation teasing him. The water in the basin stilled, the brutal image of Mitan's murder erased from the vision. Too bad he couldn't wipe away the vision from Nicole's mind. "Sh...sh...it's over now."

She drew her hand to her mouth, a soft hitch easing from her throat. Blood dribbled from a gash on her index finger. "Mitan didn't deserve to die."

"No, he didn't." Gaetan trailed his fingers along her arm until he reached her hand. He took her palm in his. "Let me tend to your wound."

She blinked, her gaze flicking to their clasped hands. "That place didn't look familiar. It wasn't Earth. Do you think it was Lemuria? Was it real?"

He drew a small cloth from his pocket, dipped the end in the water, and carefully wiped away the blood from her cut. "You have a small scrape. With your Dren heritage I suspect you'll heal in no time, and yes, I think the images were real. I suspect we saw a recording of some sort, and it appears Mitan discovered Earth first. I wonder if Alora knows about this or that Zedron murdered him."

"Can you contact her?" With a gentleness he was fast becoming used to, Nicole grazed her fingers over his brow, stopping for a moment to toy with the shock of gray. Her touch sent a rush of blood south. His inner beast growled.

"You don't contact the gods. They contact you." He turned her hand over, palm up, and brushed his fingers against hers, encouraging her to open for him.

She complied on a soft inhale.

He stroked her palm with his forefinger, tracing the outline of the letter 'M.' "At least we have an answer to this mystery. You are a descendant of Mitan, one of his characters."

She blinked, but didn't draw away from his touch. "How is that possible? I'm human."

He pondered her question, letting the implications sink in. "I'm not sure, but what would happen to his characters when he died? Especially if no one knew he'd placed them here?"

"Would they die, too?" She pulled her full, plump lower lip between her teeth, gnawing on the delicate flesh.

The urge to kiss her rippled through him, sending another rush of blood to his already engorged shaft. Surreptitiously, he adjusted his stance and returned his attention to her eyes.

The dark pupils dilated, and she drew away, her fingers skating over his marking. "Or maybe they lived…and bred with the humans."

He let her go, but a twinge tightened his chest. "That's possible and would explain the mark on your hand."

She strode to the desk, and he couldn't help but notice how her hips swung from side to side, enticing him. Brows scrunched together, she studied the open pages of an old tome. "You mentioned earlier that you found a passage about 'free will.' What did you mean?"

"From what I could gather, it means we have the ability to choose sides in this war. I thought we were bound to fight for our goddess, Alora, not that I would choose to leave her, but it looks like we have the ability to choose, hence, free will." He stroked his chin. "Kaelyn, the Ursus queen, would find that information useful I'm sure."

"That's good news." Nicole smiled, but her eyes held a hint of sadness.

An ache built inside, hardening to the point of pain. He brought his fingers to his throat and touched the skin. He couldn't see the line that circled his throat, but it was there. Nicole was his mate, and they seemed so compatible, but the solitary mark didn't lie. Their relationship wouldn't be a good one. Yet, he couldn't deny his attraction to her. He curled his fingers around his cane and shuffled across the floor to join her.

"This can't be easy for you. Your world has changed so much over the past couple of days." *...and that's my fault.* He bit down on the words. She wouldn't be here with him now if his cane hadn't knocked against his knee, alerting the Gossum. He'd ripped her from her life, uprooted her, bonded to her, but a part of him was glad, and he hated himself for it. What had her life been like? His gut churned, but he had to know.

She turned to look at him. Her blonde hair cascaded around her shoulders, accentuating her soft skin and beautiful eyes.

Craya... His chest tightened, squeezing the breath from his lungs. He didn't deserve her, never would, but that didn't stop his desire for her. "Tell me more about your brother."

She inhaled, studying him, her green eyes glimmering. After a long moment, the muscles in her shoulders relaxed, and she leaned her hip against the wooden table. "His name was Toby, and he was just like Ginnia, special."

She licked her lips, and he focused on them for a moment before returning his attention to her eyes. "Tell me more."

She rubbed her fingers over the wound on her hand. A small scab had already formed. The rhinestones in her bracelet caught the light from the sunstones lining the walls, flaring like brilliant white stars. "He was born with Down Syndrome and never progressed past the mental age of five." Her eyes sparkled, but there was a sadness in her gaze.

He swallowed the lump in his throat. What would he do if he ever lost Ginnia? She was as much a part of him as his deformed leg. "You loved him very much. What happened?"

She blinked several times and gnawed at her lip in that adorable way he'd grown to love. "There was a car wreck. My father...he..." She shook her head and looked away.

Gaetan cupped her chin, his thumb stroking her cheek. "Please tell me."

She peered at him, and the sea-green hue of her eyes held such sorrow, it called to him on a level so deep his soul ached. He cared for her, more than he should. A heat wave crested over his shoulders, accompanied by a round of regret. She wouldn't love him back. The single band around his throat was proof.

"My dad was an alcoholic. He was drunk the night of the accident, but insisted on taking us for a ride. I didn't want to go, but I was barely eighteen and couldn't stop him from taking Toby, so I went along. At the time, Toby was only twelve. I survived. They didn't." The pain in her eyes bore into him, eating into his soul like acid. Gaetan, with his pain med addiction, was too much like her father.

He couldn't breathe. *No. I won't go down that road. I care for her too much.* Yet, he wasn't sure he could fight that battle on his own. Even now, a trickle of sweat raced down his back, the need for a pill churning in his gut.

"I'm sorry for your suffering. You miss Toby very much, I can tell. What about your mother?" He couldn't stop himself and tugged a few stray strands of hair behind her ear. The silky tresses produced tingles along the ends of his fingers.

A twinge crossed her features. "She died during Toby's childbirth. I ended up taking care of Toby most of the time since father wouldn't, and I resented him for it. He was never there for me when I needed him."

"You're a strong, beautiful, caring female. Toby was lucky to have you."

A soft, relieved breath eased from her. "Ginnia, she reminds me of

125

Toby." Her attention focused on him, searching. "You said there was an accident. Will you tell me about it?"

Gods, how could he ever tell her about Ginnia and what happened that day so long ago? He pinched the bridge of his nose and sighed.

Nicole ran her fingers over the mark on his hand. The lines for benevolence and empathy burned, darkening. "Please, tell me."

He swallowed the bitterness and self-hatred rising in his throat. If there was anyone who should know everything about him, it was his mate, wasn't it? "Nicole, I don't deserve you."

Her brows drew together over her beautiful eyes. "How can you say such a thing? You are thoughtful and loving. From what I've seen, you care for others, but you won't care for yourself. Why?"

He couldn't take her scrutiny any longer and turned away.

She gripped his arm. "This starts with Ginnia, doesn't it? You became a healer to tend to others because of what happened with your sister."

The muscles in his arms tensed, but he didn't look at her.

"She told me she doesn't blame you. Whatever it is, you can tell me."

He flinched. Frustration, anger, and desire all bubbled over in a confusing, toxic brew. With a quick turn, he tugged Nicole against him, wrapping her in his embrace. "You really want to know?"

Her hands landed on his pecs, warm and enticing, as she stared into his eyes. "Yes."

"It's my fault she's the way she is." The words came out rougher than he'd intended.

"I doubt that."

"It's true."

The creases around her eyes softened, concern and empathy reflecting within her solemn gaze. "Tell me."

He clamped his jaw so tight his teeth ached, but then the words flowed and he couldn't stop them. "One night when my parents were out of our chamber, I crept into their room, found my father's sword resting against the fireplace. Ginnia snuck up on me, like she does sometimes when she plays hide and seek..."

Her breath hitched, and she moistened her lips, waiting for him to continue.

He cradled her chin in his palm and stroked his thumb over her bottom lip, tugging at the soft flesh. "When she called my name, she startled me. I yelled and dropped the blade. It sliced through my leg, damaging the tissue as well as the bone. Ginnia," he swallowed, "fell and hit her head against the fireplace."

Nikki shook her head, her gaze never leaving his. "That wasn't your fault. What happened was an accident."

"No! I *am* to blame—"

Before he could say another word, she raked her fingers through his hair and kissed him. Her soft, welcoming lips molded to his, and he couldn't stop himself, returning her kiss with a passion he'd never known before. Gods, if only he deserved her.

CHAPTER 24

$\mathcal{T}$he sharp clip of Kaelyn's shoes echoed off the corridor walls, in counterpoint to Saar's heavy boots. She curled her hand into a fist, her nails digging into her palm. The battle at Mauree's hideout had garnered good news and bad. Mauree didn't have Anlon, which was good, but he was still missing, and that was bad. In addition, they'd lost two warriors in the skirmish before retreating to the Keep.

"You're agitated, warrior queen. Planning our next steps?" Saar rubbed his hand down her back, easing some of the tension.

She peered at him, noting how the dimple in his unblemished cheek formed as he smiled. Respect and love radiated from his eyes. She gripped his hand, intertwining her fingers with his. "Absolutely. I want revenge, but Anlon and Gaetan are still out there. I fear they could be—"

"Don't say it. I'm as worried about them as you are. Scouts searched until dawn and will resume the quest at nightfall. Until then, we must wait."

Kaelyn exhaled. "We need to get to the Hall of Scriptures to see if Tanen had any more luck than we had. We could use a break in this war."

Light from the doorway cast shadows onto the corridor walls. The sunstones embedded in the rock glittered in the soft glow.

"Tanen's done an outstanding job of cleaning up the Hall of Scriptures. Perhaps he's discovered something about the new Dren and the strange symbol in their palms." At the room's entrance, Saar stepped back, letting her enter first. As she passed, he gave her bottom a gentle pinch.

"Hey, watch what you're doing." She batted away his hand, but couldn't help the smile that tugged at her lip.

A bit of golden amber flashed through his eyes. "I watched every detail."

She leaned into him and whispered, "If you like details, I have something I can show you later, close up." Before drawing away, she nipped his ear.

The rumble in his chest was his only reply.

"Saar, Kaelyn, so good to see you." Tanen placed his hands on one of the tables and rose from his chair. The legs scraped against the stone floor, the screech echoing down the long stacks of books. He wore a jacket, but his collar was unbuttoned and his hair was mussed, as if he'd run his fingers through the locks multiple times. Lines rimmed his tired eyes.

Close to Tanen, Sheri stood near a rack of books. She gave them both a comforting smile.

Demir and Aramie sat at the adjacent table, several old tomes spread across the surface. Aramie's red barrette was tilted at an odd angle. A few stray hairs protruded from between the clasp. Demir's long, dark hair hung around his ears, and the diamond stud in his nose glinted in the light. Both had weary smiles for their queen.

Kaelyn gave each of them a quick nod. "I'd ask if you've had any luck, but by the look on your faces, I'd say the answer is 'no.' "

Tanen sighed and ran his hand through his hair. "Not yet. We've been through so many texts—"

"But not the right one." Ginnia's soft voice filtered through the doorway. She peeked around the corner then disappeared from sight.

Startled gasps rose from the group.

ROSALIE REDD

Tanen closed his book with a loud slap. "What is she doing out of her cell?"

"Good question. Let me handle this." Saar took a few cautious steps toward the entrance. "Muzzie, is that you?"

"No." Her emphatic word echoed into the room.

Kaelyn stifled a laugh. She should be worried, upset that the seer was loose, but she never believed for a moment that Ginnia was harmful to anyone.

"Come now, Muzzie. You can't hide from me. Might as well join us." Saar peeked through the doorway.

Ginnia giggled and ran into his arms. The love between the two warmed Kaelyn's heart, bringing hot tears to her eyes.

Saar released Ginnia and smiled. "Muzzie, what are you doing here? How did you get out of your cell?"

Gaetan's sister gaped at the others in the room then hid behind Saar. "Nikki needed to go after Gaetan, so I helped her."

Kaelyn's pulse quickened. She took a tentative step toward Ginnia, not wanting to scare her off. "What do you mean 'you helped her.' Don't worry, hun, you're not in trouble."

She peeked from behind Saar, bits of brown hair sticking out from her head. "She needs to help Gaetan get better. I took her to see Rin, but he wasn't there, so I played with the sunstones and sent her to search for Gaetan."

"You did what?" Tanen drew closer, his brow furrowed.

Ginnia retreated behind Saar once again.

Kaelyn held out her hand, stopping Tanen. "It's okay. Let's hear what she has to say. Ginnia, please, tell us more."

"No." Ginnia voice quivered.

Saar drew her into his embrace. "It's okay, Muzzie. Just tell us what you know."

She glanced between them. "I heard you talking. I know where the book is that you're looking for."

Kaelyn's pulse spiked.

Tanen inhaled.

Sheri gripped his arm.

The scraping of chair legs against the stone floor echoed through the room. Demir cleared his throat. "You mean you've known all this time?" His brows arched over his chocolate eyes and his mouth curled. "Would've been nice to know that sooner."

Ginnia thrust out her bottom lip. "It wasn't time yet."

Kaelyn placed her hands over the seer's and gave her a gentle squeeze. "If you know where it is, please show us."

Saar led her toward the stacks. "Go ahead, Muzzie."

She placed her finger to her lips and a small grin formed. Happiness and energy radiated from her. She skipped over to the youth's section, rummaged behind some of the books, and withdrew a thick tome. "Here it is!"

Tanen gasped. "No way. We never bothered to look in the youth's area. Since we have no newbs in the Keep except for... Well, I just never thought it possible." He held out his hand. "Ginnia, may I?"

She brought the book to him and placed it in his palms.

His hands trembled. He glanced from Demir and Aramie to Saar before turning to Kaelyn. "I'll get right on this." He sat down and opened the tome, squinting at the small text. Aramie and Demir crowded around him, peering over his shoulder.

"Are you going to send me back to my cell?" Ginnia's mouth quivered and her eyes glistened with unshed tears.

Saar's gaze met Kaelyn's. Her heart ached for Gaetan's sister. As king, Noeh had imprisoned Ginnia for releasing Mauree. *Noeh is no longer here...* "Ginnia, I don't want to put you back in that cell, believe me, but as queen, I need your sincerest promise that you will behave yourself and abide by my rules. Can you give me your word?"

Ginnia scrunched her brow.

Saar trailed his finger under her chin. "Be good, Muzzie. That's what Gaetan would want you to do."

A smile blossomed on her face. "Oh, all right. I'll do it for my brother."

He drew her into his arms. "Good girl, Muzzie."

"Hey, I found something. This is unreal." Excitement laced Tanen's words.

Kaelyn approached Tanen, Saar and Ginnia, close at her heels. "What is it?"

Tanen cleared his throat. "It says here that there was a hidden chamber underneath Blue Pool—"

"Yes, I was there. That's where I found the blue sunstone," Aramie said.

Tanen shot her an impatient glance. "Bet you didn't know that there was another room at the far end of the chamber."

Her brows rose. "Another chamber?"

A lick of impatience slid through Kaelyn's veins. "Tanen, please continue."

Tanen focused on the large book. "Roan says he discovered several old tomes there and that's where he came up with much of the lore in his books. The more fascinating item, though, is that he claims Earth was first discovered by another god named Mitan. He'd had characters here, trying to figure out how to send water back to Lemuria."

"Just like Alora," Saar whispered.

"Roan indicates the entries stopped, mid-way, and he thinks something may have happened to Mitan. In any case, Roan discovered that some of Mitan's descendants mated with humans and some received a symbol in their hands, the letter 'M.' Roan believed it represented Mitan."

"Fascinating." Demir stroked his goatee. "How does this help us win the war?"

Tanen let out an exasperated breath. "I wish I knew—"

"But it explains why I, Nikki, and Melissa have the mark in our palms." Sheri held up her hand. The faint outline of the "M" was visible on her skin.

Ginnia stomped her foot. "Tell them the good part, Tanen, about what they are supposed to do."

A chill raced over Kaelyn's arms. "What do you mean, Ginnia?"

Everyone's attention drew to the seer.

She crossed her arms and pouted. "The part where the four elements destroy an enemy's army and send water back to Lemuria, silly."

"Uh…Ginnia. Do you know where that part is?" Kaelyn asked.

She nodded and glanced at the floor.

Tanen slid the book across the table, closer to Gaetan's sister. "Will you show us?"

Ginnia scooted a pebble across the floor with the tip of her worn brown shoes. "I won't get in trouble, will I?"

Kaelyn placed her hand on Ginnia's shoulder. "Of course not. You're helping us. A lot."

Ginnia peered at Kaelyn, her eyes searching, as if trying to decide if she could trust her. At long last, she took a hesitant step forward.

The pages in the old textbook fluttered, but there was no breeze.

Ginnia giggled, the sound reverberating in the space between them. "The textbook remembers me."

The chill that had raced over Kaelyn's arms returned full force, goosebumps forming in its wake.

Demir's shoulders tensed. "You read this before and didn't say anything to us about its contents?"

Ginnia met his gaze. "You didn't ask."

A slight growl eased from him. "Out of the mouth of babes…"

Kaelyn brushed her fingers over Ginnia's shoulder. "Please, continue."

"All right. I do that for you, Kaelyn, because I like you and you make Saar happy." She raised her hands over the book. As if the book understood what she wanted, the pages flipped, turning at a rapid pace. As quickly as it started, the pages stilled. Ginnia tapped her finger against the gilded-edge paper and slid the book to Tanen.

He gripped the binding and cleared his throat. "Four magical elements—earth, water, air, fire—will ignite the portal within Roan's rock sending energy to Lemuria. If anyone opposes the one who holds the blue sunstone, their army shall be vanquished." He scrunched his brow. "Says here that Roan tried to ignite the portal, but it didn't work. He said they didn't have the 'magical' elements."

Kaelyn's mind whirred. "I don't understand. Does this make sense to anyone?"

Sheri cleared her throat. "I think I might have a clue."

Kaelyn touched Sheri's arm. "Please, share."

Sheri ran her fingers over the gilded text. "I saw Nikki bubble the water in Coop's bowl, so she has the ability to control water. Through the use of her shield, Melissa could control air. My power is electricity, so that's fire. They're not the elements themselves, but manifestations, so…magical."

Silence filled the room.

"And the blue sunstone is earth. I think I understand." Tanen rose from his chair and paced the room. "These three females contain the magic. When all three of their elements converge on Roan's Rock, it will ignite the portal, destroy our enemy, and send water to Lemuria. We must get them all there to—"

Demir raised his hand. "Does no one but me see the problem here?"

"Nikki is missing and Melissa is gone," Aramie whispered.

He smirked. "Precisely, as well as Anlon."

Frustration beat against Kaelyn's temple. "What about the other Dren? Would one of them have the powers we need?"

Demir shook his head, the pointed tip of one of his fangs glinting in the light. "No. All the other Dren have telekinetic powers, not elemental."

Sheri waved her hand. "There's another problem. I saw Gaetan put the blue sunstone in his pocket, and he's gone as well."

Aramie growled. "Recommendations?"

Ginnia scraped the toe of her shoe over a loose rock, the grating noise loud in the silence. She peered from behind several loose strands of hair. "There's something else in Roan's book you should know."

Kaelyn straightened her shoulders. "There is? What do you know?"

"Let me show you." Ginnia approached Tanen and held her hand over the book's open pages. She closed her eyes, her mouth pursing into a determined line. The sheets in the book fluttered for a few moments before coming to rest on a new page. Ginnia opened her eyes and smiled. "You'll like this, Kaelyn, I promise."

"What does it say, Tanen?" Kaelyn whispered.

Tanen traced his finger over the words and read from the ancient text. "One of the gods' best kept secrets I discovered from Mitan's journal is the concept of 'free will.' Although we are selected to battle for a specific god in the war, free will allows us to choose sides. All we have to do is renounce our god and claim the free will rule."

Kaelyn held her breath as her mind raced with possibilities. "That means the Ursus can switch sides. I can convince them, I know I can."

Ginnia smiled. "I knew you'd be happy."

Demir tsked. "That's helpful to a point, but it doesn't change the fact we don't have the four elements."

Kaelyn's enthusiasm deflated. "You're right. What do we do now?"

Ginnia twirled the end of her hair between her fingers. "We wait."

The hair at Kaelyn's nape stood on end. "Wait for what?"

"There's a surprise coming. I think we're about to find out." Ginnia's soft laugh, along with dread's cool fingers, skittered along Kaelyn's nerves.

CHAPTER 25

$\mathcal{N}$icole's closeness and the feel of her silky skin under Gaetan's fingertips lit a fire deep inside. A slow growl rumbled in his chest. They only had today, for come nightfall, he'd resume his trek to find Anlon.

He slid his palm to the base of her scalp and drew her to him, giving her a blinding kiss. He poured all his love for her into their connection, letting her know without words that she owned his heart. She moaned under his onslaught, soft sighs of encouragement urging him onward.

Her firm breasts and taut nipples rubbed his chest, teasing him. He tightened his grip around her waist and tugged her closer. His erection pressed alongside her hip, straining against his pants, the material cutting into his balls.

Breaking their kiss, he growled. "My sweet Nicole, what you do to me."

"Gaetan…" Nicole tugged her lip between her teeth in that sensual way that drove him crazy. "You can't blame yourself for other people's—"

He placed the pad of his fingertip over her plump lips. "Sh…no talking."

She sighed and gave him an acquiescing nod.

Her acceptance and trust bolstered his love for her. All he wanted was to kiss her and show her what she meant to him. He trailed his finger over her chin and along her collarbone, enjoying the softness of her skin. Through her thin shirt, he grazed her nipple with his thumb and cupped her breast in his palm, the heavy weight sending a zip of excitement along his nerves.

She inhaled at his touch, and a slow moan eased from her. Before he could react, she gripped the edge of her shirt and ripped it over her head. The material landed on a pile of rocks. With a sly smile, she unhooked her bra, and it slid down her arms and landed at her feet. He sucked in a sharp breath, his arousal growing. She was exposed to him now, and he couldn't stop himself from admiring how her pink nipples hardened from the chill air.

The burning need to be with her raced through him. He placed one hand around her waist and another under her legs, sweeping her into his arms.

A small squeal rushed from her lips, and she wrapped her arms around his neck.

"Would you like to feed from me?" He hoped so, more than he cared to admit.

Nicole nodded. "If you don't mind."

"Mind? Not at all." He grazed his thumb over her bottom lip, and her fangs elongated. Pretty and white, they gleamed in the light.

He cradled her close, and she sank her teeth into the soft spot between his neck and his collarbone. A brief pinprick of pain then a rush of pleasure struck him as she tugged at his throat. With gentle caresses, he stroked his fingers against her thigh.

Joined in unison, he enjoyed the pleasurable sensation of their hearts beating as one. After a long moment, she withdrew her fangs. A blissful smile curled her lip, and her hooded eyes gleamed with happiness.

He strode over the stone floor, forcing his bad leg to carry its share of the weight. Blessedly, there was no pain. As he laid her on the bed, her hair framed her beautiful features. He leaned down and brushed his lips over hers in a barely-there kiss then drew back to study her.

The look of pure adoration in her eyes just about broke him and another knot around his heart loosened. She could never love him, not with his broken body and tormented soul, but he'd give her all his love, every last ounce.

"These have to go." He gripped the waistband of her pants.

She worked the zipper, easing it down with a quick zip. The sound echoed in the small chamber. With a firm jerk, he had her pants and underwear off in a flash.

His mouth went dry.

Completely naked before him now, her entire beauty took his breath away. Lovely, full breasts with small, tight nipples, a smooth, flat waist that flared into well-rounded hips, and long toned legs begged for a male's touch...for his touch. He kneeled on the bed with his good leg, his damaged one dangling over the edge.

Starting at her pretty toes, nails polished in a enchanting green that matched her eyes, he brushed his fingers over her soft, silky flesh. The pads on his fingers tingled.

She squirmed, and a husky laugh burst from her lips, those beautiful, luscious lips. "That tickles."

Oh, how he loved the shine in her eyes, and he wanted to tease her again and again, to burn that look into his memory. He placed his palms on each thigh and gently coaxed her to open to him.

A sense of unease flickered across her features.

His heart stuttered. "What's wrong?"

"I...I've never done that before." Her cheeks tinged a bright shade of pink.

"Never?"

She shook her head.

That he would be the first, no...the *only* one to give her such pleasure warmed his heart. An overwhelming urge to please her in this most intimate way raced through him, and the markings for empathy and patience burned on the back of his hand. He stole a glance at it. The lines reappeared, faint, but there. His chest swelled.

"My sweet Nicole, I would be honored if you would allow me to pleasure you."

She nodded once, desire sparking in her green depths.

Gaetan's throat constricted. She trusted him. He wouldn't let her down. With a gentleness she brought out in him, he slid his hands up each of her thighs, spreading her legs. The delicious scent of melons wafted into the air. He inhaled, enjoying her luscious scent. "My sweet Nicole..."

A smile tugged at her lips, blooming across her face, brightening her eyes. His heart leapt at the sight. He returned his attention to her moist, pink folds. They glistened with her desire, her want and need for him. He didn't deserve her, he never would, and that saddened him. How could the bonding only give him a single band? Being with her felt so good, so right.

Not wanting his negativity to spill over to her, he pushed the thought from his mind. He'd satisfy her until she screamed his name.

Gripping her thighs with his palms, he planted light kisses up the inside of one thigh, taking his time until he reached the juncture between her legs. With a long, languorous stroke, he licked her warm, slick creases, tasting her for the first time.

"Gaetan...please..." She gripped his hair, her fingernails digging into his scalp.

A low growl rumbled in his chest. "Not yet. I can't neglect your other leg, now can I?"

"You're torturing me." She squirmed, her hips wriggling beneath him.

Gaetan chuckled. "Perhaps I am."

He pulled back and retreated to her knees once again, trailing tender kisses up her other thigh. The need to taste her again, have her writhing from his ministrations, urged him onward. When he reached her mound, he slid his tongue over her entrance. She shuddered beneath him, her breaths fast and heated.

Her round nub hardened while he circled his tongue over the delicate flesh. She bucked against the bed, and a soft cry rose from her lips. "I'm so sensitive..."

He tightened his grip on her thighs, holding her in place. With deliberate intent, he moaned as he took her hard clit between his lips, sucking, pulling, tugging.

On the brink of her orgasm, she trembled, her legs shaking with anticipation. Her gaze never wavered from him, trust reflected in her beautiful eyes.

"Come for me, my sweet Nicole. Come for me." He laved his tongue over her folds and her hard little nub, again and again, increasing his speed with each swirl.

"Gaetan!" At last, her orgasm broke through, her muscles shuddering with her release. He kept up his focused attention, riding the crest right along with her.

Nicole gripped his hair. "Stop. I can't take anymore."

Not that he wanted to, but he complied with her request.

She stilled beneath him. The tension in her legs drained away, but a small tremble still fluttered along one thigh.

"That was amazing," she whispered.

His heart swelled. He'd pleased her in a way she'd never experienced before, and she'd trusted him, let him touch her in this intimate way. His throat constricted so tight, he almost couldn't breathe.

She slipped her legs from between his grasp and propped herself on her knees. Swift and demanding, she gripped the edge of his pants. A slow, sexy smile tugged at her lips. "Your turn. Let me pleasure you."

Gaetan's mouth went dry. If he removed his pants, she'd see his deformed leg and reject him. A sheen of sweat coated his back. He drew away, sliding off the bed until he stood near the end. "No."

CHAPTER 26

*N*ikki's heart skipped a beat. She wanted to please Gaetan the way he'd pleasured her, showing him how much she cared, but he'd backed away, fear etched in the creases around his eyes. He stood at the edge of the bed, his brow furrowed.

"No," he growled.

She slid off the bed and brushed her hands down his arms. "Gaetan, what is it?"

His leg. He doesn't want me to see his leg.

The truth reflected in his gaze.

She clasped her hand around his and brought them to eye level. "Look at me, medicine man. I care about you." She wanted to tell him she loved him, but she wasn't sure he was ready to hear those words. By the remorseful shadow darkening his eyes, he still harbored needless guilt. Besides, she wasn't sure he could kick his addiction, and long term, she couldn't deal with that.

He shook his head, the furrow between his brows deepening. "I don't deserve—"

She placed her finger over his lips, just as he'd done to her. "Shh... You care so much for others, let me do this for you."

Pain reflected in the tension lines etched in his cheeks, but he didn't look away.

She took that as a sign to proceed, so she tugged at his shirt, pulling the material free from his waistband. With a quick jerk, he drew the bit of clothing over his head and it landed next to hers with a soft swish.

She stroked his firm biceps, slowing for a moment to enjoy the strength under the taut skin. Over his shoulders and down his chest, she brushed her fingers until she reached his ribbed abs. She paused and teased the strip of hair that travelled from his navel beneath his waistband.

The muscles in his abdomen tightened beneath her touch. Pleased with his reaction, a thrilling shiver raced through her. She smiled at him then slipped her finger under his waistband. The sensitive nerves on her fingertip brushed against the tip of his erection.

He sucked in a quick breath and gripped her arms. "You tease me."

She widened her grin. "Tit for tat, my medicine man."

A brief flash of gold flickered in his eyes. "Be careful, my sweet Nicole..."

She pressed her hand beneath his waistband and slid her palm down his shaft. Oh, heavens, he was long, firm, and so, so smooth. She grasped him between her fingers and gave him a gentle but firm squeeze.

A growl, low and predatory, rushed from his lips, and his grip on her arms tightened.

Careful not to cause pain, she rubbed him, slow and steady, working him as best she could given the constraints. She wanted to get him frustrated enough to the point he'd take off his pants and let her see his damaged leg.

A tic started in his jaw. Hot, fast breaths eased from his lips.

She stroked him, squeezed him, teased him, and a wave of desire and need crested over her, sending a rush of wetness to the juncture between her legs. The musky scent of her arousal filled the air.

Gaetan's nostril's flared. "I can't take this anymore."

As he pulled away, panic flared in her gut. Had she gone too far in order to get him to reveal his injury? Would he reject her? Walk away from her and leave her stranded?

Gold flecks swirled in his beautiful aquamarine eyes, and his mouth drew into a thin line, determination tightening his features. He toed off his boots. As each hit the floor, the thump resounded throughout the room.

He gripped his waistband, unzipped his pants, and without breaking eye contact with her, let his slacks fall to the floor. With a quick flick of his foot, he tossed his trousers aside. Free from its confinement, his member jutted straight from him, proud and hard. His heavy, full balls hung below. Oh, holy hell, he was magnificent.

Her gaze swept downward, coming to rest at his misshapen leg. Twisted and gnarled, his knee bowed. Scar tissue marred the skin from mid-thigh to mid-calf. The sword had caused horrific damage.

She blinked back tears and raised her eyes to his.

His unflinching gaze bore into her. He raised his chin.

Her heart swelled even as it ached for him, for his loss, his guilt, his personal torment. He didn't deserve any of it.

Silence filled the room and it took half a second for her to realize he held his breath.

She drew her attention to his eyes.

He studied her, and tension radiated in his taut features.

Hot tears threatened to spill over her lashes. "You are so beautiful."

He swallowed and drew in a large breath.

"May I touch you?"

His shaft jerked at her words, as if eager for the attention.

Unable to help herself, she smiled. "I want to touch you there, too, but that's not what I meant."

"I know what you meant." His voice was low, controlled.

Would he let her? Fear twisted her insides into a ball.

She wouldn't rush him. Instead, she reached up and toyed with the small shock of gray hair at his temple. She trailed her finger down the side of his face and kissed him, slow and gentle.

When she broke the kiss, he whispered, "I am yours, now and forever. There is nothing off limits to you."

His faith in her, belief that she wouldn't reject him, warmed her soul. She nodded and knelt at his feet. Brushing her fingers down his thigh, she took a moment to plant a light kiss at the end of his shaft.

"*Craya!*" he hissed and wrapped his fingers in her hair.

She brushed her fingertips along the scar tissue. Although bumpy and mottled, his skin was remarkably soft. She circled the blemish, but didn't dwell on it, then turned her attention to his shaft.

Firm and long, his erection swayed with each of his breaths. A bead of moisture glistened at the tip. The sudden urge to lick the end zipped along her nerves. She clasped him, her fingers barely able to circumvent his size. With a quick flick of her tongue, she circled his crown, licking the droplet from the end.

His low and deep groan rumbled in his chest. He tightened his fingers in her hair, and he drew her closer. She eased him into her mouth, letting him slide along her tongue.

"Nicole, I can't take this. I want to be inside you." After releasing his grip, he grasped her arm and tugged her into his embrace. His warm lips met hers, and he devoured her in a bruising kiss, one that burned all the way to her soul.

She cared for him, loved him, and always would, even though she'd have no choice but leave him if he couldn't conquer his addiction. After what she'd endured from her father, she wouldn't survive another heartbreak.

His erection pulsed long and hard against her hip. "Nicole, I want you, need you."

She drew back, gripped his arm, encouraging him to lie on the bed.

His jaw tightened. "Not that way."

Faster than she thought possible, he flipped her around. With a gentleness that was branded into her soul, he gripped her hips and eased her onto the bed. Knees bent, hands on the comforter, she spread her legs for him.

He swept loving kisses across her shoulder while he stroked a few stray strands of hair away from her cheek. His compassionate touch only endeared him to her all the more.

Wiggling her bottom, she pressed against him, teasing him. He groaned and rubbed his erection along her pliant folds, taunting her in return. The sensitive nerves sent tendrils of excitement through her body. She writhed under his attention and placed her cheek against the soft pillow.

"Gaetan, please."

At long last, he entered her from behind, filling her with his engorged shaft. She stretched to accommodate his size, and when she relaxed against him, he moved with a slow grace. Blissful shudders rocked her. She met him stroke for stroke, and the bed squeaked in rhythm to their movements.

His pace increased, and a bead of sweat dripped from his brow onto her back. Ever so slightly, his erection hardened all the more. In response, a rush of wetness coated her passage and another orgasm rippled through her, sending sparks of light through her vision.

A deep, feral cry escaped from his lips. He stilled, holding her close as his release filled her with everything that was Gaetan. At his last shudder, he rolled them both to the bed.

She turned to glance at him. A slow, sexy smile tugged at his mouth. She traced over the corner then peered into his eyes.

Warmth reflected in their depths, but the sadness, the unending guilt still remained. How she longed to wipe away his pain, make him realize he wasn't to blame for others' choices, but that was something he had to discover on his own.

"Come here, my sweet Nicole." He tugged her against him, back to front. With long, smooth strokes, he brushed his fingers through her hair. The soothing sensation relaxed her, and she snuggled deeper into his embrace. She was both elated and somber. Her doubts about them overshadowed her strong feelings of affection for him. Unable to stay awake any longer, sleep finally claimed her.

CHAPTER 27

*N*ikki rolled over and buried her nose into the comfy pillow. Gaetan's unique scent filtered into her senses, and she tugged the cushion closer. Memories of their day together flitted across her mind, warming her. She slid her hand across the sheet, searching for him and wanting to snuggle once again.

Cool and barren to the touch, his place on the bed was empty. Goosebumps raced up her arm. She opened her eyes in an instant. "Gaetan?"

No response.

She pushed away from the pillow and caught a glimpse of her arm. A dark mark trailed from her left shoulder, around her elbow, and down to her wrist where it split into four lines ending at her knuckle. The mark mirrored the one on Gaetan's right arm. *I'm his mate.*

Her chest flooded with love for him, yet, a twinge of unease danced along her nerves. *His addiction was so like her father's.*

The slight swish of a page turning caught her attention.

Seated in the rickety chair, Gaetan, wearing his shirt, long pants and shoes, poured over an old text. He skimmed his finger over the page and his lips moved, silently forming the words.

She draped the sheet around her and scooted to the edge of the bed. "Gaetan?"

Brow furrowed in concentration, he didn't move.

As her feet touched the cold stone floor, a tingle of dread chilled her arms. "Gaetan, did you find something?"

He flinched. "Nicole, I'm sorry. I didn't realize you'd woken."

His gaze drew to the dark mark on her arm. He stood, and a masculine, possessive growl broke from him. "Nicole, my mate."

The deep timbre of his voice had her crossing the floor in an instant. She tumbled into his embrace, and he pressed a powerful, possessive kiss to her lips. The warmth and desire emanating from him sent a thrilling shiver travelling through her.

When she wasn't sure she could take much more, he broke the kiss, placing his forehead against hers. His cool breaths teased her cheek. "My sweet Nicole."

She glanced to her left, toward the open tome on the desk that had captured her attention. "What are you reading?"

His gorgeous aquamarine eyes flashed with excitement. "There's so much history in these books. You'd be amazed at what I've discovered."

His enthusiasm endeared him to her. She placed her palm on his shoulder and smiled. "Tell me."

"Mitan built a reactor to transport energy to Lemuria. Based on his description and approximate location, I believe that reactor is Roan's Rock."

She scrunched her forehead. "Roan's Rock?"

He exhaled. "It's a large boulder, its base larger than its tip, and sits in a meadow not far from here. We've used the place for many rituals over the centuries. I had no idea it was something more."

"Okay, so what does this information mean for our future?"

A brief flicker of disappointment crossed his features. "I'm working on that."

His stomach rumbled, the sound loud in the small cave.

She squeezed his shoulder, enjoying how his firm muscle tightened under the pressure. "I noticed some jars of fruit in the cupboard. Food sounds good to me. How about you?"

His gaze focused on the sheet wrapped around her body, lingering for a moment at her breasts before returning to her eyes. Heat flared between them, and a slow, sexy smile curled his lip. "I'd rather have you, but sunset will be here soon."

A mixture of desire, sadness, and regret swept through her like a tornado. If she didn't know better, she'd have sworn her hair moved in the breeze. Of course, he needed to get on with his mission, find Anlon. Bitterness at her own selfishness crawled up her throat.

She forced a quick smile. "I'll be right back."

After running to her clothes, she dressed as fast as possible. Her pants were still damp, but that helped ease the hot sting of rejection burning her skin. As she strode to the cabinet, she peered at him.

Hunched over the old books once again, his guilt and self-blame were etched in the lines on his face. Her heart ached for him. Focusing on her task, she yanked two jars from the shelf.

With a quick twist, she opened the first. The sweet scent of peaches filled the air. Her mouth watered in anticipation. The second jar followed suit. Several utensils lay on the bottom shelf. She grabbed two forks then picked up the jars and returned to Gaetan.

She handed one to him, and as their fingers brushed, the heat flared between them once again.

"Thank you." He ran his hand up her arm until he'd wrapped his fingers in the hair at her nape. Gently, he eased her toward him. His tender kiss electrified the nerve endings and sent a tingle all the way to her fingertips. "My sweet Nicole."

Love for him spilled from her heart. She wanted to reach into his chest and, through sheer force of will, repair his broken soul. Unable to help him, frustration burned inside. She couldn't look at him, so she motioned to the peaches. "These smell good, but I haven't tasted them yet."

He stuck his fork in one then slid a single slice between his lips. His eyebrow rose as he chewed.

She leaned against the table. "Is it okay?"

He winked at her and swallowed. "Food from the gods."

A giggle bubbled up inside, and she bit into one for herself. The sweet flavor woke her taste buds, sending them into overdrive. "This is delicious."

They ate in silence for a moment, enjoying the peaches and each other's company.

She focused on the books. "Did you find anything else?"

"I read a passage on Mitan's theoretical use of the reactor."

"Theoretical?" She swallowed the last bite of peach and set the jar on the end of the table.

He nodded, setting his empty container next to hers and returning his attention to the book. "Mitan indicated he hadn't tested the reactor yet, but that it needed all four elements to ignite."

"All four elements? You're testing my memory of my limited high school science class. Do you mean earth, water, fire, and air?"

He smiled. "Something like that. Here, let me read the next section."

She gave him a quick nod.

He skimmed his finger over the text. *"The four magical elements should ignite the reactor, sending hydrogen molecules through the portal to Lemuria. Once there, they can be combined with two oxygen molecules to create water."* Gaetan inhaled and glanced at her. "Mitan searched for water, too. Fascinating."

She leaned closer to him, enjoying his unique fragrance as it washed over her. "What else does it say?"

He swept his gaze from her breasts to her eyes. Desire sparked within his depths, and she wanted to lose herself in them. No, she already had.

He swallowed and focused on the text once again. *"A great energy burns from the rock, as if it has a mind of its own. If not used with care, it can be deadly to those that oppose it. Use caution."*

Nikki scrunched her nose. "Does that make sense to you?"

"Not initially, but let me continue." He ran his hand through his hair and focused on the writing once again. *"Initial tests indicate all elements must be present. The catalyst is the blue sunstone. Whoever possesses the magical gem shall command the other elements, Roan's Rock, and the power within."*

"The blue sunstone..." Nikki pushed away from the table, her heart pounding. "Do you still have it?"

Faster than she thought possible, Gaetan stood. His sudden movement sent the chair crashing against the stone floor. He shoved his hand into his pocket. Relief flickered over his features. After withdrawing the stone, Gaetan raised the sacred gem to eye level. Light from the sunstones lining the walls flared, refracting in the blue crystal's soft glow.

"Ginnia was right. We need this crystal." Gaetan's attention slid from the blue sunstone to Nikki. "The pieces are beginning to fit together. I believe we might have a chance in this war after all."

Confusion clouded her mind. "What do you mean?"

He grasped her hand, unfurling her fingers. With deliberate attention, he swirled his thumb over the 'M' etched in her palm. "In addition to the blue sunstone, I believe we have all the magical elements. They are bound in the new Dren. You are Mitan's descendant and your power is water. Sheri is also a descendant. Her power is fire. Air belongs to..."

The muscles in Gaetan's shoulders tightened. His features darkened. He released her hand and staggered against the table. "No, no, no."

Nikki's pulse spiked. She rushed to his side and placed her hand on his broad back. "What's wrong?"

"Melissa. She was the only other recent Dren. She had a shield power, the ability to bend air. Without her..." Ragged breaths eased from him.

The queen was dead. Nikki had never met Melissa, but she'd heard about her. "Sheri mentioned there are other Dren in the Keep. Do any of them have an air element for a power?"

"No. The other Dren all have telekinetic abilities to move or float objects. If not for Mauree, that traitorous..." Gaetan pushed away from the table. A tic pulsed in his jaw.

A tendril of fear snaked its way into Nikki's chest. "What's wrong?"

"Without Melissa, we can't ignite Roan's Rock." A tremble wracked his body, and his brow beaded with sweat.

Nikki brushed her fingers down his arm. "There must be something we can do."

"*Craya*, thinking of Melissa reminds me of the little prince. I made a vow to raise Anlon and still feel the commitment wrapped around my soul, so I know he's alive. Mauree or one of her minions must've found him. He's my responsibility. We can't do anything about the elements without Melissa, so I must save Anlon." He fumbled in his pocket and withdrew his satchel. Fingers trembling, he worked at the opening.

"Please don't." She placed her hand over his, trapping the small pouch in their combined grasp. "You don't need this. You said yourself the pain is gone. I heard you when we first arrived in the cave."

A wince crossed his features, darkening them. For several long seconds, neither moved, each evaluating the other. His jaw tightened, and he held out his palm. "Take them from me, please."

Her heart ached for him, but she wouldn't do it, wouldn't become his new crutch. She drew her hand away and shook her head. "No. This is something you have to do on your own. Toss them into the water if you must, but I can't do it for you."

His brow furrowed, pain etched within the crease. "I...I...don't know if I can."

"I have faith in you."

A keening cry erupted from him. He gripped the end of his cane, his fingers turning white from strain. A bead of sweat dribbled down the side of his face, evidence of his addiction. Jaw set, he strode toward the pool of water just outside the small room.

She followed him, hope filling her chest.

He stopped at the edge, the water lapping at the tiny pebbles. Clenched in his palm, the small ties of his satchel dangled from his fist. She stood behind him and couldn't see his face, but the muscles in his shoulders tensed.

C'mon Gaetan, I know you can do it. She wanted to voice her encouragement, say it over and over until he threw the damned medicine away, but she remained silent.

He raised his fist above the water and uncurled his hand. Ties wrapped around his fingers, the satchel dangled in the air.

Nikki held her breath. Her heart pounded in her ears.

A deep, mournful cry tore from his throat. He curled his fingers around the satchel and brought it to his chest. Working the ties, he shoved his hand into the bag and withdrew a single pill.

"Gaetan...please don't." Nikki's voice broke on a sob. Tears blurred her vision.

He met her gaze and shoved the small white tablet into his mouth. His Adam's apple bobbed as he swallowed. "I'm sorry, Nicole. I can't..."

A mixture of rage, bitterness, and grief ripped open her heart, as if smashing the fragile organ against the rocks at her feet instead of the pills she wished he'd crushed. Trembling, she turned her back on him.

"Nicole, I'm not worthy of you. There's something you need to know—"

Not willing to hear anymore, she pressed her palms over her ears. *No, no, no! This can't happen.* Her head spun, and she closed her eyes, trying to clamp down on the nausea rising in her throat.

He placed his hand on her arm.

"Don't touch me." She jerked away from him. Spittle flew from her lips.

He recoiled, pain etched in his beautiful eyes. "I'm the reason the Gossum attacked you."

"What?" Her mind spun as she processed his words.

"When we were in the woods, the Gossum attacked you because of me. It's my fault." He winced, and she couldn't stand to see that sad look on his face, the guilt etched deep in the creases in his forehead.

He cleared his throat. "The pain in my leg flared, and I knocked my cane against my knee. That's why the Gossum turned to investigate, but instead of attacking me, the damned thing assaulted you. If it hadn't been for me, you'd be home, living your life. What I've done to you is unforgivable."

Her throat constricted, tightening to the point she almost couldn't breathe. "I can't go through the pain of seeing you slip down the slow road of addiction, not after watching my father spiral down. You're too much like him."

"Nicole, please." He raised his hand, but then rested it at his side.

Steeling her heart, she used the fear, pain, and sadness flooding through her and swirled her palms over the water.

A tunnel opened, moonlight filtering through the hole.

Setting her jaw, she pointed toward it. "Go. Do what you must. Find Mauree and her minions."

"I won't leave you here." Gaetan's words slid inside, poking at the sore spot in her heart.

"Just go. Since I have your blood in me, I can contact Rin to open a portal and return to the Keep, alone."

He flinched. The agony burning in his eyes just about did her in. She bit back a sob and shook her head.

The lines around his mouth constricted. He tightened his grip on his cane and strode through the opening, taking her heart right along with him.

The crushing pain in her chest had her gasping for breath, and the urge to follow him warred with her conviction. She couldn't be with a mate addicted to drugs, no matter how much she loved him, no matter how much it hurt.

CHAPTER 28

*M*auree draped the knee-length, terry cloth bathrobe around her shoulders and tied the belt at her waist. Her skin still warm from her bath, she nuzzled against the soft fabric. Steam coated the mirror, obscuring her reflection. That was fine with her. She didn't need a reminder she was no longer beautiful.

Mauree picked up the eyepatch from the counter and, with more force than necessary, slapped it over her eye. The string snapped against her cheek, the sting bitter and swift, reminding her of the males who had betrayed her—Theron and Noeh. Both were dead. *Good riddance.*

Through the crack under the doorway, a blue mist filtered into the room, swirling with the steam.

Mauree tensed. *Zedron. What does he want now?* She tightened the belt around her waist.

The particles coalesced in the middle of the room, swirling and solidifying. Zedron, dressed in an impeccable tailored suit with wing tip shoes, met her gaze. A smile bloomed across his lips.

Despite the warmth in the room, a shiver ran down Mauree's legs. "What brings you here, my lord? If this is about Anlon, we're looking for the babe."

His attention flicked from her breasts hidden behind the robe to her bare legs before returning to her good eye. "No need. I know where he is. There is something more pressing I need you to do."

She leaned against the counter. "Of course, tell me."

"Watch. Learn." He flicked his finger to the water in the bathtub. The suds parted, and a blurry image graced the surface.

Mauree pushed away from the counter, curiosity bringing her to the tub's edge.

A waterfall appeared, a beautiful blue pool at its base. The rush of water echoed against the bathroom tile. Fresh and clean, the scent of pine, dampness, and wet foliage filled the room.

Mauree tapped one of her long red nails against the tile wall. "What am I supposed to see here?"

A rumble shook the house. Fine grains of dust fell from the ceiling.

Zedron narrowed his eyes. "Patience."

She swallowed hard. Awareness that he could crush her in an instant percolated over her skin. Yet, he'd come here for a reason. She focused on the picture.

Two figures stood at the base of the waterfall. One was a female she didn't know. The other—Gaetan, the Keep's haelen. "What is Gaetan doing outside the Keep?"

Zedron didn't reply. Not that she'd expected him to. She concentrated on the pair.

The two conversed, their hands waving in the air, but Mauree couldn't hear their words above the waterfall's roar. Gaetan tugged the female to him and gave her a powerful kiss. The female returned his passion.

A twinge hit Mauree in the chest. The intensity between the couple was something Mauree had wanted for so long and would never have. Unwilling to watch, she looked away. "Why are you making me watch this?"

Zedron tsked. "You aren't going soft on me, not now, are you?"

She clamped her jaw and snuck a glance at him. "No. Never."

"Good. If you had, I'd kill you on the spot." He winked at her.

Mauree swallowed and returned her attention to the image. The kiss broken, the female swirled her hands over the pool's edge. The water bubbled, frothing far more than the waterfall kicked up. An opening, like a tunnel, appeared, parting the water.

Mauree tilted her head. "Nice trick."

Zedron smirked. "I thought you'd like that. Look deep inside. What do you see?"

As the couple rushed through the tunnel, Mauree looked into the distance. "I see nothing but a small pool of water and a bunch of rocks. Is there some point to this visit?"

Zedron laughed, the menacing cackle growing in volume until the sound reverberated against the walls.

Perhaps this time, she'd stepped over the line. Not that she worried. She'd done far better than any of his other leaders. He'd be a fool to smack her down.

"You're always full of surprises, aren't you?" His smile seemed genuine, but she couldn't ignore the cool glint in his eyes. "Let me zoom in a bit for you."

He flicked his wrist and the picture enlarged. A small room at the back of the cavern became clear. Inside were a table, a bed, and a small basin filled with water.

She scrunched her brow. "I fail to see the significance—"

He held up his hand. "Wait."

The image flicked forward in time, in fast motion, until it stopped with Gaetan seated at the desk, pouring over the ancient texts. He read out loud. *"A great energy burns from the rock, as if it has a mind of its own. If not used with care, it can be deadly to those that oppose it. Use caution."*

The female scrunched her nose. "Does that make sense to you?"

"Not initially, but let me continue." Gaetan ran his hand through his hair and returned his attention to the old tome. *"Initial tests indicate all elements must be present. The catalyst is the blue sunstone. Whoever possesses the magical gem shall command the other elements, Roan's Rock, and the power within."*

"The blue sunstone..." The female pushed away from the table. "Do you still have it?"

Gaetan stood. The chair crashed to the stone floor. He shoved his hand into his pocket and withdrew the sacred blue gem.

"Ginnia was right. We need this crystal." Gaetan's attention slid from the blue sunstone to the female. "The pieces are beginning to fit together. I believe we might have a chance in this war after all."

The image faded, and the water in the tub returned to normal, the white porcelain reflecting the light.

Zedron leaned against the counter and crossed his legs at the ankle. "You must go to Roan's Rock and prevent Gaetan from achieving his mission."

Mauree's thoughts whirred. "...and what, exactly, is his mission?"

Zedron pursed his mouth. "If he uses the blue sunstone to ignite the portal within Roan's Rock then the backlash on all of you, my lovely characters, means you will die."

Mauree tapped her finger against the tile wall. "But I touched the blue sunstone to Roan's Rock. It slowed the Stiyaha but didn't kill them. Why would it kill us now?"

Zedron pushed away from the counter and invaded her personal space. She resisted the urge to recoil from him. He leaned in, and his breath tickled her ear. "I only showed you the most pertinent part, but the blue sunstone represents earth. The other elements—air, water, and fire—reside in three females...three Dren. Nikki, the one with Gaetan, has a power over water."

Who of the Dren had a power over air and fire? Mauree's breath hitched. "Melissa and Sheri are the other two."

"Now you're getting it. Stop Gaetan and his female before he reaches Roan's Rock. Get that blue sunstone. If he's figured out a way to start the reactor, they could win the war."

A drop of fear slid down the back of her throat. "That can't happen."

Zedron pulled back enough to meet her gaze. Steely resolve reflected in his eyes. "No, it can't, not if you want to enslave and rule the humans. That's why you're going to stop him."

The urge to please her god, beat down her rivals, and win this war once and for all, bolstered her determination. She clamped her teeth, her jaw tightening to the point of pain. "Gaetan's as good as dead. Him and that female."

Zedron stepped away, a smug smile tugging at his mouth. "Now that's the answer I wanted, no, expected to hear. Don't disappoint me."

She raised her chin. "Have I ever?"

He smirked. "That's why you're the leader of my army. Your bitterness keeps you honest."

Heaviness settled onto her shoulders. She mentally shook herself. "By the way, how did you see what transpired there?"

He winked at her. "That's my little secret."

Before she could ask him anything else, he transformed into the mist and disappeared the way he'd come.

She let out a relieved breath. Zedron had bolstered her desire to finish this war over Earth's water. One way or another, this game they played would end at Roan's Rock tonight.

CHAPTER 29

$\mathcal{M}$olecule by molecule, Alora transported into her home. Each time she propelled through space, the gnawing ache in her soul reminded her of how much she missed Veromé. *My mate.* As she solidified, she spied him leaning against the kitchen counter, his muscular arms crossed over his broad chest. He stared at the setting sun, a pensive glimmer in his eyes. She longed to trace her fingers over his smooth skin and feel his strength beneath her fingers.

"Veromé," she whispered.

His attention drew to her, and his features softened. "Alora."

He held out his arms, and she rushed into his embrace. Salty and fresh, his scent washed over her, spreading happiness within. He kissed her then peered into her eyes. A smirk played along his mouth. "Good to have you home. Anlon, that babe, has gotten into everything. He's running both Carine and I ragged."

She ran her fingers through his thick, shoulder-length brown hair. "No worries, my love. I plan to return him to Earth tonight."

"That's good. I'm not sure I could've survived another day here without you." Veromé kissed her again, his love for her evident in his passion.

When he let her go, she peered around. "Where is he?"

"Upstairs. With Carine. She's giving him a bath." He slid his hand down her waist and around her hip until his fingers grazed her bottom. "I wish we had more time together. You need to finish this war."

Before she could respond, tell him about the hidden page on the character board, and ask his opinion on whether to choose Noeh or Melissa, he dematerialized.

"I'm working on that." She sniffed and wiped at her eyes. *Oh, Veromé...*

The ding of her door chimes echoed through the room. She jerked, her legs trembling from the shock. *I must be on edge. Of course, I am. Zedron expects an answer, tonight.*

Letting out a slow breath, she headed for the front door. She gripped the handle and froze. *What if it's him?* A sour taste formed in the back of her mouth. She gritted her teeth. No way would she let him intimidate her.

With a quick tug, she yanked open the door.

"Hello, Alora." Zedron smiled, and the glint from the stud in his nose competed with his bright, shiny white teeth. "May I come in?"

She took an involuntary step back. Irritation that he'd caught her off balance sent her pulse racing. Regaining her composure, she raised her chin. "Enter, if you must."

He strode past her, his arrogance wrapped up in his cocky grin and nonchalant attitude.

"What do you want?" She spat the words at him.

He meandered over to her visus bacin and stroked his fingers along the rim. The water rippled. "What do I want?" He glared at her and raised an eyebrow. "An answer, naturally."

She fisted her hand so hard, her nails dug into her palm. The pain grounded her, gave her the strength to hold his gaze. "An answer to what?"

He tsked. "Come now, don't play games with me." He stared at the ceiling for a moment. "Perhaps that was a bad choice of words, since all we've done since this war started is play an elaborate game."

"Your point?"

"You know why I'm here. What did you decide? In lieu of going to the council and turning you in for coercion, are you giving me Carine, Anlon, or yourself?"

She held her breath. There was no way she'd send Carine back to that *Kasard*, and would she give him Anlon? A shudder wracked her shoulders.

He smirked. "Well? I'm waiting."

Hatred, hot and hard, bubbled from her soul. "Me. The answer is me."

A predatory smile slithered across his lips. His gaze drifted down her body, lingering at her breasts and then her hips before returning to her eyes.

Disgust made her lip curl.

"Excellent choice, Alora. That's what I'd hope you'd say." He strode toward her, his steps determined, purposeful. Before she could stop him, he wrapped his arm around her waist and drew her to him.

She squealed, her hands landing on his chest.

Smiling darkly, he gripped her chin and kissed her, hard.

He tasted of muldoberry wine and something vile.

With a shove, she broke the kiss. The slap of her palm against his cheek ricocheted around the small room.

"Get out," she yelled.

He tilted his head. "Have you changed your mind? Would you rather I go to the council? I can, you know."

Indeed, he could and would if she didn't comply with his demands. She toyed with the idea of allowing him to tell the council and win this war over Earth, but she couldn't give up on her characters and allow Zedron and his minions to enslave the humans.

"I hate you." Spittle flew from her mouth.

He shrugged, traipsed to the door, and gripped the handle. "You know where I live. If you don't show up before dawn, I'll know you've changed your mind. Then, I'll schedule an appointment with the council for tomorrow night. I'd like to see them sanction you for the third time, in person."

Without a second glance, he left and closed the door behind him.

The soft click echoed in the empty room.

"What have I done?" Alora's legs trembled, and she slid to her knees. Anguish, bitter and harsh, tore at her insides, ripping her heart to shreds. *Veromé...*

The soft squeak of footsteps on the stairs along with Anlon's soft coos broke through Alora's thoughts.

"Alora, are you okay? I thought I heard voices." Carine hurried down the stairs, Anlon bouncing in the crook of her arm. "Why are you on the floor?"

Alora rose to her feet and wiped the moisture from her eyes. "I'm fine Carine. It's nothing."

Carine studied her for a long moment, her mouth pulling into a thin line. "Have you decided?"

Alora inhaled. She hadn't told a soul about Zedron's demands.

Carine placed her hand on Alora's arm. "I know it's a hard decision, but Anlon deserves at least one of his parents back. Which will you choose? Noeh or Melissa?"

Alora let out a relieved breath. In all the commotion with Zedron, she'd forgotten about the hidden page on the character board. She tickled Anlon under the chin. "Who do you want, little one, your momma or your daddy?"

Anlon giggled. "Mom-ma."

Carine gasped. "My goodness. That's the first time I've heard him speak an entire word."

Alora rubbed her forehead. As much as she wanted to bring back Noeh, she couldn't imagine Anlon without his mother. "Well then, I guess we can't go against the little prince's wishes, now can we?"

Anlon clapped his hands, as if he'd understood the entire conversation. Perhaps he had.

Alora hurried to her character board and swiped her hands over the display. Red and green dots glowed softly on the screen. She narrowed her focus, concentrating on the deceased character list.

"Well, here goes nothing." Hand trembling, she pressed her fingertip to Melissa's name. Trailing her finger across the screen, she moved Melissa from "expired" to "active." The light remained dark.

Alora's pulse rose. "Did I do something wrong?"

Carine peered at the board, Anlon still on her hip. "Did you try—"

The light flared into a brilliant green, pulsing to life once again.

Alora's chest lightened, the heavy weight lifting in an instant.

"Where do you suppose she went?" Carine's wide gaze met Alora's.

"I don't know. I've never done this before and—"

"Hello?" A soft feminine voice floated across the room.

Alora and Carine both turned.

Melissa, dressed in a loose pair of slacks and a blouse, stood near the front door. Her gaze drew to her child. "Anlon!" She rushed across the room then tugged the babe from Carine's arms and held him close.

Anlon gripped a handful of Melissa's hair. Soft giggles eased from his throat.

Alora's chest constricted. The love between mother and child was a beautiful sight.

Still clutching him, Melissa peered over Anlon's head. Her brow furrowed. "Alora? Is it really you? Where am I?"

Alora strode toward her queen. "Melissa, you are on Lemuria. I was able to pull you from the character board and—"

A shimmer appeared by the door. Before Alora could so much as breathe, a male appeared. With his broad shoulders, short-cropped blond hair, and piercing blue eyes, there was no mistaking his identity.

Noeh assessed the room for a brief moment then he bolted to wide-eyed, sobbing Melissa and his son, embracing them. "My little kitten."

The happy trio kissed and laughed, their love for one another filling the room.

"How did this happen?" Carine whispered.

Alora pursed her lips, glancing at the character board. Next to Melissa, Noeh's green dot pulsed with life. "Noeh saved Melissa after Anlon's birth. They must still be tied together at the soul level." A weight Alora hadn't realized she'd carried lifted from her shoulders.

"Alora, my goddess." Noeh bent to one knee.

Melissa bowed her head.

Alora went to her king and placed her hand on his shoulder. "Rise, my son. You have returned from the character board to help me win this war." How that would happen, she wasn't sure, but she'd take this as a sign.

He stood, and Melissa straightened her shoulders.

"The war on Earth must end, soon. Zedron..." Alora fisted her hand and slammed it into her palm. "He can't win this war."

Noeh's gaze rose from Alora's lips to meet her eyes. "I'll do what I can, but where are we and why are we here?"

A small laugh caught in Alora's throat. Her eyes watered, and she wasn't quite sure if that was from the coughs wracking her lungs or her happiness at seeing her characters again. "Y...you are on Lemuria. This is my home, and this," she placed her hand on Carine's arm, "is my good friend, Carine. Through a special exception, I was able to return you to the game."

Noeh nodded to Carine in greeting then met Alora's gaze. "How do we return to Earth?"

Overwhelmed with happiness, Alora couldn't take it any longer, and she hugged Noeh then pulled back so he could read her lips. "You always were about business. I will send you there, now, so you can finish winning this war for me."

Gold flecks intermixed with the blue in his eyes, conviction lining his features. "As you command."

Alora placed one hand on Noeh's shoulder, another on Melissa's. She kissed Anlon on the forehead. "It was so nice see you, Anlon. Take care of your parents for me, okay?"

With that, Alora closed her eyes, homed in on the Keep, and sent the trio home.

As they vanished, determination built deep inside. There was no way she'd go to Zedron, throw away everything she had with Veromé. Instead, she'd let her nemesis stew, leave him hanging and take her chances with the council. There must be some way to defeat him and, council be damned, she'd find it.

CHAPTER 30

A bright flash of light filled the Hall of Scriptures, blinding Kaelyn. She covered her eyes just as a violent gust of wind whipped through the room. Several old texts crashed to the stone floor, the fluttering pages a gentle counterpoint to the chaos.

Saar wrapped his arm around Kaelyn's waist, steadying her. "Are you okay?"

She gripped his hand and opened her eyes. "I'm fine. What happened?" Without waiting for an answer, she glanced at the others and raised her voice. "Is anyone hurt?"

Dust from the ancient texts floated in the air, bits twinkling in the light. Aramie and Demir rose from the ground. Tanen and Sheri each gripped one of Ginnia's arms, helping her to her feet. In the center of the room, two figures crouched, one male, one female.

As the couple straightened, Kaelyn's pulse quickened. "Noeh, Melissa!"

At the sound of her voice, Melissa turned to face Kaelyn. Noeh followed Melissa's gaze. Anlon struggled in Melissa's arms, as if eager for release. She set him on the ground, and he crawled toward Ginnia.

"Your Majesty, what…"

"Noeh, you're…"

"Melissa, is it really…"

The others' voices echoed Kaelyn's thoughts. "You're alive. How is that possible?"

Noeh met Melissa's gaze then a smile quirked at the corner of his mouth. "It's a long story."

Sheri held out her arms and hurried to Melissa, wrapping her in a firm embrace. "I'm so glad to see you."

Saar strode to Noeh and bent on one knee. Noeh gripped him by the arm before he could make it there. "Saar, no need, my friend." Noeh clapped Saar on the back and they gave each other a quick manly hug.

Kaelyn stepped forward. "Noeh, Melissa, we thought you were dead. What happened?"

The others gathered around, as eager as Kaelyn for answers.

Noeh glanced at Melissa for several long seconds, their gazes locked as if they were in a deep conversation. Noeh then peered at each member individually. "We did die. Mauree," his jaw tightened, "killed me with a dagger, her Gossum minions finishing me off."

Melissa clasped her hand on Noeh's arm. "As soon as Noeh died, I did, too. Not all of you knew this, but we shared a soul. Which is why we are both here."

Demir narrowed his eyes. "That makes little sense and doesn't explain your arrival here now."

Noeh wrapped his arm around Melissa. "Good point. We were both on the character board on Lemuria. It was strange. I could see everyone's lights. Green for Alora's characters, red for Zedron's. I don't know how long we stayed that way, but there was a flash, and I stood in Alora's home, Melissa by my side."

Melissa inhaled. "Alora's friend Carine held Anlon. I was so happy to see him."

The small babe cooed. Ginnia sat in one of the chairs, Anlon on her lap, an open book clasped between her hands.

Noeh's eyes widened. "Why is Ginnia out of her cell?"

"Ginnia's visions have been instrumental in unraveling some

important information about Roan's Rock." Kaelyn met Noeh's disapproving stare. "She promised to be on her best behavior."

Noeh studied her for a long moment then nodded. "I regret ever placing her there in the first place."

Kaelyn exhaled. "I have so many questions, but tell us, why are you with us now? How could you come back into the game?"

Noeh drew his hand through his hair, and the ring on his finger caught the light. "Alora sent us here. She didn't elaborate—"

Demir snapped his finger. "What else is new?"

Aramie rolled her eyes and nudged him with her elbow.

Kaelyn stifled a laugh. "Please, continue."

Noeh pulled his focus away from Demir's mouth and met his gaze. He smirked. "You make a good point, cat. Alora is never forthcoming with details. All she mentioned was she ran across an exception to the rules, so she returned us to Earth."

Saar cleared his throat. "Much has happened while you were away. We've found vital information in the scriptures, thanks to Ginnia. Roan's Rock is a conduit to send water to Lemuria and it has the power to wipe out Mauree's entire army. I'll explain in more detail before we leave, but I think we can win this war. We need to get Sheri, Melissa, and Nik…"

"Except Nikki is missing, along with Gaetan." Kaelyn peered at Noeh and raised her chin. "Gaetan lost control of his beast and escaped through the tunnels. He had the blue sunstone with him. Nikki, his new mate, went after him. We suspect they are dead."

Melissa placed her hand on Noeh's arm. "Wow, a lot has happened since we were gone."

Noeh's mouth thinned. "Gaetan is alive. I saw his green dot on the character board. He was at Blue Pool. There was another green light with him, one I didn't recognize. Perhaps that was this Nikki you mentioned."

"Then we have a chance." Saar glanced at Kaelyn, one brow arched.

She swallowed. Noeh was the official king. Now that he'd returned, he would resume his duties. She bit down on the ache that built at the back of her throat. "Noeh, while you were away, I stepped into your role as leader since I am the only one with royal blood. Now that you have returned…"

Noeh regarded her for a long moment. "*Craya.*" He ran his hand through his hair. "Not sure if you're aware, but I'm deaf and am no longer the warrior I once was. In the interest of what's best for the residents of the Keep, I will step aside. You should continue to rule."

Respect for this strong, proud male made Kaelyn's throat tighten. "I could use an advisor, someone with your experience and expertise."

Noeh's eyes sparked with bits of amber. "If I've read your lips correctly, you want me to be your advisor. I'd be happy to help in any way I can and have a suggestion."

Kaelyn smiled. "Perfect. What's your advice?"

Noeh placed his hand on Kaelyn's. "We need to get the special Dren to Roan's Rock—"

"Along with the blue sunstone," Saar interjected.

Noeh nodded. "To ignite the portal and beat Mauree and her troops. You, with Saar at your side, should lead the warriors on the battlefield. If I know Gaetan, he'll do everything in his power to find Anlon, even hunting down Mauree. He'll have to go by Roan's Rock. I'll work with Tanen, Sheri, and Melissa to see if we can locate Gaetan and Nikki and meet you there."

The need to obtain their goal, to wipe out Mauree and her minions, flared within Kaelyn. Yet, some of them were her people, the Ursus. A sour taste filled her mouth, but she wouldn't let that stall her plans, her need to end this war, once and for all. Kaelyn raised her hands. "Okay, everyone. Let's proceed with the plan. Sunset is about an hour away. Demir, Aramie, gather the warriors at the portal. Tanen, Sheri, see if you can find anything else of value in that book then join us."

Noeh gave Kaelyn a quick nod. "As soon as it's dark, Melissa and I will track Gaetan and Nikki. We'll meet you at Roan's Rock."

Melissa gripped Noeh's hand. "Anlon…"

All turned their attention to the babe. He stared in rapt attention as Ginnia read from the book. "…and Roan picked up the…"

Noeh walked over to the pair and knelt beside them. "Ginnia…"

"Are you mad at me?" She peered at Noeh, her eyes flitting back and forth.

Kaelyn wanted to run to Gaetan's sister and give her a comforting hug, but she held back. This was Noeh's job, not hers.

Noeh exhaled. "Why would I be mad?"

Anlon wriggled from her arms and crawled toward his mother. Ginnia glanced at the floor. "Because I escaped from my cell. I had to. Nikki needed me to help her get out of the Keep."

Noeh exhaled and placed a strand of hair behind Ginnia's ear. "You never should've been in that cell in the first place. I should've trusted your visions. Can you forgive me?"

Ginnia's eyes widened then a smile bloomed on her face. "I love you, Noeh. Love you, love you, love you." She wrapped her arms around Noeh's neck.

"I love you, too, Ginnia." He laughed then pulled back to look at her. "Melissa and I need to leave the Keep for a while. Would you like to watch Anlon, perhaps with Bet and Jax?"

Ginnia's smile grew. "You mean I can play with him some more?"

"Yes, honey, you can." Noeh stroked her hair then rose to his feet. He met Kaelyn's gaze. "We'll meet you at Roan's Rock. May the gods be with you."

"We'll have the warriors ready to go, along with Tanen and Sheri." Kaelyn gave him a quick nod, conviction pulsing in her veins. This war would end tonight, one way or another, she was sure of it.

CHAPTER 31

*G*aetan trudged along the stream bank. The tip of his cane slid into the soft soil, mirroring the imaginary dagger plunging into his heart. With each footstep and tap of his cane, the pain worsened. Moonlight filtered between the forest's thick blanket of trees, casting shadows and reminding him of the Gossum's attack on Nicole.

He could never forgive himself for transforming her into a Dren. If he hadn't drawn the Gossum's attention to her, she would've resumed her life as a human. She hadn't asked to become part of his world, and he'd done it, knowing he'd brought her into a terrible war with an uncertain outcome. He took a deep, pained breath and continued on the path.

His goal remained the same—find Anlon. A burning sensation started in his chest, radiating down his arms until his fingers tingled. The unbreakable vow he'd given Noeh to watch after Anlon urged him onward, one foot in front of the other.

In this, he would not fail, even if it ended in his death. He would save the prince or bring down Mauree. A chill crawled down his back. *What if she doesn't have him? What if he's lost in this strange world?* He didn't know which was worse.

The urge to take a pill sent a shiver over his shoulders.

"I have faith in you, Gaetan." An image of Nicole flashed through his mind. Her moist eyes, full of encouragement and love, hadn't wavered. They'd made love in the cave, completing the bonding, binding them together.

He tugged the satchel from his pocket and gripped it in his palm. His hand shook. *I'm not worthy...*

With trembling fingers, he opened the pouch. White pills reflected the moon's glow, enticing him, calling to him on a level he couldn't refuse. His mouth watered.

"Take them from me, please." His words echoed in his mind, replaying the scene in the cave.

His gaze drifted to the stream. Water rushed over rocks and swirled in small pools.

"No, Gaetan. This is something you have to do on your own. Toss them into the water if you must, but I can't do it for you." Nicole had believed in him.

Too bad he didn't believe in himself.

He clenched his fist around his satchel, the tendons in his hands straining. His marking, the one for responsibility, burned on the back of his hand, darkening. He pulled on the strength deep in his soul and shoved the satchel into his pocket.

"No, I won't give in. I won't." As much as he'd wanted to toss the pills into the stream and rid himself of his addiction, he wasn't able to let go, but at least he'd resisted the urge to pop one into his mouth. He'd take the small victory.

A relieved breath eased from his lips. He wasn't healed, not by a long shot, but he'd taken the first step, and that was the hardest one. "I'll beat this addiction yet, Nicole, I promise."

That is, if he survived.

A crick in Nikki's neck brought her awake with a start. She inhaled, and the scent of aged paper and ink filtered into her nose. Face smashed into the old tome, she groaned and raised her head. Heat from her stretched tendon burned along her neck. With gentle pressure, she rubbed at the spot, easing some of the ache.

"I must've fallen asleep." She blinked and glanced around the small cave. The sunstones lining the walls glowed, filling the room with an eerie light. Situated in the corner, the bed's rumbled sheet reminded her of Gaetan and their time together.

An ache built in her chest, tightening around her heart. She missed him—the tug of his smile, the golden swirls in his aquamarine eyes, his gentle nature. No male had ever treated her so kindly. Yet, like her father, he couldn't give up his addiction, and she'd forced him to leave, kicking him out without a second thought.

Gaetan's not like Father. He's caring, gentle.

She shoved away from the table and stood. The chair crashed against the stone floor, the sound booming through the room. After Gaetan had left, she'd needed a few moments to calm down, and she'd sat in the chair crying herself into exhaustion. She must have fallen asleep.

The bracelet on her wrist caught the light, reflecting little pinpricks of luminescence onto the ceiling, like stars. "Where are you, Gaetan?"

"I'm the reason the Gossum attacked you. The pain in my leg flared, and I knocked my cane against my knee. That's why the Gossum turned to investigate, but instead of attacking me, the damned thing assaulted you. If it hadn't been for me, you'd be home, living your life. What I've done to you is unforgivable." His words beat against her temple.

"I'm glad you did." She rubbed the marks on her hand that mirrored Gaetan's. While at the Keep she'd met so many wonderful people, others who seemed to care about her, wanted to be with her, and trusted her. Those people had something to live for and appeared to love each other with a passion she'd only ever dreamed of, that is, until she'd met Gaetan and discovered that kind of love for herself.

He'd shown her with his caring touch and his gentle words what she'd meant to him. From what she'd seen and gathered from others in the Keep, he took care of everyone else, but never himself.

She strode to the bed and drew her fingers over the cool sheet until she gripped the pillow. After tugging the soft down close, she buried her nose in the silky material. The spicy scent of tarragon filtered into her senses. Regret tightened her stomach into a ball, clawing at her insides. "I shouldn't have forced him to leave."

She'd sent Gaetan away out of fear. Bitterness coated the back of her throat.

Although he had his own demons to conquer, he had a goal to find Anlon, and she'd be there by his side when he did. After that, they could tackle his addiction together. Tightening her fist, she tossed the pillow onto the bed and strode to the small pool of water at the cave's entrance. Using her love for Gaetan and her new resolve, she concentrated on her raw emotions and swirled her hands over the water.

Faster than ever before, the water bubbled and churned, opening the tunnel in a blink of an eye. Using the blood bond between them, she homed in on his location then bolted through the hole and into the night. "I'm on my way, Gaetan." She'd never forgive herself if something happened to him.

CHAPTER 32

A tear slid down Alora's cheek. Stuck in her dark place during the day, she had nothing to keep her company. Nothing, that is, except her tortured thoughts. *I couldn't leave Veromé. I just couldn't.*

She wiped the back of her hand over her cheek. "Damn you, Zedron."

Despite her desire to protect Anlon and Carine, she couldn't bring herself to go to him. She loved Veromé far too much to hurt him that way. Instead, she'd stewed about it all night until time ran out and she travelled to her dark place.

Now, she'd suffer the consequences. Zedron would schedule an appointment with the council and turn her in for cheating. A flash of irritation made her fingers twitch. How she hated Zedron for dragging her into this war.

The tendons in her jaw tightened. *I'm not giving up. There's still time.*

What she would do, she didn't know, yet, but she had to believe that somehow, some way, she'd find a way to defeat him. Zedron couldn't win.

The familiar tug started inside. Time to return home.

Her particles broke apart, travelling over time and space. She headed for her house nestled in the branches of a Rolmdew tree. As she materialized into her living room, smoke and the smell of burnt wood filled her senses.

Warning bells rang in her brain. Her heartbeat raced.

Her foot broke through a charred floorboard. She stumbled and her knee crashed against what remained of her couch. Her hand landed on the burnt coffee table. The charred wood gave way, crumbling beneath her palm.

Fear's cold fingers slithered along her nerves. She glanced around her home. A fire had destroyed everything in sight. Large pieces of the walls were gone. Through the openings, the surrounding tree's green canopy had turned into black, charred limbs. The remaining branches looked like sharp claws.

Alora's pulse spiked, blood rushing through her veins. "No...no...no! Veromé!" A sob escaped her lips.

"I'm right here, my love, waiting for you." Veromé wrapped his strong arms around her waist, pulling her to her feet.

She turned and threw her arms around his neck and kissed his lips, his cheek, his chin. Soft hitches eased from her chest, but she couldn't stop them.

He drew back enough to look at her. "Sh...it's all right. Carine and I are safe."

The tension in Alora's shoulders eased for the moment. "What happened?"

"A fire swept through the area. The wind," he ran his hand through his hair, "carried the flames through the treetops before we could stop it."

She swallowed. "Did everyone get out okay?"

A tic started in his jaw. He shook his head. "Two families died in the blaze. I tried..."

Alora cupped his cheek in her palm. "It's not your fault."

He gripped her fingers, drawing her hand away from his face. "I know, but I wish I could've saved them all."

"That's who you are and one of the reasons I love you so much."

"Go to my father's home. Radnor has taken us in, at least until we can find another place to live." He planted a kiss on her knuckles and glanced through the charred trees. The last rays from the setting sun turned a vibrant shade of red, reflecting in Veromé's beautiful blue eyes.

Alora's chest tightened. She didn't want to let him go, but she had to tell him what happened with Zedron. "Veromé, there's something you need to know about Zedron."

His features hardened, his mouth pursing in disgust. "Why do I have the feeling I'm not going to like this?"

Usually, his ire would ignite hers, but not tonight. She glanced at the blackened remnants of her coffee table before returning her attention to his eyes. "You were right. I should've listened to you and gone to the council with Zedron's disk."

A low growl eased from his throat. "What did he do?"

Unable to maintain eye contact any longer, she drew away from him. She turned and stepped over a broken floor board. Careful not to step on a weak spot, she glanced over her shoulder at him. "He gave me a choice. Give him one of three things and he wouldn't go to the council and turn me in for coercion."

Veromé's eyes narrowed. "What things?"

She faced him, her body trembling. "Either Anlon, Carine, or myself."

His eyes widened. "What did you do?"

"I couldn't give him the babe or Carine, so—"

"Did you go to him?" Veromé's voice boomed in the small space, echoing out into the trees.

Tears blurred her vision, and she shook her head. "No. I couldn't go through with it. I couldn't do that to you, to us."

He closed the distance and wrapped her in his embrace. She inhaled, and his cool, fresh scent filled her lungs and chased away the acrid smell of smoke.

"I love you, Veromé. I always will." She choked on the heartfelt words. "I'm so weary of being separated."

He stroked his thumb over her bottom lip, his gaze intent and hungry. "I love you, too. When this war is over, no matter the outcome, I look forward to reuniting with you. Nothing is more important to me."

Alora's breath hitched, bottling up her words.

Veromé brushed his lips over hers then claimed her with a bruising kiss. She melted from his onslaught, and she dug her fingernails into his shoulders.

The last rays of the sun faded over the horizon. As Veromé drifted away, she squeezed him tighter, but his molecules slipped through her fingers like untouchable stars.

CHAPTER 33

*G*aetan placed his hand against the cedar's rough bark. He leaned in and peered around the massive tree's trunk. The bark's familiar scent eased into his lungs, but couldn't chase away his need or his desire for his medication. His leg didn't hurt, not anymore, but the constant craving burned like fire in his veins.

He jabbed his hand into his pocket and gripped his satchel. The contents of the well-warn fabric enticed him. A bead of sweat dribbled over his brow, and he clenched his teeth.

With more force than he'd intended, he thrust the end of his cane into the moist loam at his feet and withdrew his hand. He curled his fingers into a fist.

"I won't give in. I won't give in." The mantra helped him focus, and he pushed away from the tree intent on his destination. Mauree's lake house couldn't be much farther. "I have to find Anlon."

He trudged onward. Cane, foot, foot, cane, foot, foot.

The scent of melons wafted by on the breeze.

Gaetan stilled. *Nicole...*

Light footfalls padded toward him. "Gaetan. I'm so glad I found you. I..."

He turned to face her.

Long and sleek, her blonde tresses caught in the wind, whipping over her shoulders. The moon's glow accentuated her porcelain skin, and her eyes, oh, those beautiful green eyes, etched with love, bore into him.

Like the first time he'd seen her, his breath caught in his throat. "Nicole…" Her name came out on a growl, and his inner beast bucked inside, wanting to run to her, cradle her in his arms, kiss her until she begged for more, but he held still. She'd kicked him out, wanting nothing to do with him.

She approached him as if he were a caged animal, her steps tentative. With the need for a pill sending shivers down his back, perhaps that assumption wasn't too far off base.

"What are you doing here? You said you'd return to the Keep." Fear for her snuck into his chest, tightening around his heart.

She stopped a few feet away. Her brow furrowed. "I came after you."

A flutter of hope intertwined with the fear. "Why?"

She gnawed on her bottom lip. Blood rushed south as memories of kissing those plump lips raced through him.

"I'm sorry, Gaetan, I…" She let out a quick exhale.

This was it. This was when she'd say she couldn't be with him, leave him and find another mate. She couldn't love him, not after what he'd done. He held his breath.

"…was wrong to send you away. You aren't to blame for what happened to me. In fact, I'm glad the Gossum attacked me, glad you saved me, glad I'm your female. I will do—"

He didn't give her a chance to continue. After closing the distance, he wrapped his free hand around her waist and tugged her to him.

She let out a quick gasp.

He trailed his hand up her back and rested his palm at the base of her neck. As he drew her close, he kissed her, pouring all his love for her into his kiss. Clasping her fingers around his shoulders, she returned his passion, leaning into him.

After a long moment, she broke the kiss, pulling away, but she teased the gray lock in his hair. "I love you and will do everything I can to help you find Anlon then beat this addiction."

A mixture of joy and dread skittered down his back. To hear her confess her love for him just about brought him to his knees. Never in a million years had he expected to hear those words from her. Yet, she'd brought up his addiction. She didn't want to be with an addict. He wasn't sure he could conquer the soul-sucking demon that had weaseled into every fiber of his being. She didn't want to be with an addict, that he knew.

He stroked his finger down her arm and along her marking. "Nicole, I—"

The breeze shifted. A bitter, astringent scent stung his nostrils. *Gossum.*

He turned, putting himself between the Gossum and his mate. With a tight grip, he brought his staff in front of him, ready and waiting. "Call Rin. Return to the Keep."

Branches in a nearby cedar rustled. A Gossum, then another, slid from the bough. Dressed in black with bald heads and dark, emotionless eyes, the creatures hissed. One snapped its tongue, revealing its sharp, serrated teeth.

A deep growl rumbled in Gaetan's chest. "Go, Nicole, now. I'll hold them off."

"No." She stepped around him. "We fight together."

Before he could react, she swirled her hands, drawing on the water from the small river. A thin stream of water curled toward the Gossum.

"Look! She has magical power." One of the Gossum pointed at the water as it swirled toward them. "Capture her. We have to make up for not finding that Stiyaha baby. Besides, I'm sure Mauree will be very interested in her ability."

No. Oh, craya, no. Gaetan swung his staff around and advanced on the pair. "Run, Nicole, run."

They didn't have Anlon, but Gaetan didn't have time to dwell on it because the Gossum closed in.

Loud, guttural warning chuffs, along with the snap of a wet tongue connecting with flesh, echoed from behind Gaetan.

The water Nicole had summoned splashed a few feet from their enemy. Her tormented scream ripped through the trees.

Gaetan's blood froze. Even as his staff smashed into one of the attackers, he craned his neck, searching for his mate.

A Gossum gripped her arm. His barbed tongue connected with her forehead.

Gaetan's roar ripped into the night.

The barbed sting of a Gossum's tongue hit Gaetan on the hand. His fingers numbed. He tightened his grip on his staff with his good hand. Another creature ripped his claws down Gaetan's arm. He grimaced at the stinging pain, but concern for his mate outweighed his own safety.

Nicole struggled against the creature holding her, kicking and punching. A sense of pride for her fight joined the anxiety pulsing through his veins. Blood pumping loud in his ears, he bolted toward her.

One of the two Gossum he fought jumped in front of him. Gaetan had to deal with these two before he could help Nicole. Fear for her lit a fire inside him.

He pulled on the energy and swung his staff. The end slammed into the Gossum's temple.

A loud crack rent the air.

The creature wobbled on its feet, stunned.

Taking advantage, Gaetan gripped the sunstone embedded in the handle and shoved the pointed tip into the creature's eye. The beast stiffened for a moment then transformed into a pile of goo.

The other Gossum flicked out its tongue and hit Gaetan on his bad knee. He grunted and crashed to the ground.

Nicole's scream echoed between the trees before being cut short.

Out of the corner of his eye, Gaetan caught a glimpse as the Gossum carried his mate over his shoulder into the dark forest.

"No!" Gaetan screamed.

ROSALIE REDD

The remaining Gossum leapt into the air, claws extended, serrated teeth bared.

Determination to save his mate pooled inside Gaetan. He thrust the pointed tip of his staff up, skewering the Gossum in the chest. A choking gurgle bubbled up from its mouth, along with a stream of dark blood. The creature stiffened then slid to the ground, becoming black sludge.

"Nicole!" Gaetan pushed to his feet, forcing his battered leg to cooperate.

The only reply was his voice echoing against the trees.

Nicole was gone, captured by the Gossum. The old, bitter, and familiar ache of guilt burned in his chest, squeezing his lungs until white spots formed in his vision.

His inner beast roared, eager to break free and chase the vile creature that had stolen his female, but Gaetan held the beast in check. He needed brains more than brawn. "I'm coming for you, Nicole. Nothing will stand in my way."

CHAPTER 34

*A*lora stood outside Radnor's door. Light from within her father-in-law's home cast a welcoming glow through the windows. As if on cue, the leaves in the Etila trees whispered in the breeze. At least this part of the Lemurian forest escaped yesterday's fire. She wiped her sweaty palms against her slacks and tugged on the Yandora vines.

Soft chimes echoed from within. The door opened with a low squeak.

"Alora, Alora, so good to see you." Radnor drew her in for a quick hug before gripping her arms and peering into her eyes. "Thank the gods you're all right."

"Me?" She tilted her head. "I'm thankful Veromé and Carine made it out in time."

He sighed. "Yes, me as well."

"Alora?" Carine strode from the kitchen, a cup of tea in her hands. "Alora!"

She placed the mug on the table then hurried across the room, enfolding Alora in a big hug.

Alora returned the gesture, holding on to her friend for a long moment. "I'm glad you're okay, Carine."

The Arotaar female leaned back, a sad smile blooming on her face. "I am thanks to Veromé."

Radnor cleared his throat. "Carine, would you mind giving Alora and me a few minutes?"

Alora's mouth went dry. Not only was Radnor Veromé's father, he was also the council leader. Did this have something to do with Zedron?

"Of course. I need to clean up the mess I made in the kitchen." Carine squeezed Alora's arm then shuffled across the room. Her soft-soled shoes swished against the floor's polished wood grain.

When she was gone, Radnor placed his hands on his hips. The edge of his mouth twitched along with his long dark mustache. "Zedron has requested a special council session regarding your battle over Earth. Do you know what that's about?"

Alora swallowed hard. "Perhaps, but I'd rather wait to see what he has to say."

Radnor strode to his desk and picked up a small blue disk. "It wouldn't have anything to do with this, would it?"

Her gaze flicked from the disk to his eyes. She forced a smile. "I guess we'll have to wait and see."

He laughed. "I've always liked your spunk, my dear. Say," his eyes roamed over her shirt and slacks, "you'll need something else to wear. Fortunately, Elise was about your size. There are several items in her closet. Carine has already selected a few things, but there's plenty more. Veromé's mother had a vast collection."

Alora let out a relieved breath, thankful for the change of topic. "That would be nice."

He gestured down the hallway. "It's in the spare bedroom, help yourself."

She nodded then hurried in the direction he'd indicated. As she ambled down the hallway, she passed pictures of Veromé from when he was a mid-youth through his years at the academy. She paused before one. Veromé, in what appeared to be one of his early years at the academy, sat on the branch of an Etila tree, a long fishing pole gripped in his hand. Next to him was a blond male, pointing at the small fish on Veromé's line, his golden eyes sparkling with mirth. *Mitan...*

A pang hit her in the chest. How she missed her childhood friend. As neighbors, they had grown up together, spending hours at her father's farm. When they'd gone to different academies, they'd drifted apart. At the academy, he'd met Veromé. She shook her head and continued on her path.

As she entered the bedroom, the sweet scent of Andoline perfume filtered into her lungs. Even two years after Elise's death, her scent still lingered. The antique four-post bed took up the majority of space in the small room. Perfume bottles lined the top of an old dresser next to Elise's visus bacin. Along the wall, nestled among the tree's inner bark, two doors enclosed the large closet.

Alora stared at her hands, her eyes hot and gummy. "I miss you, Elise."

Taking a deep breath, she gripped the handle and tugged. The hinges squeaked, the grating sound skittering down Alora's back.

Inside, dresses, pants, shirts, and skirts hung from several hangers. She skimmed her fingers over the beautiful clothes, pausing on a blue dress with Coletta flowers in the pattern that caught her attention. Her chest tightened. Those were her favorite flowers.

She unzipped the dress, and it slid from the hanger onto the closet floor. *"Craya."*

After pushing aside the other dresses, she twisted her fingers in the soft material and tugged it close. Nestled in the back, half-hidden behind a pair of shoes, was a large box. In bold letters across the top was a single word—Mitan.

Alora inhaled. What was a box with Mitan's name doing in Elise's closet?

A quiet knock on the door made Alora jump.

"I didn't mean to startle you, my dear. Just wanted to see if you'd found something you like." Radnor stood in the doorway. With his broad shoulders, he reminded her of Veromé. Her mate had inherited his father's build and good looks.

"Yes, I found a nice dress." She held it up.

He smiled. "Good, glad to hear that. Is there anything else you need?"

She glanced at the carton. "I couldn't help but notice. There's a box in here with Mitan's name on it."

"Oh, that. I'd forgotten it was there. When Mitan died, his parents gave a few of his things to Veromé because they were such good friends. As far as I know, he never looked at it. At the time, I think he was too stunned after Mitan's death. My guess is he forgot about it."

Alora tightened her grip on the dress, and her gaze darted to the carton once again.

Radnor cleared his throat. "He was your friend, too. You are welcome to take a look inside." He extended his palm. "Go ahead. I'll leave you to it."

Before she could respond, he withdrew into the hallway. His shoes echoed down the corridor.

Curiosity mixed with excitement rippled over Alora's arms. Mitan had died a sudden death, ruled an accident by the council. She'd never quite believed he'd slipped over the edge of his deck to the ground below. Could she dare hope the carton would provide a clue?

She placed the dress on the bedspread. With loving care, she caressed the fine material. "I'll come back for you later."

Her heart fluttering, she yanked the box from the closet, sat on the floor, and gripped the lid.

CHAPTER 35

The full moon's light filtered between the trees, casting shadows onto the path. A rich, earthy scent burned Mauree's nostrils. She scrunched her nose. In the middle of the path was a large pile of bear scat. Perfect, just perfect. With careful precision, she lifted her foot, stepped over the mound, and continued down the trail. The last thing she wanted was to add bear crap to her already dirt-covered pumps.

"I'm amazed you can walk in those things." Eldon's attention drew from her foot to her face. His dark eyes glistened and when he smiled, his white serrated teeth sparkled.

Mauree huffed. "You'd be surprised what I can do. How much longer?"

"Another minute or two." He motioned with his fingers, and a couple of Gossum sped down the path. "Scouts."

She nodded. "Once the army is in place, we wait. I suspect Gaetan won't come alone. He'll bring plenty of warriors with him. Well, the ones left anyway." A slow warmth eased into her chest, but didn't quite chase away the chill.

There was always a chance she and her brood wouldn't succeed. She fisted her hand. No, failure wasn't an option. Now that Noeh was dead, it wouldn't take much to bring down the rest of his troops. She just had to keep Gaetan and the three females away from Roan's Rock.

"Put me down!" a female's voice shouted beyond the trees.

A moment later, a Gossum slid from the forest and onto the path, a female hunched over his shoulders. She squirmed against him, pounding her fists along his back. With a grunt, he pitched forward, flinging her off his shoulder.

She landed on the dirt with a hard thud. A whoosh of air escaped her lips. With her blonde hair, green eyes, and dark mark that extended down her arm and over her hand, Nikki, Gaetan's mate, wasn't hard to recognize.

Mauree's chest expanded, giddiness filling her lungs. "My, my, look what we have here."

The female's attention riveted on Mauree. Her eyes widened. She scrambled to her feet and bolted down the path.

Mauree tsked. "Eldon. Detain her, would you, please?"

Eldon leapt in front of Nikki, wrapped his clawed fingers in her shirt, and yanked her to him. Securing her arm behind her back, he pushed her toward Mauree. "Would you like me to kill her now or later?"

Nikki struggled against him, her breaths short and fast.

Mauree tapped her finger below her bottom lip and studied the small female. "Where's Gaetan?"

Nikki raised her chin. "Far away."

"Somehow, I don't believe you. If I know anything about Gaetan, he'd never let his," Mauree glanced at the marking on Nikki's hand, "mate be out here all alone."

Nikki's mouth thinned, anger flashing in her eyes.

With a flick of her wrist, Mauree motioned to Eldon. "Take her to Roan's Rock. We'll execute her in front of her kind and take away any hope they may have of winning this war."

"No!" Nikki renewed her struggles, straining against Eldon's grasp.

He pushed her forward, forcing her down the path.

As the trees gave way to a meadow, the giant rock stood along the edge. The stream that ran around its base gurgled as it trailed into the grassy field.

Mauree studied Roan's Rock, noting the wide base and narrow tip then let her gaze drift over the meadow and the surrounding forest. Tonight, she'd defeat her enemy, win this war for Zedron, and become the ruler over the humans. She thought she'd be happy, yet the exhilaration she'd expected didn't materialize. Instead, only bitterness coated her throat.

One of the earlier scouts emerged from the trees at the edge of the clearing. He bowed low before Mauree and glanced at Eldon. "The troops, both Gossum and Ursus, are in place. We expect the enemy to arrive from the south and left them an opening. We await your orders."

"Good work. Now, about that female, little Miss Nikki." Mauree ran her hand down her short skirt until her fingers rested on the hilt of her dagger. With a quick tug, she unsheathed her weapon and studied the glinting blade in the beam of the cold moonlight.

Nikki's chest tightened, squeezing her lungs. "What are you doing?"

Mauree winked at her, and a small, wicked smile curled her lip. The dark patch over her eye matched her evil personality. "Using you as an example."

A jolt of energy rippled along Nikki's veins. She struggled against Eldon, kicking and scratching him, but she couldn't escape from his iron-tight grip.

"Eldon, bring her to Roan's Rock." Mauree strode toward the large boulder, her hips swaying to and fro with exaggerated flare.

"As you command, my lady." Eldon gave her a brief nod. His grip tightened on Nikki's arms.

She twisted in his grasp, screaming at him. As he dragged her across the meadow, her heels kicked up bits of grass and small pebbles from her tirade. None of it mattered. The evil creature wouldn't let her go.

With a hard jab, he shoved her against Roan's Rock. The rough surface scraped the skin on her arm. Blood pooled along the cut. She shoved away from the giant stone and stepped into the small creek that ran around the base. The cold water chilled her ankle, but couldn't douse the fear, anger, and hatred churning inside.

"Mauree, you bitch!" The words echoed against the trees. At her feet, the water bubbled, swirling from her outburst.

Before Nikki could react, Mauree grabbed her wrist. She yanked Nikki against her back to front and placed the knife's blade to her throat. "You're not the first one to call me that, but you will be the last. Tonight, this war ends."

In the distance, battle cries and the sound of blades clashing filtered through the trees.

Mauree tensed, tightening her grip around Nikki. "Ah, so it starts. Eldon, go battle the enemy. I can handle this little Dren."

"As you command, my lady." Eldon nodded once then raced across the clearing where a stream of warriors flooded the meadow.

Mauree breathed in Nikki's ear. "It's just you and me now, my dear."

"Don't, Mauree." As if from a dream, Gaetan stepped from the clearing. The sunstone in his cane reflected the moon's rays, casting an odd luminescence around him.

The muscles in Nikki's legs shook with relief. "Gaetan."

"Take this." Gaetan dug into his pocket and pulled out his satchel.

Mauree tittered. "You're offering me your medication? Really, Gaetan. I had higher expectations."

A tic started in his jaw, gold flecks flashing in his eyes. "This, this is nothing to me." He threw the pouch on the ground.

Nikki's heart fluttered. He'd thrown away his pain meds. Love for him filled her chest, warming her on the inside.

Mauree tightened her grip. The tip of the blade pierced Nikki's skin.

Blood, warm and wet, slid down Nikki's throat. "Gaetan…"

"Wait! This is what I have for you, Mauree." He plunged his hand into his pocket once again and yanked out the sacred blue sunstone.

Light emanated from the gem, casting the entire meadow and the fighting warriors in a muted blue glow.

Mauree's grip on the knife loosened. Nikki gulped in air, blessed and sweet.

"I offer you an exchange. The blue sunstone for," his gaze swept to Nikki, the lines around his eyes softening before he returned his attention to Mauree, "my mate."

"No, Gaetan, don't." Nikki pleaded with her eyes. If Mauree got her hands on the sunstone, she could defeat them all.

"My sweet Nicole, I would do anything to protect you." Gaetan took a step forward, the sunstone cradled in his palm.

Still holding the knife to Nikki's throat, Mauree stiffened.

Nikki's entire body shook, fear and love for Gaetan mixing with her frustration and anger. The water around Roan's Rock frothed.

"Hand it to me. Now!" Mauree held out her hand, her fingers curling with impatience.

Gaetan shook his head. "Send me my mate, then I'll toss you the stone."

"How do I know you'll do that?" Mauree hissed.

His gaze narrowed. "As long as you've known me, Mauree, have I ever lied to you?"

The blade at Nikki's throat tightened for a brief moment then resumed its resting spot under her chin. Mauree growled. "Fine. On the count of three. One. Two. Three."

Mauree shoved Nikki toward Gaetan. He tossed the blue sunstone in the air. It flipped over, again and again, as it arced over Nikki's head.

Gaetan wrapped his strong arms around her, cradling her in his embrace. Warmth filled her chest.

"Nicole, I do this for you." He dug his heel into his satchel, crushing the pills.

Tears stung her eyes. She'd never felt so loved before, so wanted and needed.

A low, feminine titter eased from Mauree's lips.

Goosebumps prickled over Nikki's arms. She turned to face the evil female.

Mauree held the sacred blue sunstone in her palm and trailed a finger over the stone's smooth edges. "Oh, how I've missed you, little gem." Her gaze rose, and she smiled, a menacing glint in her eyes. "Now, you will all die."

CHAPTER 36

*S*itting cross-legged in front of the small chest, sweat coated Alora's palms. She wiped them on her pants and placed her fingers along the box's edge. Eagerness warred with her trepidation, and with a quick push, she slid the lid off the container.

An old ball, sports trophies, and several picture frames filled the box to the brim. Memories of Mitan, his smile, his laugh, his terrible jokes, flooded her mind. Her chest constricted even as she let loose a stifled laugh. Tears threatened to fall, and she blinked them away.

She withdrew one of the frames. The picture was of Mitan when he was a mid-youth. Dark hair, cut short, accentuated the deep brown of his eyes. His smile, along with his strong jaw, had made many a young female weep. "Oh Mitan, you always were a handsome one."

She set the picture aside and retrieved another from the depths. Mitan with a curved bow in his hand, a hat on his head, and the look of sheer determination lining his features. How Mitan had loved to hunt, especially rhondo beasts.

As Alora drew the last frame from the pile, her breath caught in her throat. It was a picture of Veromé, Mitan, and Zedron wearing their formal graduation suits. They'd become friends while attending classes at the academy. She'd met Zedron and Veromé after the trio had graduated. Not long after, they'd both courted her.

She focused on the empty space above the dresser. How long ago that seemed, yet it had only been a few years since she'd bonded with Veromé. She exhaled and set the picture aside. After removing the two sport trophies, she peered into the box.

A disk, similar in size and nature to the ones she used in her visus bacin, sat in the chest's corner. She gripped the small device and held it up to the light. The round orb shimmered. "Mitan, what were you doing with one of these?"

"Find something interesting?" Carine leaned against the door-frame. The ends of her blue hair sparked as they twirled around her shoulders.

"This box contains some old photos of my deceased friend Mitan, along with this." Alora held up the disk.

Carine pushed away from the door, her eyes wide. "Hey, isn't that a recording device for a visus bacin?"

"I believe so." Alora glanced at the visus basin next to the old dresser. A sense of excitement tripped over her nerves. "Let's find out."

Alora rose from the floor and dashed to the scrying bowl. She held the round orb over the smooth water. She released the object and the disk slid below the surface with a soft plop.

Carine strode behind Alora. "You've piqued my curiosity. I can't wait to see what's in there."

"Me, too." Alora spun her hands over the water's surface. The water bubbled, roiling into a frenzy before quieting.

Situated in a Rolmdew tree, Mitan's familiar home came into focus. On the massive deck, Alora's childhood friend placed his elbows on the deck railing, his brow furrowing over his intense brown eyes.

Alora leaned forward, her chest expanding with sweet melancholy at seeing her long-lost friend once again.

"Is that Mitan?" Carine asked.

"Yes, that's him. Based on his age, I'd say this image of him is not long before he..." She swallowed.

Carine squeezed Alora's arm. "I'm sorry. You must miss him."

Alora nodded. "I do. He was—"

Zedron, wearing one of his custom suits strode onto the deck. A chilling smirk formed on his lips.

Mitan turned around and crossed his arms. "Zedron. I told you never to come here."

"Oh, Mitan. You'll come around, you always do." Zedron's menacing smile revealed his perfect set of white teeth.

Alora tensed.

"I won't be a party to your plan to win Alora's hand. She's my best friend from childhood. Once she finds out you intend to tarnish Veromé's reputation, she'll never bond to you." Mitan's eyes flashed with bits of silver.

Zedron trailed his finger over the back of a deck chair, toying with the cushion's ribbon. "Perhaps I should tell the council that a member of the neutral faction colonized a planet, a little blue one with a single sun."

Mitan pushed away from the railing. The wood creaked from the pressure. "You wouldn't dare."

Alora's pulse rose. Mitan had colonized Earth? That couldn't be.

"Oh, I would." Zedron tsked. "Neutral faction families don't support free or slave parties, so your actions are scandalous. I know how much pain that would bring your council member father. He'd lose his seat in disgrace."

Mitan's nostrils flared, and he clenched his hand into a fist. "Alora won't love you, not like she does Veromé. That's something your money and power could never buy."

Alora took in a deep breath, her lungs expanding with pride that Mitan would stand up for her.

"So, you're telling me you won't cooperate?" Zedron strode forward, that frightening smirk back on his face.

Mitan stepped into Zedron's personal space. "No, and better yet, maybe I should turn you in. I'm sure the council would be very interested in how you acquired this information. Spying is a capital offense."

Zedron's arm shook with fury. He cried out, seized Mitan's shirt, and shoved him.

Mitan stumbled and landed against the wooden rail. The wood groaned from the impact.

Alora gasped, and Carine gripped her fingers.

Mitan pushed away from the rail and bolted toward his rival. Zedron slammed his fist into Mitan's chin. Alora's childhood friend crashed against the railing once again. Wood splintered and slipped over the edge.

"Goodbye, Mitan." Zedron curled his lip, and he kicked Mitan in the gut.

The railing gave way.

Mitan yelled and disappeared over the edge.

Growls from rhondo beasts, eager to claim a meal, echoed from below.

The horrible vision faded.

Alora brought her fists to her mouth, sealing in her scream.

Carine tugged on Alora's arm, turning her around then wrapping her in a comforting embrace. "I'm so sorry."

Alora held on to her friend for a long moment, soaking up the comfort. "I can't believe it. Zedron killed Mitan."

Murderer... The ramifications flitted across Alora's mind. She drew away from Carine and paced between the visus bacin and the large bed. Her shoes tapped in rhythm with her pounding heart.

Alora stopped and glanced at her friend. "Do you know what this means?"

Carine shook her head. "Not entirely."

"Zedron will go to jail for murder, as he should, that *Kasard*." Alora curled her hand into a fist.

"And you'll win the war."

Alora took a deep breath and forced her fingers to relax. "Yes, I suppose that will be the natural outcome, except it sounds like Mitan found Earth first. If that's true, I don't know what the council will do."

UNFORGIVABLE LOVER

Carine glanced at the visus bacin. "Do you think the disk will show us?"

"Let's find out." Alora darted to the large scrying bowl then spun her hands over the water.

The water in the surface remained still, the small disk visible underneath.

Frustration flared in Alora's chest, and she swirled her hands with more force. "Show me."

Not a ripple materialized, but a few words scrolled across the water. *Enter password.*

"Mitan password protected his file. Something must've happened to it to get stuck on that one scene." Alora furrowed her brow. "I wonder what his passcode was..."

"You knew him pretty well, didn't you? Give it a try." Carine peered into the bowl.

Alora tapped her finger against her mouth. Would he use one of his parent's names? "Password, Desmond."

A light blinked over the water, and the words reappeared. *Enter password.*

Frustration had Alora clamping her jaw shut. "Password, Tanya."

The light blinked faster, and this time, new words appeared. *Failed attempt two. Disk will lock permanently after three failed attempts.*

Alora pounded her fist against the stone edge, again and again. "I don't dare try again."

The image of Mitan on the deck reappeared. As he leaned over the railing, his dark eyes furrowed. The recording device had reverted back to the original scene. Alora swiped her hand over the picture, unwilling to see his death again.

Carine placed her hand on Alora's arm. "Perhaps we should tell Radnor about this, see if he knows the password."

"Good idea." Alora shoved her hand into the cool water and retrieved the precious disk. Gripping it tight, she shook off a few drops of water from her fist and headed out the door.

As she hurried into the living room, her breaths heaved from her excitement. "Radnor!"

197

Her voice echoed around the empty space.

"Hey, it looks like he left you a note." Carine pointed at his desk.

Situated on one of the corners was a slip of paper, her name etched across the top.

She picked up the finely crafted page and read. "Alora, I didn't want to disturb you as you looked through Mitan's belongings, but I received a call and needed to leave. I'll see you at the council meeting in a few hours. Don't be late." Radnor's elegant signature graced the bottom of the page.

"Sounds like your meeting will be one to remember." Carine exhaled. "Do us both a favor, bring Zedron down."

Alora tightened her grip around Mitan's recording device. "I shall. Oh, I shall."

Despite her conviction, her stomach knotted. Zedron was no fool.

CHAPTER 37

*G*aetan held Nicole close, tugging her tight against him. Her warm, sweet scent burrowed into his senses, and his inner beast growled. She was safe and that was all that mattered to the beast, but they weren't out of trouble, not by a long shot.

He wrapped his arm around Nicole's waist, drawing her to his side so he could face Mauree. "As I promised, I've never lied to you, Mauree."

Mauree blinked. "Are you out of your ever-loving mind? You sacrificed your entire species by giving me the blue sunstone to save this one," her gaze raked over Nicole, "female?"

"I don't expect you to understand, yet I think, deep down, you understand all too well. You don't have to do this. You have a choice." His words wound around his heart, the truth hitting home harder than he'd expected. Nicole had shown him that life and love were about choices. You were responsible for your own decisions, not anyone else's. A weight lifted from his shoulders. He'd given Nicole an option to live or die. She'd chosen to live and had grown to love him in the process.

"What are you talking about?" Mauree clutched the blue sunstone to her chest. "With the sacred sunstone, I have the power to control the elements, such as you, Nikki. I could kill you in a heartbeat."

Gaetan stepped in front of Nicole, blocking her from Mauree's view. "But, you haven't. Why is that, Mauree?"

"It's not time yet, that's all." A smile crossed her face, but lines formed around her eyes.

She has regret.

A pang bloomed in Gaetan's chest. The line for empathy on the back of his hand burned, darkening. Maybe, just maybe, he could convince Mauree to change her mind. "This hasn't been easy for you. If anyone understands what it's like to live your life with regrets, it's me."

"What do you know of regret?" she spat and glared at him.

"More than you might think. I've come to realize it's never too late to make amends and change your life. All it takes is one small step to start you on the path and that begins with forgiveness."

Nicole squeezed his palm, encouraging him.

He returned the affection then took a step forward. "I forgive you, Mauree. You still have time to change your life. Trust me."

A pained expression tightened Mauree's features. She peered at the rock in her palm and shook her head. "How can you forgive me? I've done terrible, terrible things and have gone way too far down this road to ever come back."

"If I can forgive myself for making so many mistakes, then you can forgive yourself, too." He'd thrown away his medication after hiding his guilt and pain behind the small pills for longer than he cared to admit. Nicole had helped him realize he wasn't responsible for others' choices, only his own. The sense of freedom still swelled his chest. The need to convince Mauree she could do the same itched in his veins.

She met his gaze. Her eye, rimmed red with unshed tears, studied him. "All I ever wanted was to be queen...to be respected and obeyed."

Empathy for her swelled inside along with his desire to aid her. His line for benevolence warmed, darkening on his skin. Pulling on his patience, he held out his hand, as if she were a scared animal. "Give me the sunstone, Mauree. Let me help you."

If he could touch her, he could give her some of his calming influence, help her ease away from the brink.

She blinked several times, but couldn't stop the tear as it slid down her cheek. With shaky fingers, she lifted her hand toward him.

Hope soared in Gaetan's chest. He opened his palm.

"*Aiyeeee!*" The war cry boomed across the field.

Gaetan's muscles tightened.

Swords raised, warriors closed the distance, pushing back the Gossum and Ursus. Kaelyn and Saar led the charge, along with Demir and Aramie. Out of the melee, a familiar figure appeared. With broad shoulders and short blond hair, he swung his blade with a grace and experience few possessed. The warrior's identity was clear.

Gaetan's heart skipped a beat before beating double time. "Noeh... How can this be?"

Gossum and Ursus surged from their hiding spots along the tree line, approaching at a fast clip. As the groups merged, the clashing of swords and battle cries echoed into the night.

Mauree tugged the blue sunstone to her chest. "No, it can't be Noeh, I killed him." She shook from her rage, her features tightening into a grimace. "Kill them! Kill them! Kill them all!"

Kaelyn bolted toward a Gossum, her feet pounding over the meadow's tall grass. Wet from the evening dew, the blades slapped against her pant legs. She gripped the handle of her mace and swung the spiked ball over her head. The weapon hummed from the air displacement, the sound familiar and comforting.

At her side, Saar let out a bellow of rage.

They closed the distance, and the Gossum's dark eyes reflected the moonlight, eerie and chilling. Close enough to hear the creature's small cries of excitement, she swung her mace. The ball connected with its skull, crushing the bone in one fell swoop. She yanked her weapon free. The creature slid to the grass and turned into a pile of sludge.

Kaelyn's attention drew to Roan's Rock. Her nemesis, Mauree, stood before Gaetan and Nikki, a sneer on her face. Kaelyn's pulse rose as her muscles tensed. Prepared to battle her enemy, she—

"Kaelyn!"

Her gaze tracked toward the sound of her name.

Jacinth sprinted toward her, his mace twirling in the air.

She dodged as a spiked tip whipped past her nose. A low growl erupted from her. "Jacinth! Stop!"

He blinked, but continued his advance. "Why do you fight with them?"

Sidestepping his every move, she kept out of reach. "When I became Saar's mate, I chose to fight for Alora. You can fight for her, too."

He circled her, his assessing gaze searching for her weakness. "Not possible. We fight for Zedron now, we are his characters."

The desire to battle Mauree and kill the evil bitch coiled in Kaelyn's gut, but here was her chance to recruit one of her tribe and turn the tide in this war. Pulling on her love for her people, she concentrated on her tribe mate. "You can claim 'free will' and choose which side to fight on. Renounce your allegiance to Zedron."

Jacinth's brow furrowed, but his pace didn't slow. "I don't believe you."

"Aren't I living proof?" She stopped, planting her boots in the soft soil.

He flinched, holding his position. The whir of his mace beat at the wind.

She straightened her shoulders and raised her chin. "You were always a loyal warrior to my parents. Will you remain so to me?"

A tremor started in his jaw. The speed of the mace increased.

She held his gaze. "Join me, Jacinth. I know you want to. Claim your right to 'free will.' Put down your weapon."

He studied her for several long seconds, his features etched with torment. A loud scream emerged from his lips. "I...choose...Alora...

through my own...free will." He brought the mace down. The ball sank into the moist dirt at Kaelyn's feet.

"My queen." He kneeled.

Kaelyn inhaled, hope soaring inside. She gripped his arm, hauling him to his feet. "Good job, Jacinth. Your first order, help me convince the others before it's too late."

He nodded. "As you command."

CHAPTER 38

$\mathcal{M}$auree braced her feet in the soil and squeezed the damned sacred sunstone. Her fist trembled, the skin on her knuckles white with strain. Anger, bitterness, fear, regret all boiled in her veins, pounding against her skull. She focused on her rival, the male she'd once loved—Noeh. How did he still live?

He lunged with his sword, the tip piercing through a Gossum's eye. Melissa was at his side. She raised her arms, and a shimmering light encircled Noeh and grew to encompass Tanen and Sheri.

A Gossum skittered toward them, its claws extended. As it plowed into the shield, the creature bounced and fell on its behind. Its eyes widened.

Mauree took a step toward Roan's Rock. "You...you can't be here. I killed you!"

"Mauree, there's still time, hand me the sunstone." Gaetan held out his palm. Encouragement and trust reflected in his eyes.

The young Dren, Nikki, stepped toward her. "Do as he asks."

Liquid hot, bitterness rose in Mauree's throat. She was once on the verge of becoming queen. No female told her what to do. "Water girl, you'll be the first to obey me."

She held up the stone and through sheer force of will, drew Nikki toward her.

Nikki took a tentative step, then another. "Gaetan!"

He gripped her around the waist, holding her to him. Wind whipped their hair, their clothes, tugging them apart. "I can't hold on."

Ripped from his grasp, Nikki flew through the air and landed at the base of Roan's Rock. Face, arms, legs, her entire body pressed against the rough stone. A scream tore from her throat.

Gaetan bolted toward Mauree, hobbling at a fast pace, his face contorted into a mask of rage.

"Stay back or I'll kill her." Mauree shook the hand gripping the sacred stone.

Nikki's head jerked back then slammed into the giant boulder. She whimpered.

Gaetan stilled. A growl of pure frustration and anger erupted from him.

Out of the corner of her eye, Mauree caught Noeh and the others approaching at a fast clip. Unable to harm them while inside Melissa's protective barrier, her brood circled the group.

"Mauree. Don't do this. I believe there's still good in you." Gaetan raised his staff, the sunstone in the end shining.

"Don't do anything foolish, old one. You can't—"

With more force than she thought possible, he rammed the tip of his cane into the ground. The earth shook and a jolt of light burst from his sunstone, the ricochet rippling over Mauree's skin, knocking her backward.

The stone slipped from her grasp and tumbled to the grass at her feet. "No!"

Mauree dove for it, but Nikki was faster. The Dren female plucked the stone from its resting spot and rolled.

Nikki grasped the stone in her hand. Using her momentum, she tumbled over the grass.

Mauree landed hard on her. The air whooshed from Nikki's lungs. Spots formed in her vision.

Mauree ripped the stone from Nikki's grasp and shoved Nikki's face into the dirt.

Nikki struggled to breathe, fear and anger bubbling up inside. She bucked against the larger female and her elbow connected with Mauree's cheek.

"Ow!" Mauree gasped and rolled away.

The oppressive weight holding Nikki down was gone. She gulped a breath, and the cool air burned her lungs.

"Don't do this, Mauree. You're good inside. I feel it." Gaetan wrapped his arms around Mauree.

She struggled against him, trying in vain to break his hold. Quick as a cat, she raised her foot and rammed the pointed end of her heel into Gaetan's knee.

A scream of rage and pain escaped his lips. As he crashed to the ground, she pushed away from him.

A shot of adrenaline flooded Nikki's veins. She drew on her energy, and the water flowing alongside Roan's Rock bubbled. With a quick jerk of her fingers, Nikki sent a wave of water over Mauree.

The water drenched Mauree and knocked the blue sunstone from her grasp. The gem flew through the air.

Two Gossum, tongues snapping, scampered toward them. One caught the blue sunstone in his palm. They were so close, the wet slap of their tongues echoed against Roan's Rock.

Mauree gasped for breath. She struggled to wipe her wet hair from her eyes. "You...you..."

Nikki's chest tightened. *Gaetan...* They were out of time and options.

She glanced at him. Love and respect reflected in his gaze.

As one of the Gossum launched into the air, claws extended, a shimmering light enveloped her. The creature hit the barrier and fell away. It snarled, revealing serrated teeth.

"Are you okay?" Sheri placed a hand on her shoulder.

Nikki's entire body shook. She peered at her friend. "How..."

"Nicole." Gaetan wrapped his arms around her, pulling her tight. "You're all right."

Nikki slid her hands into Gaetan's hair and melted into his embrace. "Gaetan..."

"How heartwarming." Mauree cackled. "Glad to see you could all join me."

The muscles in Nikki's shoulders tensed. She glanced at the others in the strange energy bubble. Sheri was there with her mate, Tanen, along with the male she'd seen die at Mauree's hands...Noeh, and beside him was a red-headed female that must be his mate. How was this possible? Nikki wasn't sure, but she'd seen enough to know strange things could happen.

The Gossum handed Mauree the blue sunstone. A high-pitched titter eased from her mouth. "I don't know how you survived, Noeh, and I don't care," her eyes narrowed, "but you brought the exact three females I need to win this war."

Gaetan's grip around Nikki's waist tightened. Despite their circumstances, she felt protected in his arms. He'd proven himself to her, throwing away his pills, sacrificing himself for her. Love for him bottled up in her throat. She'd do anything to help him.

Kaelyn spread her feet, planting herself firmly in the meadow's tall grass. A Gossum charged toward her. His tongue whipped in and out of his mouth with a loud snap. As it neared, the creature bared its serrated teeth. Saliva dripped from the pointed ends onto its chin.

Disgust coiled inside Kaelyn, bitter and hard. She tightened her grip and swung her mace above her head. The ball whistled as it twirled, sounding eerily like the wooden carving around her throat.

With a firm thrust, the Gossum launched into the air, claws extended.

Kaelyn brought the mace down. The spiked tip hit its mark, embedding into the creature's skull.

A strangled cry ruptured from the creature's throat as it exhaled its last breath, slipping to the ground in a pile of goo.

Blood pumping through her veins, Kaelyn scanned the meadow. Warriors fought against several Gossum and a few members of her tribe. Jacinth stood between the Stiyaha warrior Quentin and one of the bears, his arms outstretched. She clenched her hands into fists. Too many had died tonight. She couldn't lose any more of her people.

Not far away, a small boulder protruded from the grass. She bolted for it. After jumping to the top, her feet landed on the uneven rock. She held out her hand to steady herself.

With quick fingers, she grasped her bear's head whistle in her palm and brought it to her lips. She took a big breath and then blew into the hole. A shrill note floated across the meadow.

Several Ursus glanced her way.

She held up her hand, palm outstretched. "Stop fighting! As your true queen, I command it!"

The Ursus soldiers held still for a moment, but then resumed their battle.

Kaelyn's jaw tightened. "Damn you, Zedron."

"Kaelyn!" Saar's voice boomed in the night air.

She turned toward him.

A Gossum launched itself at her. Its tongue snapped close to Kaelyn's ear. Spittle splattered against her cheek. She whipped her mace around and smashed it against his shoulder, pinning him against the rock. With more force than necessary, she drove her foot into his back. The crunch of bones sent a satisfying thrill through her veins.

She drew her dagger from her belt and slit the creature's throat. It disintegrated into a pile of black sludge beneath her boot.

Saar joined her on the rock and gave her a quick hug.

"Thank you, my mate." She kissed him. "Now, let's turn these Ursus to our side."

He nodded. "I'll do whatever I can to assist you."

Her heart constricted with love for him. His willingness to help bolstered her resolve. She gripped her whistle once again and blew. The shrill tone reverberated off the trees at the meadow's edge. "Ursus warriors, listen to me. Put down your weapons. The Stiyaha are not your enemy."

Several Ursus close by glanced at her. A couple stopped their attack. One lowered his weapon.

Their willingness to hear her kept Kaelyn's hope alive. "Free will is your right. You have a choice in who is friend and who is foe. Trust me. I changed sides. So did Jacinth. Join us and fight your true enemy, the Gossum."

Saar placed his hand along Kaelyn's waist. "Stiyaha warriors. Do not attack the Ursus! Repeat, do not attack the Ursus!"

Several warriors stepped back, putting space between them and their Ursus opponents. Many still gripped their swords, but the blades pointed at the earth.

Jacinth strode forward. He raised his fist in the air. "Through free will, I voluntarily chose to fight for Alora and follow Kaelyn, our true queen. You can, too. Who's with me?"

Other than the clanging of swords as a few Stiyaha warriors battled the Gossum, the meadow was eerily silent. Kaelyn peered into the eyes of her old friends, almost commanding them through sheer force of will to switch sides.

"Alora and Queen Kaelyn."

"My goddess and my queen."

"I choose you and our goddess Alora."

The spoken words of her warriors filtered into Kaelyn's ears. Her chest lightened, filling with hope. "Join us! Fight your true enemy, the Gossum."

Several cheers rang in the air. Ursus turned away from the Stiyaha opponents and attacked the nearest Gossum.

"You did it!" Saar tugged Kaelyn close and planted a quick, powerful, possessive kiss on her mouth. "Now, let's go kick some Gossum ass."

Kaelyn smiled and nodded. "Indeed, let's."

CHAPTER 39

Gaetan stared at the sunstone in Mauree's grasp. Roan's Rock rose ominously at her back, the giant stone overshadowing the small group at its base. She studied the gem, and an evil smile tugged at her lip.

Gaetan drew Nicole against him. There was no way Mauree would get close to his mate. A low growl rumbled in his chest.

"You're through, Mauree. Surrender while you still have time." Noeh's jaw tightened.

Gaetan's chest expanded even at their dire situation. By some miracle, Noeh and Melissa were alive.

Mauree's shrill laugh echoed above the battle's din. "I look forward to seeing you die, once again."

Screeee.

Noeh pointed the tip of his sword at Mauree. "You can't harm us inside Melissa's shield, but you, I can kill."

Mauree's eyes narrowed. "Oh, Noeh, that's what you think."

A tendril of worry slid along Gaetan's nerves. He held out his hand. "Mauree, don't do this. Don't—"

Before he could finish, Mauree held up the blue sunstone. The gem glowed in her palm. With a quick flick, she extended her arm toward Melissa.

Melissa's shield expanded, growing in size.

"Noeh...it hurts." Melissa hissed and winced.

"Mauree, stop!" Noeh commanded.

The shimmer enclosed Mauree, continuing until it had expanded over Roan's Rock.

Melissa shook from the force.

Tanen slid his dagger from his sheath and launched it at Mauree.

She raised her hand then flicked her fingers.

The blade swerved and embedded into the shield, held in mid-air from the force.

Strained grunts burst from Noeh. The muscles in his arms quivered, but his sword remained upright in his arms.

Gaetan tried to move his hand, his leg, any part of his body, but he, too, was immobile.

"Now, let's get down to business." Mauree's voice deepened and took on a sinister tone. She strode to Noeh and trailed a finger down the side of his face. A smile tugged at her lips. "You should've selected me as your mate."

"Never!" Noeh spat the words, a low growl rumbling in his chest.

Mauree tsked. "Come now, it wouldn't have been that bad. You always did enjoy my, well, that's neither here nor there now, is it?"

Her attention snapped between the three females. "Melissa, Sheri, Nikki, my little dears, come, join me at Roan's Rock." With a flick of her finger, the three proceeded toward the rock.

"Stop, Mauree. This won't feel like winning to you, I promise." Gaetan kept his tone gentle, encouraging, but what he needed was to touch her so he could give her some of his calming energy.

"Oh, but I can. You will all perish, and I will win this war for Zedron and claim my right as ruler over the humans." She cackled as she strode toward Roan's Rock, the blue sunstone in her palm.

Melissa placed her hand against the boulder and the shield wavered, strengthening. Sheri's fingers graced the surface, and a tendril of electricity crackled in the air. Nicole brought her palm toward the rough stone.

Gaetan inhaled. "Fight it, Nicole. Concentrate on my love for you. Believe."

His mate paused, and her fingers trembled.

Gaetan's chest swelled. His markings, the ones for benevolence and empathy, burned on the back of his hand, darkening. "That's it. Focus on me. Feel how much I love you."

"Gaetan..." Nicole cried out, but maintained her place, mere inches from Roan's Rock.

"Touch the boulder, now!" Mauree shook her hand. The blue sunstone sparked, and the ground beneath Roan's Rock shook.

Nicole inched closer to Gaetan, but she was still several steps away.

"It's working! Sheri, focus on me, try to come back." Tanen's excitement rippled through the space.

"I...can't." Sheri's heavy breaths eased from her mouth.

Noeh cleared his throat. "Melissa—"

She shook her head, a pained expression on her face.

Gaetan exhaled. "It's my benevolence and empathy marks. Only I can—"

Mauree darted to him, her high heels sinking into the soft dirt. Her slap whipped his head to the side.

His cheek stung, but Mauree had touched him. He needed her to do so again. "I forgive you, Mauree."

She choked out a laugh. "I don't need your forgiveness, Gaetan."

"You crave forgiveness more than anything. Remember, I know all about guilt and blame. Forgive yourself, Mauree. It will free your soul." He met her gaze, willing her to come to him.

Her brow furrowed, the internal battle underway.

He glanced at his open palm. "Give me the sunstone."

"No. No." She backed away from him, her lip quivering.

The glint of Noeh's sword caught his attention. Mauree headed straight for the extended blade.

Gaetan winced as her fate unfolded.

Mauree stumbled over a rock in the path. She slipped, careening toward Noeh's sword. The blade's tip slid between her ribs. Flesh ripped.

She stilled. Her mouth opened and closed. The blade's tip protruded from her chest. She coughed, and blood oozed from her lips. "I almost...won. May you all...burn in the ether, the space... between space."

The blue sunstone slipped from her fingers. The spell broke. Everyone moved at once.

Gaetan stepped forward and caught the precious gem in his palm.

Noeh withdrew the sword and cradled Mauree in his arm.

A sad smile pulled at her mouth, softening her features. "Noeh...all I ever wanted...was to be...your queen."

A moment later, Mauree's body turned to sand, the fine grains slipping through Noeh's fingers.

The blue sunstone burned hot in Gaetan's palm. A bright blue light emanated from the gem. He clenched his fist, his knuckles turning white with strain. *"The catalyst is the blue sunstone. Whoever possesses the magical gem shall command the other elements, Roan's Rock, and the power within."* The words from the ancient text rushed through Gaetan's mind. Muscles in his arms and legs tensed. "Nicole, Sheri, Melissa, hurry! Touch Roan's Rock."

Sheri placed her palms on the stone's rough surface. Melissa did the same, but the shield around them was gone.

Screeeee.

The clashing of swords rang in the air.

"Hurry, Gaetan. I'm not sure how long we can hold them off." Noeh brought his sword down, slicing through a Gossum's extended tongue. The creature screamed and its wet appendage flopped into the tall grass.

Beyond Noeh's shoulder, several Gossum sprinted across the meadow. Their long claws and serrated teeth a promise of certain death.

Gaetan gripped Nicole's hand. She peered at him, determination, love, and acceptance reflected in her beautiful green eyes. He tugged her forward and together, they darted the last few feet to Roan's Rock.

Nicole placed her palms on Roan's Rock between Melissa's and Sheri's. An eerie tone emanated rose from the giant rock.

The astringent scent of Gossum intensified, burning Gaetan's nose. They were out of time.

Pulling on his inner strength and his love for Nikki, he slammed the blue sunstone against Roan's Rock.

A rumble started under the earth, shaking the ground. He wrapped his arms around the three females, using himself as a barrier should any of the Gossum get past Noeh and Tanen.

The water at the base of Roan's Rock bubbled. Electrical sparks flickered over the rough surface.

The air shimmered, a protective barrier forming around them.

A flash of blue lit up the sky, and an audible pulse wave burst from the stone, ricocheting across the meadow.

Gaetan's ears rang, blocking out all sound. His labored breaths rushed in and out of his lungs. He glanced behind him to Noeh.

The king held his sword over his head, his fingers gripped around the hilt. His eyes widened for a moment then he blinked.

Gaetan's gaze tracked beyond Noeh into the meadow. Warriors glanced around, shocked expressions on their faces.

There wasn't a single Gossum in sight. Their enemy was gone, destroyed in an instant.

The war was over.

Hard and fast, a wave of relief travelled along Gaetan's nerves. His legs shook from the force.

Still pinned against Roan's Rock, Melissa and Sheri stirred. Nicole turned around, and he tugged her into his embrace, holding her tight.

Another pulse erupted from Roan's Rock, followed by a second then a third. The energy waves rippled over the meadow. A slow reverberation shook the Earth.

Gaetan drew Nicole away from the boulder. Noeh and Tanen approached, each embracing their mates.

Shouts from the warriors in the meadow and Noeh's deep voice penetrated through the cotton in Gaetan's ears.

"Look!" Noeh pointed upward, toward the tip of Roan's Rock.

His gaze rose along with the others. From the boulder's top, a blue shaft of light trailed into the atmosphere, disappearing into a small pinpoint of light.

"It's beautiful!" Nicole pressed into Gaetan's chest, and the sweet aroma of melons wafted into his senses. He breathed in, enjoying her unique scent, the one branded into his soul.

Cheers, whoops, and hollers erupted from those in the meadow, as well as from those standing near him.

"We did it, didn't we?" Nicole brushed a finger down his cheek.

A sense of well-being and happiness swelled his chest. He gripped Nicole's hand and planted soft kisses along the back of her knuckles. The little rhinestones in her bracelet picked up the light, shining like small stars. "Yes, I think we did."

She smiled. "Just like Ginnia said we would."

His chest constricted for a moment, the old guilt pinging against his heart.

"What is it?" Nicole gnawed on her lip.

"Ginnia—"

She placed her finger alongside his mouth. "Shh…Gaetan. She told me to tell you she doesn't blame you, that she enjoys being the seer."

He stared into Nicole's eyes, assessing her, searching for the truth in her words. His calming influence wound into her and rebounded back to him tenfold. She told the truth. Ginnia didn't blame him.

The heavy weight he'd borne for most of his life lifted from his shoulders. He'd never felt so relieved, so free. "Thank you."

"Oh, Gaetan—"

He tugged her close. She melded to him, her breasts pressing against his chest, lighting up his nerves. Blood pumped through his veins, his desire for his sweet Nicole filling him. He cradled her head in his palm and kissed her, telling her without words what she meant to him. She returned his kiss, opening up to him, giving him all that he'd ever wanted, ever needed. He loved her more as each moment passed and would never have enough of her.

Noeh cleared his throat.

Nicole drew away, a soft sigh easing from her lips.

He met Noeh's gaze.

"You've done well, old friend. We couldn't have won this war without you." Noeh yanked him into a big hug, patting him on the back with one arm.

Rawness coated the back of Gaetan's throat. He closed his eyes, accepting the affection from the one male he loved like a son.

Noeh pulled away. His gaze slid to Gaetan's neck then flicked to Gaetan's eyes. "Seems you've claimed a mate. This confirms what I suspected. The mating bond is what allows us to connect with our beasts. Congratulations, by the way."

Gaetan's mind spun. "Wh...what?"

"Your bands. Looks like you have a good relationship." Noeh winked at Nicole.

Gaetan touched his throat. "Bands. Plural?"

Noeh blinked. "You have two."

How did that happen? He'd only had one before. A tingle raced up Gaetan's arms. Maybe he'd earned the second one after the physical claiming. He peered at Nicole and the mirror image of his marking on her left hand. Yes, the bond connecting them tightened.

Melissa placed her hand on Gaetan's arm. "Congratulations. Anlon will be glad to see you as well."

Gaetan raised his eyebrows. "Anlon?"

"When he went through the portal, he ended up on Lemuria. Through a special, um, circumstance, Alora was able to send all three of us back to Earth."

Although Gaetan had searched and searched, never to find the prince, the little babe had been safe all along. The last hollow in Gaetan's chest disappeared, filling with relief. A realization hit him, sending a ripple over his shoulders. His quest wasn't for naught. Along the way he'd found Nicole, himself, and a love everlasting.

Happiness swirled inside, and he drew her close, holding her tight, never wanting to ever let her go.

Noeh wrapped his arm around Melissa's waist. His brow furrowed, tension lines forming around his eyes. "Speaking of Alora, now that we've won the war for her, shouldn't we return to the character board?"

A painful ache started in Gaetan's chest and radiated down his arms. He'd just found Nicole, his mate, the love of his life. There was no way he wanted to leave her now. He tightened his grip around his cane, and he pounded the tip into the dirt. "No, no, no...this can't happen."

Yet, deep inside, he couldn't ignore the truth. The war was over, and it was only a matter of time before they all returned to Lemuria.

CHAPTER 40

*A*lora dashed across the platform surrounding the largest Rolmdew tree in the Lemurian forest, her feet skimming over the wooden planks. A tratee fly buzzed around her head. The small creature provided extra illumination along the path. Out of breath, she didn't bother to wait until her heart rate calmed. Instead, she rammed her knuckles against the wooden door.

The hinges squeaked as the door opened. Light from inside cast the greeter in darkness. Even still, she recognized his form.

"Alora, glad you could make it. You're late, as usual." Radnor's mouth twitched, and his mustache curled, yet his eyes were full of warmth. "Come in. We were about to start without you."

Alora smoothed her dress, the one she'd picked from Elise's closet with the beautiful Coletta flowers. As she stepped inside, the murmurs silenced.

Several council members sat around the revered table. All drew their attention to Alora.

She swallowed and raised her chin, refusing to let them see her unease.

"Alora is here. We can start the meeting now." Radnor held out his hand for her to proceed.

As she drew further into the room, the sharp sound of glasses clinking stopped her. Standing next to the elaborately carved bar along the far wall, Zedron raised his goblet in mock salute.

"Hello, Alora." He smiled. His white teeth contrasted with his dark suit, which matched his blackened heart.

Alora fisted her hand around Mitan's recording device. "The game isn't over yet."

He arched an eyebrow, shrugged, then sipped the red wine from his glass—muldoberry wine.

Radnor sat in his seat at the head of the table and rapped his mallet against the aged wood. "Zedron, you requested this meeting. Bring forth your charges."

"Wait!" Alora raised her hand. "I have—"

Radnor's mouth thinned. He brought the gavel down once, twice, three times. "No interruptions, Alora. Your turn will come. Now, sit." Although he was her father-in-law and loved her dearly, he was a stickler in council meetings.

She exhaled a frustrated breath, her pulse pounding behind her eyes. After a forceful strut, she sat in one of the chairs lining the room. Her heel tapped against the floor, beating with her nervous energy.

Council member Tomra cleared her throat. "I have a hair appointment in," she glanced at the clock on the wall, "forty-five minutes. Let's get on with it, shall we?"

"Yes, dinner is waiting for me at home." Betain, a muscular male council member with short brown hair and a cleft chin, pursed his lips.

Alora furrowed her brow. How could the council members be so callous? The fate of humankind rested on the outcome of this meeting. She bit her tongue to prevent herself from lashing out at them. Instead, she tightened her grip around the disk.

Zedron set his glass down on the bar and swaggered toward the character board. His dark suit, with its fine weave and tailored sharp lines, lent him an appearance of authority. He met her gaze and winked.

She hated the arrogant male all the more.

With an air of nonchalance, he roamed his gaze over the nine council members. After he'd looked them all in the eyes, he pointed to the character board. "If I may, Council Leader Radnor."

Radnor inclined his head.

Zedron swiped his hand over the table. The wood expanded in breadth and width, displaying the characters in the game in the form of small dots—red for him, green for Alora. He pressed his finger to a single green dot and the image of an Ursus female with long dark hair, a yellow cloth interwoven in her braid, emerged onto the screen. "This female character, Kaelyn, is an Ursus female. Note that she bears a green emblem, an indication she is on Alora's team."

Radnor raised an eyebrow. "I fail to see the significance. State your claim or we'll disband this meeting."

"Forgive me, Council Leader." Zedron gave Radnor a slight bow. "The issue here is that after Alora's second offense at cheating, she transferred the Ursus to me. Kaelyn should be my character, but as you can so clearly see, she isn't."

Alora leapt to her feet. "You dirty *kasard*—"

"Quiet!" Radnor slammed the gavel against the table. The wood shook from the force.

Gasps and soft cries erupted from the council members.

Radnor pointed at her, his gaze narrowing. "Don't say another word until I ask you to speak. Otherwise, I'll award the game to Zedron. Do I make myself clear?"

She swallowed, nodded, and sat down once again. The ache in her chest burned.

A smirk curled Zedron's lip, and the urge to punch him there made her fingers flinch.

"Alora cheated. She coerced me to give up Kaelyn in exchange for one of my recording devices Alora obtained through theft. This is her third offense. I graciously ask the council to name me as victor in the war over Earth."

An eerie silence settled over the council chamber.

Alora stood and opened her mouth, eager to tell them her story.

Radnor held up his hand. "Just answer my question and only my question."

Her heart sank. She closed her mouth, biting down on the words.

Radnor stood and approached her, pain etched around the lines in his eyes. "Did you or did you not use coercion to obtain Kaelyn in the game?"

She exhaled. "Yes, but—"

"That's your third offense, Alora." He shook his head. "The council has no choice but to cast an immediate vote that Zedron is the win—"

"Wait!" Alora's pulse spiked. Something happened in the game, she was sure of it. Before anyone could stop her, she ran to the character board and cast her palm over the screen. Green lights filled the display. There wasn't a red dot in sight. The war was over. "I won..."

Zedron cleared his throat, drawing her attention to him. "No, you did not. You cheated. I won the war!"

"Silence! The council will vote—"

"No. I have proof here," Alora held up Mitan's recording device, "that Zedron is a murderer."

Loud gasps erupted. Several council members rose from their seats, chairs scraping across the wooden floor.

"Nonsense!" Zedron yelled.

"Order! Order!" Radnor banged his gavel, silencing everyone in the room. He focused on her. "Be careful, Alora, false accusations carry a heavy penalty of one hundred consecutive days in your dark place."

"My claims aren't false." She held the disk between her fingers so everyone could see. "This is Mitan's recording device. It will substantiate my charge."

"Not possible!" Zedron strutted toward her, his expensive tailored shoes pounding against the floor. He raised his hand as if intending to snatch the disk from her hand.

She palmed the small object just as his fingers whisked through the air. Zedron's sneer revealed his true nature, and a shudder ran down Alora's spine.

Radnor clamped his hand on Zedron's shoulder, preventing him from invading her personal space. "Sit down. I, as I'm sure the rest of the council, am eager to hear what Alora has to say."

Murmurs of assent rose from the council members as they reseated themselves.

Zedron strode to a nearby chair, but didn't sit. Instead, he crossed his arms and leaned against the wall. A malevolent glow ignited in his eyes.

Alora wiped her palms down her dress, straightening the fabric. The Coletta flowers reminded her of Veromé and his love and support for her. As she inhaled, the walls of her chest expanded, giving her the courage and determination to see this through. She prayed the device would work.

"Council members, Radnor," she raised her chin and strode before them, "in this device is all the proof I need that Zedron killed my childhood friend Mitan."

The visus bacin in the corner of the room, with its large hand-carved rock bowl and beautiful clear water, was the largest one she'd ever seen. A mirror hung from the wall above the bowl, so the council members could watch what transpired below. Never had she been given the privilege to use the sacred scrying bowl. She pointed toward the basin. "May I?"

Radnor nodded. "Of course."

She approached the bowl, forcing herself to walk at an even pace. There was no way she'd let Zedron make her nervous anymore. She placed her hand on the basin's worn edge, the polished rock smooth to the touch.

Without any further delay, she tossed Mitan's recording device into the bowl. It sank to the bottom, and a ripple undulated across the water until a small splash of water careened over the basin's edge.

Alora closed her eyes and swirled her hands over the water, concentrating on the image she'd seen, willing it to come to life. After a long moment, the water bubbled, the familiar sound feeding Alora's drive, fueling her need for retribution.

Some of the council members whispered amongst themselves.

Alora opened her eyes. The image of Mitan and Zedron appeared in the water, reflecting in the mirror. She turned to look at the council members, studying each one as the scene progressed.

Along the wall, Zedron edged toward the exit. His gaze darted around the room before settling on her. She shook her head. As much as she wanted to bring Zedron down, the death of her friend, Mitan, was a high price to pay.

When Mitan's final scream reverberated through the chamber, Zedron bolted for the door.

"Stop him!" Radnor shouted.

Several of the council members lurched from their seats. Betain tackled Zedron to the ground.

A loud cry burst from Zedron's throat. Trapped under the larger male, Zedron struggled to free himself.

Radnor approached Betain. "Drag him to his feet."

Betain gripped Zedron under the arm and yanked him to a standing position. Her nemesis jerked his arm, but Betain refused to release him.

"Zedron. Based on the evidence presented by Alora, I place you under arrest for the murder of Mitan." Radnor motioned to the doors. "I've called for guards. They'll arrive any moment, so—"

A knock on the chamber door reverberated through the room.

"Allow me." Tomra strode to the door and tugged on the handle.

The door squeaked open and two guards stood in the entryway. "You called, Councilor?"

Betain hauled Zedron toward the door. "Take this scum to the holding cell."

A guard unhooked a length of Yandora vines from his belt. The magical plant slid around Zedron's wrists, tightening into an unbreakable band.

Zedron turned his head, his glower focusing on Alora. "I have the final laugh, Alora. You won't win the game. Mitan discovered Earth first. See what the council has to say about that."

As they dragged Zedron from the room, goosebumps chilled her arms. What would become of Earth and the humans there?

CHAPTER 41

*A*lora leaned against the visus bacin, her legs shaking. The war was over, yet she wasn't sure she'd won. The council members reseated themselves around the council chamber's elaborately carved table. Radnor stood at the end, his palms planted on the polished surface. She twirled Veromé's bracelet around her wrist, wishing he were here.

"Alora, where did you get that disk?" Radnor arched his brow.

Alora's adrenaline spiked. "I found this in the box in your closet, the one you said I could look through."

A few titters from the council members erupted in the room.

Radnor's eyes sparked with mirth. "I guess I should've had Veromé do that long ago." He waved a hand in the air. "No matter. It's clear from the recording Mitan discovered Earth. Is there more on that device?"

She bit the inside of her cheek and glanced at the small orb lying at the bottom of the visus bacin. Even under the water, the smooth surface glinted in the light. "I suspect there is, but it wouldn't play anything else for me. It's locked and requires a password."

Radnor toyed with the ends of his mustache, twirling them

between his fingers. His gaze drew to his peers seated around the table. "Council members, I'd like an immediate vote."

Alora's pulse picked up speed.

"Since Zedron committed the ultimate crime, his claim to Earth is void. The question remains on whether Mitan had first rights or Alora. Since the war is over, I put forth for a vote that the sanctions against Alora and her mate, Veromé, my son, should be lifted. All in favor?"

"Aye!"

"Aye!"

"Aye!"

Radnor cleared his throat. "Any opposed?"

Silence filled the chamber except for the shuffle of a few shoes against the stone floor. Tomra glanced at Alora, a smile tugging at her lips.

Radnor placed his hand on her shoulder and gently squeezed. "As council leader, I lift the sanctions against you and Veromé."

An image shimmered in the middle of the room.

Alora inhaled, a nervous, excited energy pulsing through her.

As Veromé's molecules reformed, Alora couldn't wait any longer. She rushed to him, throwing her arms around his neck. His fresh scent of salt and ocean burrowed into her senses. He wrapped her in his tender embrace, holding her close.

"Alora, my love." His rich baritone rumbled in the space between them. The muscles in his arms and back stiffened. "What am I doing here?"

She pulled away enough to look at him. "The war is over. Zedron killed Mitan and—"

He furrowed his brow. "What?"

Radnor clamped his hand on Veromé's shoulder. "It's true. We saw it all happen on Mitan's recording device. Welcome back, son. The sanction over you and Alora has been removed."

A smile bloomed across Veromé's face. He picked her up and spun her around.

Alora squealed, the sudden movement catching her off guard. Her lungs expanded, love for him filling her chest. She couldn't believe he was home.

Veromé set her back down and gave her a quick, sensual kiss then focused on the council. "I don't understand. How did Mitan have a recording device? Those are used by colonizers, which are only allowed for either slave or free faction groups. Mitan and his family were from the neutral faction."

"That's what we want to know and hope you can help us. We cannot rule on the fate of Earth until we resolve this issue." Radnor pointed to the visus bacin. "Mitan's recording device is there, but it's locked on one scene, the one of his death. Since he left you his belongings, maybe you can unlock its secrets."

Alora squeezed his hand. "We both knew him well. I'm not surprised he would do something like this. Are you?"

Veromé shook his head. "He loved his family and would never outwardly dishonor them, but he always had a penchant for discovery."

Alora exhaled, a wave of sadness for her friend washing over her. "If we find the proof he did discover Earth, perhaps its best that his parents aren't here to witness it."

Veromé kissed her forehead. "Why don't you try again. I think he'd want you to find out."

Alora's throat tightened. "I don't know the password. It will only authorize one more attempt before shutting down."

"I think I know what it is." He tugged her close and whispered, "Alora."

With a quick inhale, she pulled away. "Really? My name? No, it couldn't be that simple."

"Mitan always thought of you as his little sister. He confided in me once that he used your name as his gaming password. I'd bet he did the same for his recording device." Veromé shrugged. "It's worth a try."

A tingle of hope travelled over her shoulders. "All right, I'll do it."

Veromé turned to his father. "Do you mind if Alora gives it another try?"

Radnor inclined his head. "Not at all."

With firm determination, Alora concentrated on the visus bacin once again. As she swirled her hands over the still water, she thought of her childhood friend. His gentle nature, easy going attitude, and zest for adventure had drawn them together from the first moment they'd met. In many ways, he was the brother she'd never had.

The eerie light blinked over the visus bacin... *password...*

"Password, Alora." Her stomach knotted.

A ripple skipped across the water, then another. Her chest lightened, the water's tempered gurgling urging her on. She increased her pace, her fingers flying over the water. Bubbles formed along the surface, frothing into a frantic pace then stilled.

An image of Mitan, sitting at a desk in a small cave came into focus. He pushed away from the table, the chair crashing against the stone floor. His eyes widened, and he ran his hand through his hair. "This will work, I know it will!"

The image wavered. Alora's heart skipped a beat, and she doubled down on her effort, concentrating on the picture. A bead of sweat formed on her brow.

Mitan paced between the desk and a small bed. "Once the four elements—water, air, fire, and earth combine with my creation, my stone, it will ignite a chain reaction, sending hydrogen to Lemuria, where we can combine it with two oxygen molecules to create water."

He stopped, his brow furrowed. "The problem is the byproduct. Carbon is pulled from the air and turned into a solid. What to do, what to do... The last thing I want is to alert the humans and drag them into intergalactic politics." With a brisk step, he resumed his pacing.

Converting hydrogen to water through the portal would be so much easier than transporting the water via ship. Alora furrowed her brow. Perhaps there was a way to still come out of this a winner.

Radnor held up his hand. "Halt the recording."

Alora steadied her palm over the visus bacin. Mitan's image froze, his mouth curled into a smile.

"This is conclusive proof Mitan discovered Earth, yet he was from the neutral faction, so that was against the law. Even though Alora defeated Zedron in the game, she can't claim the planet because she wasn't the first to discover it. The circumstances are unprecedented." Radnor directed his attention to the council. "Suggestions."

Murmurs and heated voices erupted from the council members.

Nervous energy coursed through Alora. She pushed away from the visus bacin and strode toward the council. "I have a suggestion, if you'll allow me."

Tomra placed her hands on the table and rose from her seat. A lock of gray hair tumbled around her shoulders. "I'm willing to hear your idea, but this better be good."

Several other council members nodded in agreement.

Radnor held out his hand as he lowered himself into his chair. "Alora, go ahead."

Taking a large breath, Alora lifted her chin and approached the council members. One by one, she met their gazes. "Earth has what we desperately need—water. I believe we can do a mutual exchange with the humans while honoring Mitan's wishes to keep Earth neutral, free from interplanetary interaction."

Tomra scoffed. "Impossible."

Alora crossed her arms. "I disagree. It is possible."

Radnor leaned back in his chair, assessing her. "Please, continue."

Out of the corner of her eye, Alora caught Veromé's gaze. He smiled and gave her an encouraging nod. His love and support spread elation deep inside. She pulled on her determination and paced the small room. "Earth has a global warming problem. Their use of fossil fuels, coal burning, and other pollutants will destroy their planet. If we fire up Mitan's portal and send hydrogen to Lemuria, the byproduct of removing carbons from the atmosphere would be a great benefit."

"What do you plan to do with the byproduct, the solid carbons?" Tomra shook her head, her lips pursed in disdain.

Here it was, Alora's big leap of faith. "I'd like to recommend that some of my characters remain on Earth to monitor the portal and bury the carbon deep in the Earth. There are several tunnels under the Keep and—"

Tomra slammed her palm against the table. "Nonsense! Characters don't remain on a planet after a war. They return to the character board."

Alora raised her chin, tightening her lips. "I care for my characters. They are like children to me. Free will is the first rule in the game, isn't it?"

"Indeed. Free will is the primary law." Radnor glanced from Alora to Tomra before returning his gaze on her. His mouth thinned. "But Tomra has a good point that characters return to the character board. What makes you think this will work?"

"Recently, several of my characters exercised free will, making choices that went against the norm." Alora turned toward Veromé. "Would you agree?"

Veromé pushed off the wall and strode toward the council members. "Yes, starting with Alora's king, Noeh. He chose a Dren female for his mate, breaking centuries of custom in the process."

"...And Demir, Panthera leader. On his own he broke from tradition and allowed his mate, Aramie, to remain a warrior." Alora's pulse increased, her excitement building. "Tanen, the council leader, fell in love with a human, bringing her and her dog into the Keep."

Veromé placed his hand around Alora's waist. "Saar, the Commander of Arms, fell in love with his enemy..."

"And let's not forget the most recent one, Gaetan, the Keep's haelen." Alora gripped Veromé's hand, intertwining their fingers together. "He saved a human from a Gossum and fell in love with her. Each of these characters made a choice that changed their lives forever. I'd like to offer them a chance to continue to live with their chosen mates, and I believe they will jump at the opportunity to stay on Earth. Of course, I'd watch over them and ensure the exchange progressed accordingly."

"I'd gladly help." Veromé kissed her on the forehead.

Radnor cleared his throat. "Your points are well made, Alora."

Alora swallowed, her pulse spiking. Here it was, the final determination.

"Council members, I'd like to put this matter to an immediate vote." Radnor scanned the group. "All in favor of allowing Alora's character the right to choose, of their own free will, to stay on Earth and monitor the exchange, say 'aye.'"

"Aye."

"Aye."

"Aye."

Tomra shook her head. "I will only give my assent if the individual characters who don't wish to stay can return to the character board to await another war on a different planet."

Alora let out a relieved breath. "Yes, of course. Free will."

"Then it shall be done." Radnor rapped his mallet against the table. The sound echoed around the chamber. "Alora, you have officially claimed Earth as the first neutral planet. Congratulations."

Alora turned toward Veromé and wrapped her arms around his neck. He placed his hands on her waist, and picked her up, twirling her in the air. She laughed, a sense of happiness lightening her spirit. Now, to visit her characters. She hoped they'd make the right choice.

CHAPTER 42

*G*aetan draped his arm around Nicole's shoulder and took a step, urging her forward. Savory and sweet, the scent of roast beef and potatoes permeated the Grand Hall. The line for this evening's repast wound out the door and into the corridor. Good thing they'd arrived early.

The clink of silverware and solemn voices filled the large room. For many in the Keep, elation over winning the war ended as soon as realization set in that they'd soon be sent back to the character board on Lemuria. Gaetan shared that sentiment. His time with Nicole would be brief.

She leaned into him, mirth sparkling in her eyes. "I'm glad we went to our quarters after returning from Roan's Rock."

He couldn't resist, and brought his lips to hers, stealing a brief kiss. A slow groan eased from him.

She placed her hand on his chest, breaking the kiss. "How much longer do you think we have?"

"Who knows. I stopped trying to figure out our goddess long ago." He took another step forward, his palm tightening around the sunstone in his staff. Although the pain in his leg was gone, he still needed the support.

"Gaaa...taaa." Anlon grabbed Gaetan's pant leg and hauled himself to a standing position. He glanced up, his grin lighting up his eyes.

Gaetan laughed and placed his palm on Anlon's shoulder, giving the babe a gentle pat. "Hello, little prince, you have no idea how happy I am to see you."

"Anlon!" Melissa strode toward them, a slow smile forming across her features. "I set him down for a minute and he's halfway across the Grand Hall." She scooped him up in her arms.

"Gaaa...taaa." Anlon clapped his hands together, a drop of drool sliding down his chin.

The child's infectious smile warmed Gaetan's heart, and he tickled the little guy under the chin.

"I have to meet up with Noeh. We'll talk more later." Melissa squeezed his arm and headed toward Noeh. Deep in conversation, he stood in a group with Tanen, Demir, and Saar.

The line moved forward. Gaetan inched toward the plates, hand extended.

"Gaetan!" Ginnia's voice pierced the air.

Gaetan turned to look.

She bolted toward him from the Grand Hall's large entryway. Bits of her brown hair blew around her ears.

He gripped Nicole's wrist and drew her from the line. As he opened his arms, heat radiated through his chest, expanding with each breath.

Ginnia leapt into his embrace, wrapping her hands around his neck, squeezing tight. "You're back. I'm so happy."

"Angel, I'm glad to see you, too." He held her for a long moment then released her.

She peered at him, her eyes twinkling with happiness. "I knew you'd do it. You and Nikki both."

He blinked a few times. "Do what, Angel?"

She glanced at Nikki then returned her attention to him. "Win the war for us. My visions are never wrong."

Nicole rubbed her hand down Gaetan's back. "When I went to see

Ginnia in the strong room, she mentioned that you and I would win the war."

"See! I'm a good seer." She crossed her arms in front of her chest and nodded. Pride radiated in the glint in her eyes.

"Ah, Ginnia..." He shook his head, the thoughts and memories of long ago were still present, but the guilt was gone.

He wrapped one arm around Ginnia, the other around Nicole, and drew them close. Tears burned his eyes, and he choked on his words. "My two females. I don't know what I would do without you."

"I love you, my mate."

"Love you, brother."

He held on, never wanting to let either of them go ever again.

The temperature in the room dropped. Gaetan's breath became visible in the cold air.

Oh no...Alora.

A loud blast of air whipped through the room. Tables rattled, chairs flipped over, plates crashed against the stone floor. Grunts and cries filled the Grand Hall.

Gaetan tightened his grip on Nicole and Ginnia and waited out the storm.

Alora materialized into the Keep's Grand Hall and surveyed the room. Pushed to one side, tables lined the walls. An upended chair, with one of its legs broken, stood near the room's entrance. Several of her characters, including Noeh and Melissa, Demir and Aramie, Tanen and Sheri with Coop, Saar and Kaelyn, and Gaetan and Nikki, were in attendance. Good. She could get down to business.

Beside her, Veromé squeezed her hand. His support meant the world to her, and she smiled, thankful the war was over and they could be together again.

She smiled and turned her attention to the crowd. "My children. You have done well, winning the war over Earth. Per the rules of the game, all warriors are to return to the character board to wait for war on another planet."

Quentin and a few of the warriors beamed, their eyes lighting with pride. Many others cast their gazes to the ground. Noeh's attention drew to Anlon cradled in Melissa's arms, and his mouth tightened.

Alora held out her hands. "For those that wish to return to Lemuria, you may do so. However, I have an opportunity for those that elect to stay."

Hushed whispers and the shuffling of feet whisked across the room.

Noeh glanced at Melissa for a long moment as if they had a private conversation. His eyebrows rose, and he twirled the ring on his finger. "There's an opportunity to remain on Earth?"

Alora smiled. "We need several Lemurians to remain behind to monitor the portal at Roan's Rock, ensure the hydrogen transports to Lemuria, and dispose of the carbon byproduct. I don't suppose I have any volunteers here, do I?"

Shouts and cheers bounced off the walls.

Noeh wrapped his arms around Melissa and Anlon.

Gaetan kissed Nikki and Ginnia on the cheek.

After several long moments, the crowd quieted.

Noeh cleared his throat. "You mentioned a carbon byproduct. What's the disposal method?"

Veromé wrapped his hand around her shoulder. "The process to transport the hydrogen to Lemuria takes carbon from the air and converts it to a solid, like ash. This will need to be buried underground. You have several unused tunnels in the Keep, perfect for storage."

Gaetan hobbled forward until he stood next to Noeh, his cane tapping against the stone floor. "What of the humans? Are they part of this?"

Alora shook her head. "As I see you learned for yourself, Mitan, another...god...from Lemuria, discovered Earth first. He was from the neutral faction. To honor his wishes, humans will not be involved in the exchange, so the work must be kept secret. The process will help Earth reduce global warming, so it is a mutually beneficial arrangement."

Saar cleared his throat. "Sounds good, where do I sign up?"

Several chuckles and shouts of agreement filled the room.

Alora held her breath. "In a show of hands, how many, with their own free will, elect to remain on Earth?"

Noeh raised his hand, followed by Melissa and Gaetan, Saar, Sheri, Tanen, and several others. Soon, everyone in the entire room had their hand raised.

A weightlessness lifted Alora's spirit. She clapped her hands and smiled. "Well done. I'm so very proud of you all. Oh, and before I forget, there's one other little tidbit I should share. Now that the war is over, you can go out in the sun."

Cheers and claps erupted from the group. The happiness in the room was like a wave, overtaking Alora in its depth and intensity. Tears misted her eyes. "I'll stay in touch. Until then, enjoy your newfound freedom."

She glanced to Veromé and held out her palm. "Let us go, my love." She still couldn't believe she'd won the battle and beat Zedron. Her world was complete again.

Veromé clasped her hand and they returned to Lemuria, to their new life together.

∼

Want to know what's coming next? A new shifter paranormal romance series - Feline Shifter Mates! Keep reading for a sneak peek of book 1, *Snaring a Snow Leopard...*

Could you find your mate at *The Windows*?

Snow leopard-shifter Celia's biological clock is ticking and she must go to *The Windows* to find a suitable volunteer to take care of her calling. She's forced to breed to stave off the madness, but because she's been burned by love she vows to keep the walls around her heart firmly in place.

Mason has had his eye on Celia for quite some time, but has kept his distance from the hardened female until they are thrust together at *The Windows*. What he desires most is within his grasp if he can break down her defenses and show her the true passion in his heart.

~

Chapter 1

Seattle, Washington
One year ago...

Mason stepped into the courtroom, and the scent of his enemy burned the fine hairs in his nose. He clenched his teeth, tamping down the urge to growl. One of Mason's recent captures, Antoine, a lion shifter, sat in the courtroom's witness box. His long blond hair, straggly at the ends, splayed over his bulging shoulders hidden underneath his three piece suit. He met Mason's gaze. A cocky grin curled his lip. The suspected Slayer had murdered a young human female and her child.

A tic formed in Mason's jaw, and he fisted his hand. As a Protector who defended humans, he couldn't wait to see the asshole pay for his crime.

Packed with humans and shifters, the stifling temperature in the old building only added to his frustration, and a bead of sweat rolled down the back of his neck. He slipped into the back row, sitting next to an elderly man. Creases lined the man's face, but his eyes were filled with wisdom. He gave Mason a quick nod.

Over the past few decades many shifters had moved from their homes, hidden by ancient magic in the surrounding forests, into the cities. Unbeknownst to the majority of humans, the shifters remained hidden in plain sight, working alongside their human neighbors without issue.

"This knife isn't yours?" The female prosecutor's voice echoed across the room.

The determination and animosity in her tone caught Mason's attention, and he glanced at her.

She faced the podium, her back to him. Dark, silky hair cascaded around her shoulders, covering the top of her blouse. Her slim waist flared at her hips, accentuated by her tight pencil skirt. Long, shapely legs ended in a pair of red high-heeled shoes.

His inner cat roused, and he leaned forward in his seat.

"Nope, not mine." Antoine smirked, his gaze focused on her.

She slapped her hand against the wooden pew. "Then, tell me, why are your fingerprints on the murder weapon?"

His face tightened. "You better watch your back."

"That sounds like a threat. Are you one of Kylar's boys?"

Gasps rose from the crowd.

His snarl was his only reply.

The female turned and Mason glanced upon her features for the first time. He held his breath and couldn't look away. Her dark hair caressed her chin and accentuated her luscious lips, but her eyes, a beautiful shade of hazel, captured his interest. Self-confidence and spunk radiated from their depths. In the middle of her neck chain was a white stone. She was a snow leopard shifter, just like him. A spark of irritation flashed through her eyes, and she pursed her lips.

"Sit down." The old man next to him pulled on Mason's arm. "You can't interrupt the proceedings like this."

Mason tore his gaze from the female. Sure enough, he'd stood. The veiled threat had spurned his protective side. As a member of the elite Protector squad, he couldn't help his natural reaction. The tic in his jaw tightened. He glanced at her once again and returned to his seat.

The proceedings continued, but he didn't follow the questioning. He couldn't pull his focus from the female prosecutor. Conviction lined her pursed lips and the fire in her eyes called to him. They had a common goal, a common passion to stop the Slayers from killing the remaining humans who'd survived the super bug immune to antibiotics. Respect for her burned inside.

He turned to the elderly man. "Do you know the prosecuting attorney?"

The old man's gray eyebrows drew to a point over his eyes. "Sure, everyone knows Celia. She's the best prosecutor in town."

Celia, he'd heard of her. She had a reputation all right—cold as ice, strong-willed, and independent. A few of his co-workers had joked about trying to bed her, but they'd failed.

Mason thrust out his chin. Their failure wouldn't stop him. His inner cat purred in agreement.

The loud bang of the judge's gavel filled the courtroom, dragging Mason's attention back to the activity.

"Recess! The court will reconvene in fifteen minutes." As the old judge stood, he placed his hand on his back. A grimace crossed his grizzled features.

"All rise." The bailiff's voice broke through the silence.

Chair legs scraped against the wooden floor, and the sound of shuffling feet echoed around the chamber. All were quiet as the judge shuffled from the courtroom.The door to the judge's chamber closed, and the spectators headed for the exit.

"Excuse me." The man next to Mason gave him a quick smile and nudged toward the end of the pew. He was one of the few humans in the room. After the super bug wiped out two-thirds of the human population and the shifters outnumbered their counterparts, many more shifters came in from the wild, eager to live in the open without fear.

Mason stepped into the aisle and let the old man and the rest of the bystanders leave. When the row emptied, his focus returned to Celia.

Her male counterpart whispered in her ear. A tinge of jealousy Mason didn't quite understand played along his nerves. The male pointed toward him, and Celia glanced his way.

Her penetrating gaze bore into him, and he straightened his spine.

With his heightened senses he inhaled, trying to determine her scent among the diminishing crowd. She pushed through the small hinged gate that separated the courtroom from the pews and headed toward him.

"Are you Mason?" Her warm peaches fragrance invaded his senses, lighting up his nerves.

He nodded. "And you are Celia."

She raised an eyebrow.

"The man next to me mentioned your name." It'd been a while since he'd found himself attracted to a female. His Protector job kept him busy, leaving little room for much else.

"Jordan, my partner on this case, tells me you're the one who captured Antoine and brought him in. I wanted to thank you."

The weight on Mason's chest lightened, and he gave her a quick smile. "Part of my job. I don't normally watch the proceedings, but this case…" He fisted his hand.

Mason and those in the Progressive faction wanted to co-exist with the humans while the those in the Partisan faction wanted to relegate humans to slave status. With tension escalating, two radical groups had formed within each faction, Slayers and Protectors. Where the Slayers wanted to wipe out the humans from the face of the planet, the Protectors guarded them, often times with their lives.

The disparate goals had clashed, pushing the conflict to a boiling point, and the feline shifter wars started four years, eleven months, and twelve days ago. Fortunately, the Progressive faction had the upper hand, and Mason would do everything in his power to ensure that remained so. His tense shoulders loosened as he forced himself to relax.

"I'm going to nail that bastard to the wall for slaying that mother and child," she hissed. Passion and determination radiated from her and rushed over him like a heatwave. His fingers twitched with his sudden desire to touch her, be a part of that passion. He held the urge in check, barely.

"The more Slayers we can pull off the streets, the safer for all of us." He admired how her hazel eyes sparkled in the light. Her cheeks reddened, and she licked her bottom lip, moistening it.

Mason clamped his teeth together as a sudden rush of blood raced south.

She glanced at the clock on the wall, but not before he'd caught the slight rise at the corner of her mouth. "I have to go over my notes before the defense makes his final speech for the judge. Thank you, again."

As she turned to go, he gripped her arm, stopping her retreat. Her warm skin lit up the sensitive pads on his fingers. His inner cat howled with delight. "Wait…"

She glanced from his fingers to his face. Tension lines formed around her eyes. "Yes?"

He let her go, and a rock formed in his gut. "Seems we have something in common, our disdain for Slayers. Would you meet up with me later for dinner?"

She blinked, but then her features hardened once again. "Sorry, I don't think so."

She turned on the ball of her foot and headed toward the prosecutor's table. He couldn't pull his gaze away from her behind swiveling back and forth as she walked. A seductive yet graceful movement. She was tough and ruthless, and lived up to her reputation, the Ice Queen. Indeed, but if he ever got the chance, he'd work on thawing her out.

You don't want to miss out on this sexy shifter romance series! Find **Snaring a Snow Leopard** at your favorite retailer <<here>> or visit www.rosalieredd.com.

ALSO BY ROSALIE REDD

Books in the *Warriors of Lemuria* series:
Untouchable Lover - book #1
Untamable Lover - book #2
Unimaginable Lover - book #3
Undeniable Lover - book #4
Unforgivable Lover - book #5
Unforgettable Lover - novella
Alora's Love Potion - short story collection
Marked by Love - novella

Reviews

Enjoyed *Unforgivable Lover*? The best gift you can give an author is an honest review. Please consider leaving a review on your favorite retailer to help spread the word and support an author.

Newsletter

Want access to free reads, special offers, and giveaways? Sign up here for my newsletter on my website and you'll receive a **free ebook**. Don't worry, your information won't be shared with anyone but my muse. You can visit me at my website at www.rosalieredd.com or contact me at Rosalie@rosalieredd.com. I love to receive email from readers!

GLOSSARY

Antorro stalks: A green, leafy vegetable imported from the planet Antorro.

Aridis: Lemuria's largest moon

Arotaars: People from the planet Arotin. Held as slaves on Lemuria. They have blue hair that sparks with electricity when they are emotional.

Craya: An expletive.

Dren: Short for "chil*dren*." Originally human adults, but were transformed into Dren through a Lemurian's bite. During the "turning," all Dren receive a unique, special power. Dren must drink blood at least once a week from the opposite sex or they become weak and lose their powers.

Gossum: Human converts turned by another Gossum through their bite. They have black eyes, and are hairless, with rough, scalelike skin down their neck and back. Gossum have a spur at the end of their long tongue which they use to paralyze their prey.

Haelen: Healer

Jixies: Small, dwarf-like characters that voluntarily serve the Stiyaha. Jixies tend to be quick, resourceful, and are great planners.

Despite their short stature, they can go amongst the humans to obtain special items not made within the Keep.

Kasard: An expletive.

Keep: The underground home of the Stiyaha and Jixies, located in the mountains of the Pacific Northwest. The Keep is sentient and reacts to her inhabitants with minor tremors and/or by warming or cooling the environment through the sunstones embedded in the walls.

Lemuria: A planet in the Orion constellation. Lemuria is slowly dying and its people must rely on natural resources from other planets to survive.

Lemurians: Refers to both the people on Lemuria, as well as, the characters on Earth. The people of Lemuria appear as gods to the characters in the war on Earth.

Matronin colony: A Lemurian trade partner from planet Matron in a nearby galaxy.

Newbs: Young children

Panthera: Sleek and muscular, these highly skilled fighters are known for their speed and agility. They transform into black panthers and are highly arrogant and confident. They respect strength and cunning and will only follow a leader who can command them.

Porte stanen: The massive stone structure in the Portal Navigation Center used to transport characters in and out of the Keep through the portal gateway.

Qithan: Betrothed

Rhondo beasts: Fearsome creatures that terrorize the surface of Lemuria. They have black, oily skin with disproportionately long arms and short legs. A small amount of hair runs down its spine. They have a long tongue and sharp teeth, including tusk-like fangs.

Stiyaha: Stoic and just, Stiyaha are noble warriors. Tall and strong, they transform into large beasts, between eight and nine feet tall, covered in fur with large, protruding tusks.

Sunstones: Magical stones that line the ceilings and walls of the Keep, providing heat and light to its inhabitants. Sunstones are used in trade and have some healing abilities.

Tratee flies: Small flying insects on Lemuria that have translucent wings.

Ursus: A tough, burly species that shape-shifts into large bears. Tenacious and vicious, they are fierce warriors.

Visus bacin: Scrying bowl

Yandora vines: A trailing plant the lives on the bark of the Etila trees. The leaves have a melodic tingle when touched.

ABOUT ROSALIE

After finishing a rewarding career in finance and accounting, it was time for award-winning author Rosalie Redd to put away the spreadsheets and take out the word processor. She pens paranormal, science fiction, and fantasy romance in her office cave located in Oregon, where rain is just another excuse to keep writing.

www.ingramcontent.com/pod-product-compliance
Lightning Source LLC
Chambersburg PA
CBHW061614170626
46811CB00001B/424